MISSION ACCOMPLISHED
High praise for *New York Times* and
USA Today bestselling author
CINDY GERARD
and her scorching alpha hunks!

"I'm hooked on Gerard's tough-talkin', straight-shootin'
characters." —Sandra Brown

"A true master!" —*RT Book Reviews*

"Slam-bang romantic suspense." —*Fresh Fiction*

"Kicks romantic adventure into high gear."
—Allison Brennan

"Just keeps getting better and better." —*Romance Junkies*

RUNNING BLIND
Book Two in the thrilling One-Eyed Jacks series

"My, oh my, can this lady craft a story." —*USA Today*

"Gerard's name has become synonymous with high-
stakes and high-action adventures that don't skimp on
either the romance or the thrills."
—*RT Book Reviews* (Top Pick!)

KILLING TIME
Book One in the thrilling One-Eyed Jacks series

Nominated for the *RT Book Reviews*
Best Romantic Suspense Award!

"Cindy Gerard writes such fun books. Full of tons of
action, witty lines and plenty of sexual tension, *Killing
Time* totally lived up to my expectations." —*USA Today*

THE WAY HOME
A captivating One-Eyed Jacks novel with some sizzling Black Ops Inc. heroes

"A story readers can't help but fall in love with."
—*RT Book Reviews*

"Smart, romantic, exciting, and so emotionally satisfying. I hugged myself for hours after reading it. Cindy Gerard really knows how to bring it home!"
—Robyn Carr

"A really sweet read about second chances, finding love, and the path that leads you to your happily ever after. Gerard continues to impress me."
—*Smexy Books*

"An interesting meditation . . . on the changing foundations of love. In many ways it challenges the first and only soul mate concept that is so prevalent."
—*Dear Author*

"I anxiously await every new Cindy Gerard release. I've always thought there was nobody who wrote romantic suspense better, able to seamlessly blend romance and action while creating strong heroines and macho, yet caring heroes."
—*Fiction Vixen*

"Gerard is an author whose stories I always have an easy time falling into and thoroughly enjoying. . . . You can never go wrong with the Black Ops world."
—*Happily Ever After-Reads*

"Gerard simply excels when it comes to writing action-packed scenes that are highly detailed and infused with passion and fun. Similarly, her heroes have been some of the hottest in RS that I've read."
—*Under the Covers Book Blog*

Also by Cindy Gerard

CINDY
GERARD

TAKING
FIRE

Pocket Books

New York   London   Toronto   Sydney   New Delhi

Pocket Books
An Imprint of Simon & Schuster, Inc.
1230 Avenue of the Americas
New York, NY 10020

Copyright © 2016 by Cindy Gerard

First Pocket Books paperback edition March 2016

POCKET and colophon are registered trademarks of Simon & Schuster, Inc.

For information about special discounts for bulk purchases, please contact Simon & Schuster Special Sales at 1-866-506-1949 or business@simonandschuster.com.

The Simon & Schuster Speakers Bureau can bring authors to your live event. For more information or to book an event, contact the Simon & Schuster Speakers Bureau at 1-866-248-3049 or visit our website at www.simonspeakers.com.

Manufactured in the United States of America

10 9 8 7 6 5 4 3 2 1

ISBN 978-1-4767-3951-9
ISBN 978-1-4767-3953-3(ebook)

Acknowledgments

I would like to thank my readers old and new, who have read and praised my books so enthusiastically over the years. Without you, there is no reason to write.

My editor, Micki Nuding, and my publisher, Louise Burke, I thank for your kindness, expertise, and support, and for letting me write the books the way I want to write them. Thanks also to my agent, Maria Carvainis, who has been the bedrock on which I stand for both guidance and business decisions. I'm proud to call all of you amazing women my friends as well as my business partners.

The longer I'm in the business, the less I'm surprised by the friendships that are forged, nurtured, and remain among the strongest bonds I've ever known. Glenna McReynolds, Susan Connell, Rossella Re, Leanne Banks, Kim Bahnsen, Roxanne Rustand, Rob Browne, Debra Webb, Peggy Webb, and so many, many more authors who have been there with me and I with them, through the good, the bad, and the ugly. You are among the special blessings in my life.

Joe Collins. What can I say that I haven't already said? You help add the boom to the bang, the grit to the grail, the method to the madness. Thank you, friend, for teaching me so much about warfare, weaponry, and medical trauma.

Tommy, Tommy, Tommy. You're my rock. My fill-in chef, shopper, laundry service, chocolate supplier—you name it, you do it for me while I'm dug in on a deadline. I couldn't do any of this without you.

TAKING
FIRE

PART I

Betrayal

"Each betrayal begins with trust."

—Phish

1

Kabul, Afghanistan, six years ago

Talia Levine sat at the bar in the dingy Mustafa Hotel lounge, wiping the dirty rim of her wineglass with her shirttail. Three nights in a row, she'd landed in this beat-up old bar, ordered a glass of cheap red, and hoped for the best.

The best never happened. It never did in Kabul.

She damn sure wouldn't have picked the Mustafa as her watering hole, but the American military contractors stationed in the city had, staking out the bar for their own. *She* had staked out an American contractor. Just one out of all the bad boys doing the same thing she was—nursing a cheap drink and wilting in the heat.

Like her, the men were a long way from home. Unlike her, they were in the bar seeking like-minded company and a relatively quiet place to drink away the physical and emotional dirt from the day.

Many were bored. Some were lonely. But none were easy. Especially not her target.

She took a long swallow of her wine, gaze dead ahead on the hazy mirror behind the bar, studying his reflection through the drift of smoke skimming the room. His back was to the wall, his eyes on his whiskey as he absently flipped a playing card back and forth between his fingers and listened to the conversation at his table.

Even if she hadn't read his file, she'd have known he'd once been Special Ops, just like the men with him. Men who were now private military contractors, most of them with the Fargis Group. To a man, they all wore battle-hardened looks and a clear air of danger.

This man in particular relayed a coiled readiness, an underlying situational awareness that told anyone within striking distance that he was no easy mark. No one was going to get the drop on him. Anyone coming after him was going to die. No hesitation. No regret.

She'd be playing with fire once she engaged him, and as she watched him expertly flipping that card, she knew she regretted volunteering for this op. But the endgame was what drove her, and she'd take the same chance again if it meant getting what she was after.

When he looked up and made eye contact, she gave him a slow blink before averting her gaze from the mirror to her almost empty glass. This part of the plan required patience. And finesse. She couldn't appear too eager, so they'd been playing this little game of peekaboo for a while now. All she had to do was wait. If all worked as intended, she'd get what she wanted and get out within a week.

Overhead, a slow-moving fan barely stirred air heated by a long, miserable day and fouled by strong cigarette smoke. She lifted her heavy braid, arched her back, and used a napkin to wipe away the perspiration dampening her nape. The action was mostly for his benefit. He was watching her again.

For three nights straight, she'd kept her distance but subtly relayed her interest with quick, well-timed glances or the hint of a self-conscious smile, until he'd finally started playing along. It was clear he was attracted to her but hadn't yet decided how things were going to roll out between them.

She tipped the last of her wine to her lips and let him think about it a little longer.

"Buy you another?"

For a big man, he moved fast. He'd slipped into her personal space without making a ripple in the air around them. And while she was irritated that she'd let him catch her off guard, she was also relieved they'd finally moved past square one.

She glanced up at him. "Sure. If you don't make me drink alone."

He caught the bartender's attention, made a circle in the air with his finger signaling for another round, and eased down onto the bar stool beside her.

"So . . . come here often?" His smile surprised her as much as the corny line.

He knew this was her watering hole. Just as she'd known it was his before she'd ever set foot inside. His, along with all the other mercs, spooks, and journalists who called it their home away from home.

"Can't seem to stay away." Her smile said, *What's a girl to do?* "Must be the homey atmosphere."

He grunted and made a cursory glance around the room—smoke-stained yellow walls, cracked marble floors, years of abuse and wear. "Yeah. Or the cheap booze. Any port in a storm, right?"

"What about you?" She nodded her thanks to the bartender when he slid a fresh glass of wine in front of her and a whiskey in front of her new friend.

"When the pickings are slim, you take what you can get." He smiled again. Surprised her again. He had the look of a hard man, and everything she knew of his background said that he was. Yet when he smiled, there was nothing hard about him.

"Are we still talking about the hotel?" she asked, reacting to that smile.

He laughed. "Well, we're not talking about you, ma'am. You class up the place."

"Ma'am?" Whether it was an old-fashioned endearment or a holdover from his Army days, it charmed her more than it should have.

"Best I could do since I don't know your name. Mine's Taggart."

Robert Andrew Taggart, to be exact. Known to his coworkers as Bobby or Boom Boom. It was the boom she had to remember to be careful of. He'd been Special Forces, but a mission had gone south a few years ago, and he and two of his fellow team members got tagged for the screwup. All three were given less-than-honorable discharges. Bitter and with no place to go, he'd signed on for military contract work and ended up back in Afghanistan.

His military history and his fall from grace might work for her. That and something as inherently basic as the difference in their chromosomes. She needed information. He had it. She'd do whatever she had to do to get it.

"Talia Levine." She extended her hand.

His palm was warm and rough, and she held on long enough so he'd understand she had something more in mind than drinking together.

"You're American, right?"

Another engaging grin. "What gave it away?"

She pushed out a flirty laugh. "Only everything about you."

"Yeah, I need to work on that." He leaned a little closer. "What about you? Can't place the accent."

"I was hoping I didn't have one." She smiled again. "I'm from D.C., actually. But of late, Israel, London, Baghdad . . . anywhere my assignments take me. War correspondent," she clarified when he cocked a brow. It wasn't a lie, but it wasn't what had brought her to Kabul. *He* was.

"Of course. Why else would a beautiful woman spend time in a sweatbox like this unless she was forced to?"

"Not forced," she corrected. "I volunteered for this assignment."

He sipped his whiskey, studying her face in a way that made her feel like a mouse in a trap when *she* was supposed to be doing the trapping. "So you're one of those."

She crinkled her brow. "One of *those*?"

"An 'all for the sake of her career' woman. Always ready to take reckless chances to get your story."

"Now, how would you know if I was reckless?"

"Not to point out the obvious, but you're in Kabul in the middle of a war zone. And you're coming on to a stranger in a bar."

"Wow." She feigned insult. "That's harsh."

"That's life," he said with a shrug. "No insult intended. Maybe a little wishful thinking, though. You *were* coming on to me, right?"

She sipped her wine, aware of his gaze on her face. "I was still deciding."

He chuckled. "And now?"

"And now I think I need to know more about you."

He lifted a hand. "Me? I'm an open book."

"Of course you are," she said, letting him know he wasn't fooling her.

He was good at this game. Just not as good as she was.

"Are you really any different from me in the reckless department?" she asked, now that the door was open. "You were military, right? I'm guessing Spec Ops. Most likely served more than one deployment in the hot zones. That would have been enough for most men, yet now you're a civilian contractor."

She wasn't stating anything that wasn't general knowledge around Kabul. The bulk of the Americans who ended up here had military backgrounds, and most were employed by civilian contractors.

"Seems to me that in the reckless-chances department, you're way ahead of me."

"So I guess it's settled. We're both a little crazy." He lifted his glass in salute.

She did the same. "But you can't say it's not exciting."

Another smile from the man who kept surprising her. "Yeah. This is definitely my idea of excitement. Watching the paint peel off the walls of this run-down bar."

She toyed with the stem of her wineglass, then tilted him a measured look. "You're not watching the paint peel now, are you?"

He wasn't stupid. And he wasn't slow. She'd just let him know she'd made her decision about him, and he turned that charming grin on her again. "No, ma'am. I certainly am not."

According to his file, he was a man who kept to himself, and if he fit in anywhere, it was with men just like himself. Judging by his pleased look, however, that wasn't altogether true. He wanted *her* company now. Which was exactly what she'd been counting on—but for an entirely different reason.

This was all business on her part. She'd taken an

oath, and she'd do what was expected of her. Yet a surprising awareness arced between them, and for a moment, she let herself see the man, not the assignment.

Square-jawed, hard-edged, and tough as leather, his sandy-brown hair in a military cut. Still had the look of the Bronx street brawler he'd been in his teens.

And he had the most watchful green eyes.

He wore rugged and muscular like a tailored suit, and the truth was, he was very easy to look at. Especially when he smiled. When he smiled, it was oh-so-easy to romanticize and even picture him in another era. An adventurer, crossing the rough Atlantic on a tall-masted ship, braving the danger and uncertainty of the rough passage, and finally landing at Ellis Island with his fellow German, French, or Irish immigrants.

An electric silence had stretched out between them before she managed to fall back into her role. She glanced up at him. "Just so you know, I don't make a habit of doing this."

His gaze was intense but not judgmental. "So why me? And why now?"

She looked away, and when she looked back at him, tears pooled in her eyes. All she had to do was recall today's horrible memory to rouse them. "Why you? Because you look about as lonely as I feel. Why now? I don't know. Maybe . . . maybe because life—this life—is risky, and today I narrowly escaped with mine. Maybe because today I need human contact."

"To remind you that you're human?" His tone suggested he might need that reminder as well. And his eyes had warmed just enough to tell her she'd struck a chord—struck it hard enough that she might have felt a twinge of guilt for exploiting it if this mission weren't so crucial.

"To remind me that humanity isn't dead . . . even in the thick of this inhumane war."

He studied her face and then his whiskey before knocking the rest of it down. Then he stood, dug into his hip pocket for his wallet, and tossed some cash onto the bar. "My room or yours?"

2

She'd surprised him, this Talia Levine, or whatever her real name was. He'd been certain that his über-crude "My room or yours?" would make her bolt, telling him this was a bad idea and then telling him to get lost.

But she hadn't, and now here he was. Following her and her exceptional ass up three creaky flights of stairs after she'd gone to the trouble of staking him out in the bar. And he'd love to know why, because if she was a journalist, he was a frickin' nanny.

She clearly wanted something from him that she thought only he could give her. He'd sensed it the first time he'd seen her and was convinced of it when she'd started giving him the sultry eye.

If she was playing him, what did she really want?

And how far would she go to get it?

How far would he *let* her go?

He checked out her ass again. Pretty far, no doubt about it.

He'd noticed her three nights ago. Even looking

worn-out and thirsty, her khakis covered in dust, her black hair bound in a thick braid, she'd been striking as hell. Hadn't taken but one look, and he'd wondered what her hair would look like falling free. What it would feel like when he combed it through his fingers, when it brushed across his naked skin.

Oh, yeah. She'd had him interested way before *hello*. One look, and he hadn't been able to stop thinking about her. Which was pointless as well as stupid. And worse, she was a distraction that could get him killed. Women and war zones didn't mix. Especially conspiring women.

So he knew he shouldn't be here, he knew he should be beating feet back to his own hotel, but he was curious. And hell, yeah, a part of him hoped she wasn't playing him, because damn, the woman was fine.

In Afghanistan, every day was a crap shoot. And sometimes the need for human contact in the midst of all the brutality got a man in a choke hold and wouldn't let go.

So despite his second thoughts, he followed her down the hot, dimly lit hallway and stopped when she did at room 309. Three was his lucky number, and he could make four threes out of 309, which quadrupled his luck, good or bad.

The key clicked when she slid it into the antiquated lock. She stepped inside and flipped a switch, and small lamps on either side of the bed lit up, casting a pale glow over the room.

"Home sweet home." She walked to the bed and tossed the key onto a nightstand.

He followed her into the room and glanced around. A ceiling fan turned lazily over a double bed covered with a red-patterned spread. Two side tables flanked the bed. An open laptop sat on one of them. A camera with a big bulky lens sat beside it along with a well-used paper notebook.

Nicely done, he thought. Her props supported her story. Still unconvinced, though, he walked to the wooden wardrobe that substituted for a closet, opened the doors, and checked inside. Empty except for more drab khakis and a pair of sandals. Same thing with the bathroom—no terrorist lying in wait to whack an American.

She looked amused when he checked under the bed. "So . . . what do we call this? Paranoia or a basic distrust of women?"

"Call it anything you want," he said agreeably as he straightened up, dusting his hands together. "Mostly, it's called life lessons."

Her deep brown eyes weren't exactly smiling, but clearly, she felt entertained. "And do I pass inspection?"

"The room does." He stalked slowly toward her. "But I haven't thoroughly inspected *you* yet. Got any explosive devises hidden under that ugly shirt?"

Because he was taller than her by a head, she had to tilt her head back to look up at him. "No IEDs. Hope that doesn't disappoint you. And I'm so sorry

I didn't dress for the occasion." She smiled as he gripped her hips and eased her up against him.

When she looped her arms around his neck, he pushed a little harder, just to see how far she'd let this go. "Dressing is highly overrated. Now, undressing"— he started tugging her shirt up and out of his way— "that's something I could get into."

She didn't resist, but she didn't exactly melt against him, either. He, however, was about to go up in flames. She was slim and compact and soft where a woman was supposed to be. Especially where her breasts pressed against his chest. It had been a damn long time since he'd been naked with a woman; his job didn't allow time even for one-night stands. Didn't make him much of a long-term prospect, either.

He smiled into her eyes, then bit back a groan when he slipped a hand beneath her shirt and touched warm, bare skin. Smooth and silky and gloriously alive. And that wasn't all. Her lean body coiled tightly in anticipation as he worried a thumb back and forth across the skin above her waistband.

Just before he reached the point of no return, while he still had it in him to think straight, he called her out. "It's not too late to back out, Talia—if that's really your name."

She frowned, then flattened her palms on his chest. "What? Of course it's my name."

When he said nothing, she looked at him through narrowed and suddenly wary eyes.

"Wait. You think I'm lying?" Her expression shifted

from beleaguered amusement to a simmering anger. "Oh, my God. You do. You think I'm lying to you."

"What I think is that you've gone to a lot of trouble to get my attention and make contact with me."

"Excuse me? Did *I* move into *your* space and offer to buy you a drink?"

"No, but you would have if I hadn't made the first move."

She glared at him. "You know what? You're an ass-hole."

That shocked a laugh out of him. "You're not the first woman to suggest it."

She shoved against his chest, but he held her right where she was.

"Look. It's no big deal. Just tell me who you really are and what you want from me. Then I'll tell you I don't have anything of value, and we can—"

"Screw you."

"I wasn't going to put it *that* way, exactly—"

"God." She cut him off with a disbelieving glare. "You really don't trust me?"

If she *was* playing him, she was damn good at it.

That was fine. He could play with the best of 'em. "With my heart? Oh, you're going to steal it for certain. And I'm okay with that. With my life? That I'm not so sure of."

Her eyes cooled from fiery anger to Arctic cold. "I thought we both understood what we wanted from each other. My bad. But I warned you that I've never done this before. Apparently, I really suck at it."

Embarrassment joined her anger, and this time, when she pushed, he let her go.

"Here's something you can trust." She walked to the door and opened it. "I'm out of the mood. Please leave."

That was when he noticed her limp. He'd seen it earlier when she'd slid off the bar stool and headed toward the stairs. But he'd been busy watching her ass and wondering what she was up to, and he hadn't processed it. Truth was, he hadn't really wanted to know about it then. Now he did. He wanted to know real bad.

"What's with the limp?"

"I asked you to leave."

"*Why* are you limping?" he asked in a tone that demanded an answer.

She stood stiffly, her grip tight on the doorknob. "I told you. I had a close call today."

Yeah. Yeah, she had said that. He'd pretty much ignored it, too, because he'd been so busy trying to get a read on her motivation. But now he had an unsettling idea of where that close call had been. "How close?"

She lowered her head on a long breath, and when she met his eyes again, she wasn't nearly as steady as she wanted him to think she was. "Close enough to need a few stitches. No big deal."

He walked up beside her, pried her hand off the knob, and closed the door. "Sounds like a very big deal. Let me see."

"Why? Because you think I'm lying about that, too?"

"Because I want to see."

Her dark eyes snapped with anger. He was pretty close to pissed now, too, and not altogether sure why. He gripped her upper arm, walked her over to the bed, and, cupping her shoulders, sat her down.

"Take 'em off." He nodded toward her pants.

She glared up at him.

"Don't get shy on me now. A few minutes ago, we were about to strip each other naked and do the big nasty."

"I repeat. You're an asshole."

He could glare, too, and evidently, he got his message across—either she'd take them off, or he would—because she finally unbuttoned her pants and undid the zipper.

"Where?" he asked.

"Right leg. My calf."

He knelt in front of her, propped her right foot on his thigh, and undid the laces on her boot. Once he'd gotten both it and the sock off, he helped her tug down her pants so her entire right leg was exposed, except for the white bandage wrapped around it from just below her knee to her ankle.

She said nothing during this process. She sat there, eyes pinched in anger. Her ugly shirt gaped open just above her navel, revealing a smooth wedge of olive skin between it and the band of her bikini panties. Flesh-colored. Practical. Sexy as hell without meaning to be.

A visual of him taking them off with his teeth shot through his mind and straight to his dick.

He dragged his attention back to her bandaged leg. "Lie down. Roll over."

"I'm not a damn dog."

He grinned. "True—you look more like a defiant bunny. So stop with the glares, and just do it."

She muttered something under her breath but hitched herself lengthwise on the bed, then rolled to her stomach.

He sat down beside her and carefully undid the gauze wrap, forcing his gaze away from her luscious ass. When he uncovered the wound, he swore.

A four-inch gash, ragged and mean and still seeping blood, ran down her calf. Clumsily made stitches bit into the raw flesh.

"What happened? And what quack stitched you up?" He laid his hand over the wound. It didn't appear to be infected. Her skin was only slightly warm to the touch, but it was clearly sore, because she winced as he continued his examination.

"An Army combat medic stitched it and field-dressed it for me," she said, as he carefully rewrapped the dressing. "He was too busy trying to save lives to worry about tidy stitches."

His anger and mistrust deflated on a long breath, and he realized just how weary he was. Of this country. Of this damn war.

He lay down beside her, not liking that he let her get to him. Crossing his hands beneath his head, he stared at the ceiling. For a long, long time, the fan spun overhead, and his thoughts spun out over how much he hated this place.

"You were there? At the school today?" he finally asked.

He'd heard about the ambush. Taliban fighters had opened fire on a group of children, specifically targeting the girls who dared go to school. The death toll was staggering. Inconceivable.

He felt her shift beside him, sensed her gaze on him. And he knew before he turned his head what he'd see on her face.

"They massacred them," she whispered through tears she couldn't hold back. "They killed those innocent children."

He'd survived this long by listening to his instincts. But even though he might be wrong in discounting them now, he gathered her in his arms and pulled her against him. He'd worry about lies and trust later.

Her tears fell, hot and wet against his shoulder, where they seeped through his shirt and dampened his skin. She was so tense she trembled. And for the first time in a very long time, he felt empathy. Not the sympathy he felt daily for the Afghan people who were besieged by this endless war, but compassion for a single, fragile soul.

A fragment of their conversation in the bar played back in his mind.

Because today I need human contact.
To remind you that you're human?

To remind me that humanity isn't dead . . . even in the midst of this inhumane war.

And what had been his sensitive response? *My room or yours?*

He closed his eyes in self-disgust and pulled her closer.

Was she who she said she was? Maybe yes, maybe no. And maybe he'd turned into a callous, cynical bastard who no longer knew how to trust.

Most likely, he'd simply lost it. Everything about her skewed his judgment, and he knew he should be careful. But right now, he didn't give a damn about caution. He just cared about comforting her as she cried.

3

The room was dark when he woke up. The power must have gone out again—nothing new in Kabul—because the bedside lamps were dark and the overhead fan was still. Along with the heat, random scents and sounds drifted in through the open window. A slim band of moonlight snuck in through the darkness, painting pale shadows on the walls, on his boot tips at the end of the bed, on her arm draped across his chest.

His internal clock told him it was the middle of the night, and he was still holding Talia Levine. Him in his dusty fatigues, her half dressed and sweet-smelling, her breathing deep and slow.

He dragged a hand across his jaw. How, in this shit-hole country where the softest thing he ever encountered was the powdery dust that stung his eyes every day, had he ended up in a bed with her soft, warm body nestled against him?

She stirred and snuggled closer in her sleep, and he quit asking questions. He indulged in her heat and her softness and her ill-advised trust in him. A stranger who could have robbed her, raped her, or just badgered her to death with his dogged disbelief in her story. And it made him wonder. Could a woman who was capable of such trust also be capable of a deceitful game he'd been certain she was playing?

In his world, anything was possible. Case in point: he'd just slept with the woman, and he'd laid nothing but an altruistic hand on her. Mark *that* one down in the record books.

It hadn't been easy, either. Especially when the rutting-bull part of his brain kept coming up with excellent reasons to just take her.

He breathed deep, pressed the heel of his hand against his swollen dick to relieve a little pressure — and realized he wasn't the only one awake.

He didn't say anything, hoping she'd go back to sleep so he could slip away before the rutting bull got the upper hand. But when it became clear that wasn't happening, he knew he couldn't dodge the bullet any longer.

"You doing okay?" he whispered into a night that had suddenly shifted from self-assessment to acute awareness.

She rolled onto her back and out of his arms, and damn if he didn't feel a chill despite the still, dry heat of the night.

"I'm fine." She didn't sound fine. "Considering I keep managing to make a fool of myself."

It didn't take a psychic to know where this was

going, but he wasn't touching it. She was embarrassed that she'd picked him up and then botched their hookup by crying—an act she thought was weak.

"I don't cry," she announced, with an edge in her voice that spoke of defensiveness and anger but, most of all, mortification.

"You had good reason." It came out before he could stop himself.

She hiked up on an elbow and looked down at him. In the shadowy darkness, he could make out every contour of her delicately sculpted face. The curve of her full lower lip. The thick, satiny tail of the black braid lying against her neck.

"You don't understand. I. Don't. Cry." She repeated it emphatically but without the anger this time. This time, there was something in her tone that told him flat out: she'd had reason to cry many times in her life, but she considered giving in to that self-indulgence inexcusable.

"Everyone cries, Talia. Not everyone gets caught."

There'd been a time when he'd been too broken to be ashamed of his tears. He'd watched his team die in an ambush not far from here. And later he'd listened in painful disbelief as his best friend sold out not only himself but him and Coop, too.

Less-than-honorable discharge.

It was pure bullshit. Stink-to-high-heaven bullshit. But his world as he'd known it was suddenly gone with the slam of a military judge's gavel. A world he'd bled for and would have died for. And now he was an outcast in that world.

He breathed deep. No good would come from mourning everything he'd lost that day. And no good would come from getting soft over a woman he'd cast as Mata Hari less than four hours ago.

"I should go," he said abruptly. He didn't like the turn his thoughts had taken.

He sat up and swung his feet to the floor in one quick motion. He hadn't yet gathered the where-withal to get up and walk out the door when her slender fingers touched his arm and her soft whisper stopped him.

"You should stay."

Nothing real should feel this good. And yet as he held his weight on his elbows above her, with nothing but perspiration and heat between their naked bodies, he knew this was as real as it got.

You should stay.

Desire and need shot straight to his core with those three words. She'd meant it. And to make sure he knew it, she'd sat up and tugged his shirt over his head. He was already gone by then. Already twisting around to return the favor.

Somehow, despite their frantic rush, they man-aged to get rid of their clothes without hurting each other and fell naked together on the bed.

He didn't ask if she was sure. The way her mouth

tracked hot, brazen kisses across his skin, the way her lithe and toned body moved against him, was all the answer he needed.

Could he trust her? Did she lie? He didn't know. Didn't care. Not now, as he moved over her, kissed her deeply, and pumped his hips against hers, so hot and ready for her all he could think about was sliding inside her.

She ran greedy hands over his shoulders, down his back, fingers splayed, as if to touch as much of him as fast as she could. "Please."

The single word fractured his lust-crazed mind and stopped him from pushing into her.

He pulled away from her soft, swollen lips and groaned. "Condoms. I don't have any condoms."

She twisted to the left, reached into a drawer of the bedside table, and produced the one thing he'd have given a year's pay for.

He didn't want to know why she had it. He just wanted to be inside her. Now.

She pushed him onto his back, rose to her knees, and began unwrapping it. Then she straddled him, took him in her hands, and rolled on the protection.

He almost came before she had him suited up. If he didn't slow things down, this was going to be over before he could beg for mercy. And he didn't want it over. Not when they'd barely gotten started. Not when everywhere he touched her—with his hands, with his mouth—came alive like a lightning storm.

He didn't ask if he could unbraid her hair. He'd wanted to get his hands in it since the first time he'd seen her. And he languished in the feel of it as he combed it out with his fingers, freeing thick, silken strands to fall loose around her face.

He knotted the lush mass of it in his hands and tugged her toward him. He wanted her mouth. Needed her mouth, and her tongue, and took them both without apology. Then he gave his own as she matched his hunger and shot them to another level of urgency.

He sat up abruptly, lifted her to her knees, and took a firm, perfect breast in his mouth. He swirled his tongue around her turgid nipple, sucked until she arched against him. When she cried out, he was afraid he'd gone too far and hurt her.

"I'm sorry." He kissed the stiff peak of her nipple in apology.

She cupped his head and pulled him back against her, her thick hair making a curtain that cocooned them in desire. "More."

Oh, God.

The frayed rope holding him together snapped. He lifted her, tossed her onto her back, and covered her. Out of control with need, he hooked her left leg behind his knee and tipped her hips up toward him. She reached between them, gripping him in ravenous hands, and guided him home.

It was as much hell as heaven when her breath escaped in gasps and he pumped into her. Rough. Raw. Deep and hard, pushing them both up the bed with each powerful stroke. On his third thrust, she came with a muffled cry that triggered his own blistering release. He exploded with breath-stealing pleasure, aware only of how tightly she gloved him, how liquid and spent she felt beneath him, and how consumed he was in the raw honesty of her release.

4

He slept like a stone, like a man who was physically drained and sexually spent. It would be light soon, and Talia still had tasks to complete. Yet she couldn't get herself to do anything but lie here in this nest they'd made of passion and deception and tangled sheets.

She'd never thought of herself as sexual, had never anticipated that a man could make her lose control as she had with him. He was an assignment. A duty. She had no reason to feel shame that she'd let him use her body. Her mission was vital, and sacrifices had to be made.

Yet she did feel shame. Shame at the weakness that made her feel guilty for using him. Shame that his tender attention had made her forget about the school shooting. And shame because she had enjoyed him and his body and his desire, and nothing about what they'd done felt remotely like a sacrifice.

She rolled onto her side so she could see him. He lay on his back, naked and beautiful. Undeniably a warrior, even in sleep.

He'd flung an arm up over his head, revealing a tattoo on the inside of his right forearm: a helmet bearing the letters *RIP* hung over the tip of a rifle barrel supported by a pair of worn combat boots. A tribute to his brothers in arms who had died in battle.

Like her, he was no stranger to war or to loss. And she had no business thinking about that. Or about guilt. This scene had played out thousands of times in hundreds of wars. Two strangers in a war-torn country, reaching out for human companionship. Needing something to make them feel alive when their lives could be taken in a heartbeat. By a sniper's bullet, by artillery fire.

By a betrayal that ripped their world in half.

The thought finally jolted her back to her mission.

As the night teetered on the edge of daybreak, she slipped silently out of bed, careful not to jar the mattress. She felt around under the bedside table until she located the radio-frequency identification tag she'd taped to the bottom of the drawer and tugged it free. She'd already memorized the creaking spots on the old floor and avoided them as she tiptoed around the bed and searched for his clothes.

A quick glance over her shoulder assured her he was still sleeping as she found his pants and dug his phone out of a hip pocket. Checking again to make certain he hadn't awakened, she removed the back cover of the phone and piggybacked the RFID tag to the battery. Cell-phone location via GPS monitoring alone, especially in Kabul, wasn't going to do the job. The RFID tag would make it possible to track his phone and locate precisely where he was from up to a quarter of a mile away.

After quickly returning the phone to his pocket, she laid the pants on the floor where she'd found them and headed for the bathroom. If he woke now and found her up, he'd think nothing of it.

A few minutes later, she opened the bathroom door. He was still sleeping. She breathed deep and had started gathering her own clothes when two strong hands gripped her by her hips and pulled her back into bed.

"You're very busy," he murmured, nipping at her ear when he'd dragged her close against him, curling spoonlike behind her. His erection pressed hot and hard against her back.

"A girl's got . . . to . . . oh, God . . . work to . . . eat," she managed around her rapidly beating heart, as he cupped her breast with one hand and coaxed her legs apart with the other.

Then she quit thinking and just felt—the expert strokes of his fingers against her swollen flesh, the boldness of his domination, until finally he rolled her to her back, slid down the bed, and tilted her hips to his mouth.

"Speaking of eating," he murmured. Then, with his busy, busy tongue and erotic and thorough suction, he drove her beyond the ability to do anything but writhe in pleasure, until she came with a soft cry.

Boneless, delirious with satisfaction, she lay catching her breath and riding the aftershocks.

"That," he whispered, kissing his way up her body, "was to make up for my quick trigger earlier."

She pushed out an exhausted laugh. "Apology . . . accepted."

"Did I break you?"

An amused male voice woke her as a gentle, callused hand skimmed along her bare hip.

Talia opened her eyes and saw him standing by the bed, smiling.

He appeared to be fresh out of the shower; his only nod toward modesty was a towel wrapped low on his hips.

She took a leisurely visual stroll up the length of his beautifully honed body to his intriguing face, his smiling green eyes, and back to the tenting towel.

"I can't believe I fell asleep again."

"I thought you'd passed out."

She yawned and stretched languorously. "You don't have to sound so smug."

"Oh, I think I do. I think I ruined you." He leaned down and pressed a kiss against her lips, then straightened and started getting dressed. "Your leg okay? We didn't rip any stitches, did we?"

"My leg is fine."

She watched him dress in silence. Couldn't help but watch him. She'd learned his body well in the dark. A body that gave as well as took pleasure to extremes and was as pleasing to see as it was to touch. And taste . . .

And that was a train she had to derail.

She needed to seal the deal. To find out if he was corruptible and, if not, make certain he'd begun to trust her. Enough to keep coming back.

"You were right," she said, sounding guilty with little effort, because she did feel guilt. And something more that she'd never planned for and didn't want to dwell on. When he looked back over a broad, bare shoulder, she lowered her gaze to the sheet she'd drawn over her breasts. "I do want something from you."

He chuckled. "Sweetheart, I don't think I have any more to give. At least, not right now." Then he pretended surprise, a hard glint in his eyes. "But we're not talking about sex anymore, are we?"

"For God's sake, it's nothing sinister. Not like I want state secrets or anything." Only it was.

He sat on a side chair, tugged on his boots, then finally lifted his head, waiting.

"I want to go on a mission with you."

His slow smile wasn't very pleasant. "You can't seriously think that's going to happen?"

No, she didn't. But it had been worth a try. "I've been covering combat zones for years. Mostly after the fact. I want to be there on an operation. In the front line as it goes down."

He reached for his T-shirt and pulled it over his head.

"You still don't believe me?" she asked when he didn't respond.

"It doesn't matter what I believe," he said, tucking and zipping.

"It matters to me." She sat up, dragging the sheet with her, and reached for her laptop. "Here. Look at this." She shoved the laptop toward him after booting it up and finding the file she wanted him to see.

He glanced from the laptop to her face and shook his head. "I've got to get going."

"Please," she begged. "Just look at it. It won't take long for you to get the message. I'm not a danger to you. I'm not a threat to anyone."

That brought a reluctant smile. "Trust me, you *are* a threat. To my peace of mind. I'm going to think about you all day. You know that, right? I'm going to be distracted, thinking about all the things I want to do to you." He leaned down to kiss her, and melting heat pooled between her legs.

She made herself pull away, then shoved the laptop into his chest with shaking hands. "It'll only take a minute."

He eyed her, eyed the laptop, and with forced patience sat down on the bed beside her and started reading, then scrolling through the articles—complete with photos of her and bylines and commentaries about how important her voice was in spreading the human side in her war stories.

He was quiet for a moment, then shut the laptop and set it on the table.

"Is that why you were at the school yesterday? You were writing a story?"

"I'll still write the story," she said, determined to do so. "But the question is, are you convinced now that I am who I say I am?"

He sat for a moment longer before looking at her. "Gettin' there."

"That's something, I guess."

His eyes and his voice changed when he lifted his hand and ran a single finger along the curve of her bare shoulder. "What do you say we continue this discussion tonight?"

She clutched the sheet tighter around her breasts, feeling inexplicably vulnerable instead of victorious. "Tonight," she agreed, sounding way too breathless and way too pleased.

Yes, she was pleased he'd started to trust her. Yes, she was pleased he wanted to see her again. It was what she'd planned, but planning suddenly took a backseat to anticipation and arousal as he leaned into her, knotted a hand in her hair, and pulled her toward him for a long, searing kiss.

"What you do to me," he murmured. After a deep, searching look, he stood and walked to the door. "I'm gone. While I still have the upper hand over my better judgment. Oh, and about that ride-along?" He swung open the door and looked back over his shoulder. "It's not going to happen. Never. End of discussion." He left, shutting the door firmly behind him.

She lay back down and stared at the ceiling, torn

between self-disgust and a humming physical arousal. She'd done what she'd set out to do. She'd made contact. She'd successfully engaged her target. She'd never really expected him to agree to let her go on a ride-along. She only suggested that to cement her cover—the eager journalist, willing to do anything to get her story.

So, yes. Everything was going as planned.

Everything but this disconcerting skip in her heartbeat that had nothing to do with nerves and everything to do with him as a man, not an assignment.

Ashamed suddenly and determined to move past these unexpected feelings of exposure, she slipped out of bed. After making certain that he was out of the hall and on his way, she dug into the wardrobe and carefully removed a loosened board from the wardrobe's base. She pulled out the SAT phone she'd hidden there and punched in a number only she had access to.

"The RFID tag is planted," she told her unit commander when he answered. "If he meets with the target, we'll know exactly where they are."

"We're already receiving a signal. Good work. And you, Talia?" he asked after a telling pause. "You are all right?"

His concern rang hollow. He'd asked her to prostitute herself for this mission if necessary, something he'd never asked of her before. And he'd known she would, no matter what it cost her. He'd known she would do it to get retribution for those who had been murdered.

"I'm fine. I'll notify you when I'm certain he is en route to the target. It may be several days, but I will know when he makes his next move."

"You've done well. We don't undervalue the sacrifice you have made," he added quietly.

She closed her eyes, reminded herself why she was here.

"In the meantime, the tracker alone may not be enough to accomplish the mission. Keep your eyes and ears open for other leads."

"Of course."

"Be careful, but remember, we're counting on you." He disconnected.

She stayed on her knees, stared at the phone a moment longer, then tucked it back into its hiding place. Many people were counting on her. Her country was counting on her. And no matter what transpired, no matter what she had to do to complete her mission, she would not let them down.

She was Mossad, a member of the Israeli Special Forces. She must follow orders. There was no choice. She could *not* let them down.

5

Bobby fished his battle-worn jack of spades from his breast pocket, kissed it for luck, and tucked it away before he climbed into the Jeep's shotgun seat and they headed out on patrol.

He'd carried the card since the One-Eyed Jacks unit had been formed all those years ago. All the guys had. Now all but three of them were dead. He had no idea where Brown and Cooper hung their hats these days. Didn't care. Once they'd been best friends. Pretty boy Cooper. Mike Primetime Brown. The betrayal still hurt—even more than the leg he'd broken when their chopper had gone down. Now it only ached in the cold or if he'd been on it too long. Or if he thought about Brown.

Jaw clenched, he stared out the window of the Jeep he had helped armor with the skins of a decommissioned Humvee. Soon the base was several miles behind them, and they were rumbling over the rough terrain well outside of Kabul. It was hot, it was dusty, and sweat ran down his face and beneath his Kevlar

vest. A pair of sand and brown camo binoculars hung
around his neck; an M4 rifle lay across his thighs.
The other squad members were a little less traditional
with their choice of weaponry.

The men in the Fargis Group had all been through
the wars playing on Uncle's team. Now that they were
out from under military rule, they tended to carry
oddball weapons that worked for them. Gomez and
Wagoner, who occupied the Jeep's backseat, were
perfect examples.

"You can never bring too much ammo or big
enough guns to a fight," was Gomez's motto. Today
he lugged a heavily modified M14 that could hit hard
at long distances.

Wagoner loved his ancient and battered H&K G3,
even though the trigger pull was like trying to open
a barn door. "As long as it goes *bang* when I want it
to, that's good enough for me," he'd said when Bobby
had taken one look at the gun and said, "What the
hell?"

Two up-armored Humvees, each with a crew
of four, had come along for the sightseeing expedition, sandwiching the Jeep between them. Both were
equipped with belt-fed automatic grenade launch-
ers in roof-mounted armored cupolas. The big guns
might be relics of the Cold War, but they were hard-
core, and Bobby was damn glad for these men and
their expertise with this particular type of fire power.
If they found their quarry today, they were going to
need it.

A ragtag group of Taliban had been playing havoc with the U.S. military's supply lines. Most likely, they were the same bastards who had attacked the school yesterday. Fargis had been tasked with finding and taking them out. That was why they'd ventured deep into Taliban country today and were on the hunt—and most likely being hunted.

So now was really not the time to be thinking about Talia Levine.

Yet there she was, filling his head, screwing with his mind. Small, perfect breasts. Hips nicely rounded but still slim. Skin so soft it defied description. A libido fueled by fire and a wanton abandon that was as big of a turn-on as the silk of her hair that he loved to lose his hands in.

Only after he'd left her bed this morning had he been capable of getting his head on halfway straight and remembering what had made him wary of her in the first place.

When, he wondered, as he raised the binocs to search a ridge ninety meters away, had he stopped feeling suspicious about her?

So he'd seen and read the articles on her laptop. So she'd provided "facts" that said she was who she said she was. A cover story could be easily faked, especially using her own equipment.

Now, however, he wanted to believe her. Now, after last night. Which made him an idiot to the nth degree.

The Jeep bounced over a crater-sized hole, and he

lowered his binocs. Still thinking, still off his game. If one of his teammates came to him with a story about a beautiful woman, a few tears, great sex, and a request to ride along on a patrol, he'd have told him to wake up and smell the honey trap.

And what happened last night was textbook honey trap. Straight out of the *Spy for Hire Handbook*. The operative picks up a beautiful woman in a bar, surprised that she asks him to come back to her room so easily. In the morning, she's vanished, along with important documents, and the cell phone is missing . . .

Okay, so she wasn't gone, and neither was his phone. That hadn't stopped him from heading straight for the Fargis field HQ and tapping a buddy in the intelligence office before he'd set out on patrol this morning.

"Run this name up every flagpole and back down again. No hit is too small, okay? And no, I'm not going to tell you why. I'm calling in a favor."

P. J. Granger, an experienced operative and all-around good guy, had squinted up at him from his bank of computers. "I didn't know I owed you any favors."

"You will if you hang around me long enough."

"Oh, well, in that case," Granger had muttered.

Bobby had grinned. "And let's keep this between the two of us."

"Never figured you'd want it any other way. When do you need it?"

Bobby had given him a look.

"Yesterday. Got it. You trigger pullers sure know how to pick your moments."

Bobby had clapped Granger's shoulder. "Thanks, bud. I'll pick it up when we're back from patrol."

"And you'll come bearing?"

"A big smile of gratitude?"

"Cheap ass." With a grumble, Granger had turned back to his keyboards.

"Okay, a six-pack," Bobby had promised, sweetening the pot.

"There ya go."

One way or another, he was going to get the truth about Talia Levine.

When they came in from an uneventful patrol later that day, doused in dust and sweat and empty-handed, Bobby cut a beeline straight for the intel shack.

Without even looking up, Granger held a manila envelope in the air.

"Thanks, bud. Knew you'd come through." Bobby snatched the packet, handed Granger a scribbled IOU for the six-pack, and headed out the door to the sound of Granger's curses.

When someone called his name, he looked across the compound and spotted his immediate supervisor walking toward him. He bounded down the steps and walked out to meet him.

Wes Bridgedale, a combat veteran of both the Iraq and Afghanistan wars, was a well-respected leader among the men. Bridgedale had turned in his Army uniform two years ago because he'd felt betrayed by an administration that attempted to micromanage the military from behind pristine Washington desks instead of letting the generals in the field make the calls.

If it hadn't been for Bridgedale, who'd thought he'd gotten a raw deal from the Army, Bobby wouldn't be working for Fargis now.

"Sir." While Bobby didn't salute, he showed Bridgedale the respect his position in the company warranted. They might no longer be in uniform, but members of the Fargis Group still adhered to the U.S. military's chain of command as their model.

"What's the latest on al-Attar?" Bridgedale asked.

"I wish I knew, sir."

A few months ago, intel had come down the pike that Mohammed al-Attar was hiding out in or near Kabul after fleeing Israel to escape retaliation from Mossad, Israel's elite Spec Ops unit, for bombings that had killed innocent citizens. Fargis had been tasked with getting the goods on al-Attar, and Bobby had been designated the leader of the team of operatives who would make it happen.

Al-Attar was an important get, because with the drawdown of U.S. troops on the horizon, Uncle needed more intel fast. The word on the streets was that al-Attar, a vicious rogue Hamas leader, had no love for the Taliban and was willing to provide information on the locations, numbers, and firepower of Taliban fighters in exchange for cold cash.

So Bobby had sent out feelers, letting al-Attar know he wanted to make contact. It hadn't been difficult to root him out, especially with Bobby playing the part of the disgruntled and disgraced U.S. Army Special Forces who'd been cut loose from the military for dishonorable acts. Not much of a stretch, he thought grimly.

Since that first contact, Bobby had been working al-Attar for information. The Hamas leader was a gold mine of intel, but he was slow about dishing it out. So Bobby was happy as hell when Uncle Sam had recently decided to get the Hamas war chief in custody, where they could mine the scumbag for every piece of information they could dig out of him.

The problem was, al-Attar had gone to ground.

"I haven't heard from him in almost two weeks," he told Bridgedale now. "Last time I met with him, he'd finally agreed that our next meet would be at his secret headquarters instead of some random coffee shop. I was pumped. I've been trying to get access to his hiding spot from the beginning. Maybe he got cold feet. Maybe he was just blowing smoke up my ass. But I don't think so."

"I'm getting some heat from up top," Bridgedale said. "They want him pulled in before he gets antsy and heads for Pakistan, where we'll never get access to him again."

"I'm as frustrated as you are," Bobby said. Al-Attar was too valuable a resource to lose. "I could put out more feelers, but I'm afraid he'll think I'm too eager and question his decision to take me into his confidence."

"So what's your plan?"

"Wait him out," Bobby said. "He's going to be hungry for cash again soon. That's our ace in the hole. Al-Attar knows that if he wants money in exchange for ratting out his Taliban enemies, he has to keep in touch with me."

"All right," Bridgedale said with a resigned look. "You know what you're doing. And you know what to do when he next makes contact. Let's hope for everyone's sake that he does it soon."

"Yes, sir."

"Looks like you've had a long day, son," Bridgedale said, taking in Bobby's sweat-soaked shirt and dirt-streaked face. "Get out of here. Call it a day."

"Got a cold one waiting for me," Bobby said with a grin, and headed toward the motor pool.

He managed to hitch a ride on a transport truck that took him back to the antiquated hotel where Fargis put up the senior operatives.

He tossed the manila envelope onto the small bed in the small room and snagged a beer from the small fridge he'd bought for a *small* fortune from a local vendor. Groaning in pleasure when the first deep swallow was ice-cold, he set the bottle on the nightstand. As much as he wanted to read the intel on Talia, he wanted a shower more.

As usual, the water was lukewarm, but at least it was running, and the pressure didn't give out until he'd scrubbed the dirt away. After wrapping a towel around his hips, he tracked water across the floor and grabbed his beer. Then he lay back against stacked pillows and opened the envelope.

Ten minutes later, he decided that his suspicion meter needed some serious tweaking. Grim-faced, he whipped off the towel and started getting dressed.

6

Talia watched Taggart walk into the bar, glance around until he spotted her, then walk straight in her direction. He looked relentlessly sexy in khaki pants and a snug black T-shirt that emphasized how huge his biceps were. He also looked mad, and he looked mean. A thick knot tightened in her stomach. Had he somehow found her out? Maybe he'd found the tag she'd planted in his phone?

She forced a smile and held back a twinge of panic. "Now, *there's* a scowl that tells a story. Bad day?" she asked when he pulled out a bar stool and signaled the bartender for his usual.

"You were born in the U.S. New York City, specifically," he began without preamble, and the knot in her stomach tugged a little tighter.

She'd anticipated that he'd go digging. The question was, how deep? Had her cover held up?

"Your Israeli parents—a history professor and a linguistics professor—were quite affluent and emigrated to the States thirty years ago to escape the chaos of the

Israel-Palestine conflict." He stopped when his drink arrived, took a sip, and turned back to her.

"A-plus for research work," she said, holding on to her calm by a thread. "Which one of us gets the gold star?"

"Drink your wine. I'm not finished yet. You were an only child and were ten when your parents moved to D.C. After you graduated from high school, you left for Israel and attended university in Tel Aviv."

"Because I wanted to become more familiar with my Israeli roots," she said, careful not to sound defensive.

"You studied journalism and photography, and once you started working, you made a big name for yourself."

"I believe that's what I've been trying to tell you."

"So big," he continued after another sip of whiskey, "that you've won a ton of awards and are on every major news publication's speed dial. When they need a heavy hitter to cover a war story, they call you."

"Maybe half a ton of awards," she said, attempting to defuse the tension with humor. Everything he said was true—and provided an excellent cover that had held up for several Mossad operations. "At the risk of total redundancy, I *did* try to tell you."

"Yeah," he said with a long, appraising stare, "you did."

"So . . . that was an apology?" She made herself hold his gaze.

He scratched his jaw, his hard eyes still on her face,

then reluctantly nodded. "Yeah. That was an apology."

She lifted an eyebrow to disguise her deep relief. "So, then, what's with the mad-dog glare?"

"That's me being ticked with myself for giving you such a hard time."

She turned back to her wine before she could blurt out something stupid. Like a confession. "So now you know it all."

"So it would seem," he agreed.

Yes, he knew it all—except for two vitally important pieces of information that would cause him to hate her. She was a Mossad agent using her journalism credits as cover. And she was using *him* to get to Mohammed al-Attar, the Hamas terrorist who had massacred so many of her people.

She pushed down the recurring urge to feel guilty. She wasn't sorry that he would unknowingly lead her to al-Attar; there would be justice then. She wouldn't be the one to pull the trigger, but she would facilitate al-Attar's death. She felt nothing but satisfaction that this monster would soon pay for what he'd done.

What she *would* be sorry for, she admitted as she silently sipped her wine, was the hatred Taggart would feel toward her if he ever found out she'd deceived him.

"How about we go upstairs?" he said, running the tip of his index finger along her arm and making her shiver. "I'll show you just how sorry I am."

His wicked grin was pure temptation, and the

memory of last night fired through her erogenous zones. She'd follow him up those stairs no matter what the reason. No matter what the cost.

"Dinner? I can't go out like this," Talia protested when Taggart asked her to go out with him several days later. "I've been out in the field all day. I haven't even been up to my room yet. I need a shower and clean clothes."

"Then go. I'll wait. I want to take you somewhere special. Someplace we can get a real meal," he insisted, and that was the end of the discussion—almost.

His eyes were never hard or cold when he looked at her now. They'd softened to warm and intimate when he reached out and tucked a strand of hair behind her ear. "Wear your hair down for me."

His voice compounded the sexual awareness. Gruff and gritty and sounding very much as he did every night in her bed, where they'd spent the last six nights together. He loved her hair. She'd even teased him about having a fetish for it. He'd agreed without remorse that he loved burying his hands in it. Loved to fill those callused but oh-so-giving hands with it, then tug her down to kiss him. Loved the feel of it trailing over his body.

And she'd loved the way he groaned in deep, almost primal pleasure, the way he made her moan. One particular memory was so visual she got lost in it. And it frightened her to realize this man had such a hold on her.

"Talia?"

"Yes," she said breathlessly, and found his hungry eyes focused on hers.

He knew. He'd been there, fantasizing right along with her. "You were going to shower?"

"Right." She eased off the bar stool, working hard to appear collected. "Give me fifteen."

Then she headed up the stairs to her room, telling herself the same thing she did every day. There was nothing wrong, just because Bobby Taggart knew how to engage her libido. With a word. With a look. With a touch.

Nothing wrong with the weakness in her knees, either, or with the flush of heat surging through her body and the sweet gnawing ache that gripped her when she thought of him. Nothing wrong with spending as much of each day and all of her nights with him.

He was a striking man. A battle-hardened warrior yet a generous and giving lover. The contrasts were fascinating, and she wasn't immune to the sheer excitement of being around him.

Going into this, she'd known she might have to seduce him.

What she hadn't been prepared for was that he hadn't been the only one seduced.

She wore her hair down, as he'd asked, telling herself it was all part of the game. She was so used to braiding it immediately after her shower that when she finished brushing it and had taken the time to look in the mirror, she'd been shocked at how long it had gotten. If she'd been wearing a bra, the ends would have hit several inches below it.

As thick as it was, it was also arrow-straight, so it didn't take long to dry in this heat. Still, it was a little damp beneath the delicate white shawl she'd chosen to wear over a long, lightweight teal slip dress. It was her standard packs-like-a-dream, ready-to-wear-at-a-moment's-notice dress. She'd dragged it across several continents in the event that she'd need to dress for a dinner with some muckety-muck who could help her with a story. Or with a mission.

Tonight she found herself wishing she had a new dress. One she'd never worn before and had bought just for him. Which was as foolish as the skip of her heartbeat when Taggart spotted her walking down the stairs.

"Look at you." He swallowed hard, then walked straight to her. "If you're wondering, I like this way better than your ugly shirts."

"And if you're wondering," she said, attempting to keep her voice steady behind her smile, "I still have time to change back into one of them."

"Yeah." He touched a hand to the small of her back and ushered her toward the door. "Like that's going to happen."

"Where is this restaurant?" she asked after they'd walked a couple of blocks.

"Not far now." He steered her into a lantern-lit

alley and in the pale evening light, with the lanterns flickering like fireflies, it actually looked pretty. Almost magical—a rarity in Kabul. Although the night was warm, a chill of awareness feathered down her spine when he reached for her hand and entwined his fingers with hers.

She didn't even think about resisting. She thought about both the strength and the gentleness in his long, strong fingers. About how small and protected her hand felt surrounded by his. And about how wonderfully easy this moment was, when she should be much more alert for signs of trouble.

"It's been a while since I held hands with a woman." He grinned down at her. "In fact, the last woman's hand I held was probably my mother's."

She glanced up at him. "That long?"

"Actually, it was just last year, when I went home for a quick visit. She still won't let me cross busy streets by myself."

She smiled down at her feet as they walked, too amused, too charmed, too careless. And far too comfortable after only a few days and nights spent with him. "And he's a comedian, too," she managed.

He chuckled and squeezed her hand. "Too?"

What the hell. She was going to let herself play. She never got nights like this; she never met men like him. And she'd forgotten how delightfully heady a man's interest could be.

"Fish all you want," she teased, "but you're not going to get a compliment from me."

He stopped and, with their hands still linked, grinned down at her. "Was I fishing?"

"I recognize bait when it's dangled in front of me."

"Ah. And if you *were* biting?" he asked with mischief in his eyes. "What kind of a compliment would I catch on this fishing expedition?"

She made a show of zipping her lips.

"Oh, woman, did you pick the wrong guy. I never back away from a challenge."

It was fun, this flirty and nonsensical back-and-forth between them. And she firmly blocked rising feelings of guilt for enjoying his company too much and for deceiving him in the process.

"Still not talking?"

She remained stubbornly silent.

"Maybe I need better bait."

Very slowly, he backed her up against a wall that was still warm from the heat of the sun. Warmer still when he leaned into her, freed his hand from hers, and drew her against him. Full lips brushed lightly against hers, and when she attempted to open her mouth to protest, he slipped his tongue inside and convinced her it was exactly the thing she wanted. Her knees were rubbery when he pulled away, looking very pleased with himself.

"Was that it?" His silky whisper was mere inches from her lips. His eyes were slumberous and sexy. "Were you going to compliment me on my kisses?"

She opened her mouth again, shut it, tried to pull

her thoughts together around her racing heart and the liquid heat between her thighs.

He laughed, then tugged her away from the wall. "I'll take that as a yes."

Draping his arm casually over her shoulders, he started walking again.

What kind of man was this? He'd seen the savagery of war and yet voluntarily put his life on the line in a part of the world where life had little value. He carried a well-worn playing card to honor his fallen brothers. Despite being dishonored by his own country, he still had the capability to trust someone.

And he was still capable of whimsy and of stealing kisses.

He had more than enough reasons to be bitter, jaded, and angry at life. Yet he wasn't.

He would be, she reminded herself, breaking the spell. When she was through with him, he would be all of those things.

She was thankful when they reached the restaurant before she had more time to anguish over her assignment. And after spending several enjoyable hours in a place where the walls were covered with beautiful Afghan carpets and the doors were magnificently carved works of art, where they'd relaxed on colorful cushions and eaten a delicious meal from low tables, they walked hand in hand again back to her hotel.

This time, when she took him to her bed, she took him there with a single-minded purpose that had nothing to do with deceit and missions and calcula-tion. She took him to bed to please him. To be with him. To enjoy the wonder he brought to her body and to her heart, which had been numb for so long.

Afterward, when he slept, she lay awake listening to him breathe, absorbing the heat radiating from his body, wishing they could lock themselves away here and never leave.

But there could never be more than this between them. It was idiotic even to dream that somehow, some way, there could be more. Because after she got what she needed, she would leave him—and what was left of her heart would be numb once more.

7

An irritating buzz woke Bobby from a deep sleep. The next buzz had him shooting straight up in bed. He'd left his phone on the bedside table, and the screen alerted him to an incoming text.

Talia stirred sleepily beside him. "What—"

"Shh," he whispered, silencing the phone. "Go back to sleep."

Then he slipped out of bed and walked to the window, hoping to catch a little night air to wake him up. He checked the time—2:17 a.m.—before pressing the key to accept the text.

"Game on. Fifteen minutes." The text went on to name two cross streets as his destination.

Al-Attar's coded message told Bobby that he wanted to meet. Finally. This was it. The bastard liked to play games, but Bobby had a gut feeling that this was the real event. It was significant that al-Attar had called a zero-dark-thirty meeting out of nowhere. And if he was at the location suggested by the cross streets, al-Attar had been under his nose all along. What a kick in the ass.

He deleted the text and set his mind to what would happen next. They were finally going to nab this bastard and his thugs and put him out of business. Bobby just hoped he wasn't heading into a trap.

He glanced at Talia, her black hair spilling across the pillow. No matter what happened, he would make it back to the best thing that had ever happened to him.

The thought hit him like a tank. Then it backed up and rolled over him again.

The best thing that had ever happened to him.

Shit. He dragged a hand over his head, wanting to deny it. But there it was. Unfiltered and as real as daylight.

When in holy hell had *that* happened? *How* had it happened? He'd only spent seven days with her—most of them involving wild, delirious sex—and he was already thinking long term?

He went into the bathroom, turned on the cold-water faucet, and splashed the sleep from his eyes. Then he faced himself in the mirror.

This was so not happening. Falling in lust was one thing, but falling in love? In a week? No freakin' way.

But with the initial shock ebbing, after he'd gathered his clothes from the floor and dressed in the dark, the idea didn't feel as unbelievable.

In fact, he kind of liked the way it fit. Maybe it was time he had something good in his life. Something like a woman who entertained him with her wit, engaged him intellectually, and made him remember a part of himself he thought he'd lost in the murky fog of year after year of war.

"Come back to bed," Talia whispered, in that husky *I'll do anything you want* voice. And he damn near dived back in with her.

"I've got to go out for a while," he said softly, hating that he had to leave her. Hating it a lot.

"But it's the middle of the night," she said sleepily.

"It's important, or I wouldn't be going."

With a soft groan, she rolled over and checked the time on her phone. "Good God." She turned back to look at him. "So important it can't wait until morning?"

"Yeah," he said. "It's something I've been trying to tie up and get out from under for a long time."

Her brow furrowed, and she started to rise, but he leaned down and pressed a kiss to her forehead, then smoothed her hair away from her face.

"Don't get up, babe. Just go back to sleep. Everything's okay."

God, she was beautiful, her eyes now clear and focused on him, her gaze filled with concern, with worry for him. *Best thing that had ever happened to him.*

"Everything's going to be okay," he reassured her again.

"Bobby . . . I . . . Bobby—" Her voice caught on a short breath, and she reached out and cupped the back of his head, drawing him into a sweet, desperate kiss. Her mouth opened over his, her other hand coming up to hold him close, as if she couldn't get enough, as if she'd never get enough.

"Hey. Hey," he whispered, breaking off the kiss when he touched her face and felt tears. "What's this? What's going on?"

She shook her head and got herself back under control. "I don't know. I don't wake up well, I guess."

When she smiled for him, he kissed her again and felt a deep, urgent need to get back to her as fast as he could. "I'll be back before sunrise. Save my place, okay?"

This time, she managed some sass. "Well, I *was* expecting Habib around five . . ."

A mental picture of the ancient Afghan man who hung around the bar and bummed smokes made him chuckle. "Tell him hello for me. And make sure he drags his bony ass out of here before I get back."

"Be safe," she said, her eyes imploring.

"I always am," he promised, and after stuffing his phone into his pocket, he took off.

Talia fought back tears as the knot in her stomach became a wrenching ache. This was the moment she'd waited for. And the moment she'd begun to dread.

God, she'd almost compromised the operation. She'd almost told him who she was and what would happen tonight.

Treason echoed through her mind like a death knell.

She was not a traitor. But she'd hoped so much to have more time with him.

Tonight all came down to one choice. Betray her country or betray Taggart.

She stared at the ceiling and made herself focus. This was what she'd worked for. The success of the mission had come down to the RFID tag she'd planted in his phone and her ability to get close enough to her target to read between the lines—which was exactly what she'd done.

Yeah. It's something I've been trying to tie up and get out from under for a long time.

She'd known what was going down the moment he'd said those words. Only one thing could provoke him to go out into the dark streets at this time of night. Mohammed al-Attar.

She forced herself to sit up, lowered her head to her hands, and reached deep for the strength to make the call. Finally, she stood, dragged her hair away from her face, and walked to the wardrobe.

The SAT phone felt ominously heavy in her hand as she dialed.

"Talia," her commander said before she could speak. "We see that he's on the move."

"Yes." She knew they'd been tracking his movements since she'd hidden the tag seven nights ago. "I believe this is the opportunity we have been waiting for."

"Believe? You are not certain?"

"As certain as I can be, yes."

"Good work," her commander said, then hesitated. "Talia . . . you are all right?"

She pinched her eyes to force away the tears. "Yes. Yes, I'm fine."

"I'll alert the team. They are ready for this. You know what to do now."

"Yes. I know what to do."

But first, she did something that shamed her, something that went against the service she'd pledged her life to uphold. She asked her commander something she had no right to ask. Something that would jeopardize everything that made her who she was.

Bobby shoved his hands into his pockets and walked at a fast clip down the darkened Kabul streets. He was oblivious to the beggar asleep in a pile of rags on the walkway. Didn't register the day-old scents of garbage and exhaust and unwashed bodies spilling out of windows and doors.

He focused on two things only: staying alive and finally getting access to al-Attar's secret den. The terrorist had had his uses, and those had kept him alive and free. But now al-Attar and his band had accommodations waiting for them at Gitmo, compliments of Fargis and Uncle Sam.

Bobby could have picked him up the last time they'd met. He hadn't done so because Uncle wanted to capture not only him and his minions but also his computers and files, all rich with intel. The only way to accomplish that was for Bobby to enter al-Attar's base of operations, which he'd never been able to do before. But the time had finally arrived.

"Should there not be trust between us, after all of the commerce we have successfully executed together?" Bobby had asked at their last meeting. "I grow weary of this game of hide-and-seek. It insults me. I can always take my money somewhere else."

Apparently, the veiled threat of losing his main source of revenue had made al-Attar reconsider, because he'd assured Bobby that their next meeting would take place at his headquarters.

Not even a stray dog moved on the street as Bobby approached the rendezvous spot. It made him a little itchy. Going into a meet with al-Attar unarmed went against all of his instincts. But those were al-Attar's rules, so, as always, he had nothing on him but his phone. Adrenaline pumped through his system, revving him up like a muscle car running on high-octane fuel. He wasn't Captain America, however, and he wasn't a cowboy. He would keep his head, and he wasn't going in completely alone. Before he'd hit the streets, he'd texted a coded message to his team leader, letting him know that the meet was finally on and giving him the street names so they could find him.

Apparently, he'd walked a little faster than he'd thought, because when he arrived at the spot, no one from al-Attar's camp was there. That was fine. It would give his team more time to arrive and get into position. They'd had a plan in place for the day this big meet finally came. Still, this was where blind faith came into play. Even when the boys got here to provide backup, he wouldn't see them. No one would, until they wanted to be seen. But it was good to know they'd soon be here, guarding his back.

He moved into the shadows and leaned against the corner of a spice store, wondering which of the nearby buildings housed al-Attar's HQ. A little wind gust sent a plastic bag skittering down the street, but otherwise, all was quiet. Then an old Toyota Hilux pickup careened around the corner and braked abruptly in front of him.

The Hilux was the go-to vehicle in Afghanistan. This one was beaten and battered, but Bobby suspected some tweaks had been made under the hood. These guys were going to make certain they could always get away—fast.

The few working streetlights were dim, but Bobby recognized the man riding shotgun from previous meets as Ghulam, one of al-Attar's top lieutenants.

Four more men were similarly dressed like locals in white khats and wearing pakuls on their heads. One was the driver. The other three carried AK-47s like Ghulam and each one sat in his own corner in the truck box. The fourth corner was empty, and Bobby suddenly had a very bad feeling about this.

"Get in," Ghulam ordered. Yep—the last corner was reserved for him.

"Get in? We're not meeting near here?"

"Get in," the man repeated.

Shit. This was not good. He'd expected to be led to a building nearby, where al-Attar would be waiting.

"Where's your boss?" Bobby asked.

"We will take you to him."

Not good at all.

And unless he came up with a believable stall tactic, he could kiss his backup good-bye. Fargis's home base was around twenty minutes from his current location. Even if the team had assembled immediately after he'd alerted them, they were still three to four minutes away. If he didn't come up with something fast, they weren't going to get here in time to help him. The Hilux—with him in it—would be long gone.

"Get in now, or we leave, and the meet is off."

He gave a millisecond of thought to letting them drive off without him, but he'd worked too long and too hard on this op to blow his chance of pinning down al-Attar's nest now. Somehow, he'd get a message to the guys, and they'd find him. Or maybe—if these goons weren't smart enough to block transmission— the team could track his phone via GPS. Even then, by the time they figured out exactly where he was, it could be all over but the eulogy.

With a resigned breath, Bobby walked around to the back of the truck, then hiked himself up inside. He'd barely sat down, with his back to the tailgate and his eyes on the boys with the guns, when the Toyota took off.

They traveled several blocks through a city that was in turns decrepit and crumbling and newly modern. He was hot as hell from the adrenaline buzz, and the dusty wind generated by the speeding truck didn't make it easy for him to find the zone.

The Hilux suddenly braked, and he figured they'd arrived.

No such luck. Thug One tossed a black hood at his chest. "Put it on."

Bobby caught it and narrowed his eyes. "What the fu—"

"Put it on!" the guy yelled, and three Russian rifles rose, all pointing at his head.

"No need to get testy, boys," he mumbled, and put on the hood. Then tried to keep from gagging. It smelled like goat shit.

The Hilux tore off again. He was as good as blind, with no backup plan or team in place. This was going south fast, and he could very well be dead tomorrow.

And the thought that bit harder than anything else was the possibility of never seeing Talia again.

8

As the old Toyota roared down the cratered streets, turning, braking, slowing, then racing several times, Bobby could no longer get a feel for what direction they were going. It felt like a good half hour before the driver finally stopped, but they could be miles or mere blocks from where he'd been picked up.

The engine died with a cough; two truck doors opened and then slammed closed. Someone jerked the hood off his head. It took a few seconds to get his eyes to focus, and when he did, the tailgate was already down, and he was the only one left in the truck.

He took it as a good sign that they'd gotten rid of the hood and hadn't bound his wrists, but he was a long way from confident that he'd live to see the sunrise. When you played games with men like al-Attar, if you got too confident, you soon got dead.

He sucked in the fresh air, said, "My compliments to the driver," then jumped out of the truck and tried to get his bearings. It was still dark, and very few streetlights burned in this neighborhood. He took in everything he could see as fast as he could and spotted a blue banner hanging from a wall outside the entrance to a market. What market, he had no clue.

"Follow," Thug One ordered. To make certain that he did, he tapped him none too gently with the business end of the AK. They walked only a couple of blocks, then ducked into a narrow alley before stopping at a walled adobe compound. One of the gunmen pounded on the door. Not long after, a peephole opened. An exchange of words in Arabic followed, before a man opened the door and they all trooped inside.

The new guy led them into the house and a central receiving area that was spacious and well lit, with wide-open windows and several worn but comfortable-looking chairs. Wood bookshelves ran along one wall and overflowed with books and antiques. The Hamas leader clearly liked his creature comforts.

"Spread," the gunman ordered.

Knowing the drill, Bobby planted his feet wide and held his hands in the air while the man searched him and then held out his hand.

"Phone."

Having no choice, Bobby handed over his one and only lifeline.

A hand gripped his shoulder and pushed. "Sit."

Bobby sank into the nearest chair.

And then al-Attar entered the room, welcomed him as though he were a long-lost friend, and, playing the gracious host, served him tea.

Bobby smiled and fought the urge to spit in his eye.

His only play was to punt and hope the team could somehow find him. But the odds of that happening were zilch, and it was looking as if al-Attar and his men were not going to be taken into custody tonight. That was the bad news. That and the fact that he'd finally gotten into the den, but he had no idea where it was located.

The good news was, it didn't appear he was going to die tonight.

He drank the strong, bitter tea and made nice while twenty of al-Attar's top lieutenants gathered in the receiving room, listening quietly as al-Attar and Bobby discussed a deal for the new intel that the Hamas leader stated was his best information yet.

After al-Attar named his price, Bobby said, "That's a lot of money, my friend."

"Have I not always delivered what I promised?" Al-Attar lounged regally in his chair, a master accustomed to hard-core negotiating.

"Just as I have always held up my end of the bargain," Bobby said, maintaining his own casual façade. "And yet you found it necessary to have your men hijack me at gunpoint and hood me."

Al-Attar lifted a hand, swatting the issue away. "I

promised you a meeting in my home. I did not promise the circumstances of your arrival."

Because al-Attar smiled, Bobby smiled. "We'll have to get more specific the next time."

"More tea?" his host asked, dodging the subject.

"I need to get back to base before they know I'm gone." Bobby stood.

"And my price?" his host wanted to know.

"I'll see what I can do."

"Do not keep me waiting long. There are others who would also pay for the service I provide."

It was a bluff, and Bobby knew it. He didn't call al-Attar on it, though, and risk angering him. "How will I contact you?"

It was an old game between them.

Al-Attar nodded to the guy who had taken Bobby's phone. He reached into his robes and handed it to him.

Relieved to have the cell phone back, Bobby pocketed it quickly before al-Attar could change his mind and take it back again.

Al-Attar smiled. "I will contact you. Do not wor—"

A blinding flash of light exploded inside the room. A series of loud bangs and choking smoke followed.

"Sonofabitch," Bobby swore, and ducked for cover. The cavalry had arrived after all, and they'd brought their flashbangs with them.

He must have missed a memo, though, because he didn't remember the part about the shemaghs; the black hoods with narrow slits for eyes and mouth, however, were a nice twist. And they infiltrated the house exactly as they had drilled. Fast and decisive. Excellent. He didn't know exactly how they'd found him; he only cared that they had.

"Hands in the air! Drop your weapons!" The guys yelled in Arabic and English as they stormed through the room in choreographed precision, employing the "slicing the pie" method to clear the room, then immobilizing their targets quickly and efficiently by shoving rifle barrels to the backs of their heads. It took only minutes, and they'd flex-cuffed the lot of them with their hands behind their backs.

"Hey. Take it easy," Bobby grumbled when he was hauled roughly to his feet and shoved against a wall. "I'm one of the good guys, remember?"

He got a hard push and ducked—just not fast enough. Instead of cracking open his skull, a rifle butt grazed his jaw.

Pain exploded inside his mouth, along with the taste of blood.

That was when he realized it wasn't the cavalry after all—and for the second time that night, he figured he was a dead man walking.

They wore Afghan military uniforms, and they very well could be military, but then why had they shouted their orders in Arabic and English but not Pashtu? Something was off here, but whoever they were, they knew what they were doing as they roughly lined al-Attar and his men up against the wall with Bobby.

He stood beside al-Attar, staring at the business ends of twenty automatic rifles, waiting for the bullets to rip through him.

Al-Attar wasn't going down without a fight. "Whatever it is you want, you need only ask."

The leader of the group walked up in front of him, hauled back, and rammed the stock of his rifle into al-Attar's face.

He screamed in pain and dropped to his knees, his nose bleeding heavily.

Bobby measured his breath and kept his mouth shut, looking for a way out. Seeing nothing.

The leader walked down the line of men, studying their faces one at a time through the slits in his face mask. When he stopped in front of Bobby, cold black eyes seemed to cut straight through him before he turned away and nodded to his men.

Two of them broke rank; each one grabbed an arm and dragged Bobby toward the door.

Shit. He knew where this was going. He was an American in Kabul. They were taking him outside to execute him.

Now, though, at least he had a glimmer of hope. His odds had just dropped from twenty-to-one to two-to-one.

He knew exactly how he'd take them down—except, as one held the rifle dead center at his heart, the other stepped behind him and cut off his flex cuffs. Then they shoved him out into the alley and slammed the door closed behind him.

What the hell?

He didn't know what had just happened or why he'd been released, but he wasn't going to hang around and ask questions. Adrenaline pumped so hard his chest ached. He drew several deep breaths, cleared his head, and ran like hell.

When he'd put several blocks behind him, he ducked into an alley, bent over, and puked his guts out. Then he fumbled around for his phone and hit speed dial.

"Taggart, where the hell are you?"

It was Bridgedale himself, manning the SAT phone for the operation.

"Just listen." He quickly told Bridgedale what had happened.

"Tell us where you are."

"If I knew, I'd already have told you."

He stuck his head out of the alley, saw that the streets were still empty, and took off running again until he hit a cross street.

"Taggart, you still there?"

"Hold on." He caught his breath, then gave Bridgedale the names of the two intersecting streets.

In the background, he heard Bridgedale shout at Leavens to plug them into their on-board nav system. Fargis had top-of-the-line electronics that would pinpoint his location and map the most direct route.

"Get your ass out of the street, and find concealment," Bridgedale barked. "We're looking at twenty minutes, but we're on our way."

Bobby had started running toward a deep, shadowed doorway before Bridgedale broke their connection. He ducked into the cover of the wide, tall threshold and made himself small. No one would spot him unless they walked right past him, and even then, he figured he had a fifty-fifty shot that they wouldn't see him if he held still as stone.

His adrenaline finally dropped to the manageable zone. A good thing and a bad thing. Good because his heartbeat and respiration had slowed to those of a Sunday jogger instead of a sprinter hitting the finish line. Bad because without the adrenaline rush, his jaw hurt like hell, and so did the leg he'd broken in the chopper crash several years ago.

He was pretty well wired again, though, when the team's twenty-minute ETA turned into twenty-five and then thirty. He had a sudden craving for a cigarette—and he'd never been a smoker.

Finally, he heard the growl of the up-armored Humvees roaring toward him.

The first Hummer braked to a stop, and Bobby sprinted toward it, barely hauling himself inside before it took off again.

Bridgedale looked him over as Bobby gripped the M4 rifle Gomez handed him. "You sure you're up for action?"

"When am I not?" He got Leavens's attention and gave him directions to al-Attar's nest from there. "Look for a market flying a blue banner."

Then he sat back, breathed deep, and hoped they would get to al-Attar in time. He'd worked the bastard for months, worked him hard, taken a helluva lot of chances. He wanted to close the deal. He did not want some team of ninja assholes doing it for him. He wanted al-Attar in custody, and he wanted to be the one who put him there. Wanted him to know that he'd been played and who had played him.

"Got a bad feeling we've already lost him," Bridgedale said into the darkness of the Hummer.

"Which is going to royally screw up my day," Bobby muttered, and cupped a palm to his aching jaw. "Whoever those guys are, they weren't playing patty-cake."

A few moments later, within three blocks of the compound, a monster flash of light electrified the sky ahead of them. The driver slammed on the brakes and asked God to save him.

The blast that followed rocked the Humvee, as pieces of adobe and wood and glass rained down on them like Vesuvius spitting fiery rocks over Pompeii.

"Sonofabitch!" Bobby pounded his fist on the back of the shotgun seat. "Son. Of. A. Bitch," he repeated in total defeat, as smoke and flames boiled up from the ground where al-Attar's compound used to be.

The blast had destroyed any opportunity to gather

intelligence for analysis—documents, hard drives, whatever. Bridgedale ordered the small convoy to turn around and head back toward base. There was no point in going farther.

Whatever was left of al-Attar would have to be scooped up with a shovel, along with all the other debris.

9

"Better have Hutchinson take a look at your jaw," Bridgedale advised Bobby after they'd all finished the debriefing.

"I'm fine," Bobby assured him. "Just need some shut-eye." His ears would be ringing for a week from the explosion.

He sat in the chair after everyone else had filed out of the room.

"You got something you need to say?" Bridgedale asked, watching Bobby carefully.

He hoped not. He hoped to hell he had nothing to say that his boss would want to hear.

"About who did it? Or why they let you go?" Bridgedale pushed.

They'd already hashed this over at the debriefing, and, like a lot of bombings that took place in Afghanistan, in the end all they had was speculation.

Taliban warlords bent on retribution for al-Attar's betrayal? Al-Qaeda unhappy when they'd found out he was helping the Americans? Al-Attar's competition wanting him out of the picture so they could get a bigger cut and wanting to keep Bobby alive so they could make deals with him?

But none of those explanations washed. He was still stuck with the disaster's biggest damn question: Why had they let him go?

He looked up at Bridgedale, who held his gaze, and finally shook his head.

"You have no ideas?"

"Not one."

Then he walked out of the briefing room, hoping he hadn't just lied. Because if what he feared was true, he wasn't certain he could live with the guilt.

One of the guys gave him a ride to Talia's hotel. The sun was almost up, and a few merchants were starting to set up their shops on the sidewalk by the time he got there. His eyes felt gritty from lack of sleep; his jaw throbbed. Above all, a tight knot of dread clutched his chest as he sprinted up the stairs to Talia's room.

For a long moment, he stood outside her door, hoping like hell he was wrong. He really didn't want to believe the worst. Not of her, and sure as hell not of himself—that she'd taken him for a fool.

Finally, he opened the door and felt the last of his hope die, along with a piece of his heart. The room was empty. Stone cold empty.

Jaw hardening, his emotions turning to ice, he strode past the bed and wrenched open the bathroom door. There was nothing—not a toothbrush, not a comb.

He did the same to the wardrobe, swinging the door wide, only to find more nothing.

No laptop. No camera. No ugly shirts.

No note explaining where she was. That she'd been unexpectedly called away to cover a bigger story somewhere else.

No note telling him she was sorry.

Because, of course, she wasn't.

She'd gotten exactly what she'd wanted—and he'd gotten played. It took everything he had just to stand there and keep breathing.

He looked around the room again, making sure he hadn't missed anything, some small *something* to tell him she'd be back. But all he saw were memories— of her naked body stretched out beneath him on the bed, her skin so soft, her hair a wild mane, her voice with his name on her lips.

He hadn't dreamed her response. He hadn't dreamed how good they were together.

His cell phone rang, and, like a fool, he felt a rush of hope and yanked it out of his pocket. Then he saw the message and felt gut-shot. It wasn't Talia with explanations and innocence. It was a reminder he'd sent to himself days ago about a briefing scheduled for this morning.

Fuck! He threw the phone against the wall, and it fell to the floor in pieces. And then his day hit rock-fucking-bottom.

Disbelieving, he leaned over and picked up a piece of metal about the size of the battery. An RFID tag. He'd planted plenty of them over the years while tracking bad guys.

And it had fallen out of his phone.

He closed his eyes, and his head fell back in absolute misery. *Honey trap.*

Because of his stupidity, not only was al-Attar dead, but so was all the information the intelligence community could have gathered from him. Important information. Lifesaving information.

He thought back to all the signs that he'd missed.

He'd seen her passport, and she maintained dual citizenship with the United States and Israel.

Al-Attar was a known Hamas leader with a price on his head in Israel.

Now al-Attar was dead.

And Talia was gone.

It felt as if she'd hammered a stake clean through his heart. Talia Levine was dead to him now.

As dead as he felt inside.

PART II

Retribution

"The more you trust, the greater the betrayal.
The more you love, the greater the harm."

—Unknown

10

"Lord love a duck." Looking shocked and pleased, Ted Jensen pushed back his desk chair and stood when he saw Bobby Taggart standing in his doorway. "Would you look what the cat dragged in."

Jensen was the principal security attaché to the U.S. Ambassador in the American embassy in Oman, but when that grin split his face, Bobby saw traces of the Alabama farm boy he knew and loved to hassle.

"Thought someone woulda killed you by now," Jensen added, his grin widening.

Bobby gripped the rough hand his old friend extended across a sleek, lacquered desk. "So did I. Trust me, it's not for lack of trying on their part."

Jensen laughed, rounded his desk, and trapped Bobby in a hard bear hug.

Bobby hugged him back, truly glad to see him. Back when he and Ted had been Special Forces, they'd served together on many deployments. Saved each other's ass more than once, too.

"Damn, it's good to see you, man!" Jensen finally released him. "I really was afraid you were dead."

"Highly exaggerated rumors," Bobby assured him.

"You look damn good, given that ugly mug of yours."

"Says the man with the face like a waffle iron."

Jensen chuckled. "So how've you been, Boom Boom? I heard about the exoneration. I always thought those charges were bogus; it never made sense that they charged you in the first place."

Jensen's expression invited both venting and a sympathetic ear if he needed it. Maybe if he were good and drunk, he'd indulge in a little info share. But when he was sober, he rarely talked about the Operation Slam Dunk debacle.

"Water. Bridge," he said with a dismissive shrug. "In the meantime, I'm good. Apparently, not as good as you." He made an appreciative scan of the lavishly furnished office. "You're clearly top dog in these parts."

Jensen sank down into his cushy desk chair. "The doghouse may be fancy, but I'm still guarding a junkyard."

"So I've heard. That's why I'm here."

Jensen narrowed his eyes and studied Taggart's face as if he'd mistaken him for someone else. Then he figured it out. "No shit? *You're* the big-shot, hush-hush badass the Department of Defense sent to bust my chops?"

"Drew the short straw, yeah."

"Huh." Thoughtful, Jensen reached into his top desk drawer, pulled out two glasses and a bottle of Scotch, then poured them each two fingers.

"All the straws seem to come up short these days," Bobby added after tossing back the Scotch. "You okay with me trying to poke holes in your operation?"

Oman wasn't exactly a hotbed of terrorist activity, but given its strategic importance at the mouth of the Persian Gulf and the volatility of the entire Middle East, the State Department wasn't taking any chances. So the DOD had deployed the International Threat Analysis and Prevention team to assess the embassy's security, recommend upgrades if necessary, and authorize the resources to ensure that it got done. Because Mike Brown and the rest of the ITAP team were running training maneuvers in Central America, Bobby had caught the first flight over. And since Jensen was in charge of security here, Bobby was going to be tromping mud all over his nice, clean floor.

"Well," Jensen said, "I've got a good team here. We've got a solid plan in place. But if I've got problems, I want them found. I don't want a Benghazi disaster on my watch."

"Ditto." Bobby leaned forward. "So where do you want me to start?"

"You mean right this minute? Well, that's a big hell no. We haven't seen each other in five years, it's almost six o'clock, and we need to catch up. So you can attack the defenses first thing in the morning. Tonight we're gonna go tie one on for old times' sake."

"All right," Bobby agreed, although if he wasn't going to work, he'd rather get some shut-eye. "I guess I'm in."

"Great. Just give me a minute to deal with some of this paper."

Bobby sank back into the chair as Ted rifled through the stack of paperwork on his desk. Maybe his friend was right. Maybe a stiff drink, some "good ol' days" conversation, and then a good night's sleep were in order. Especially after the ridiculously long flight with the requisite delays and jet lag.

It was funny how they'd ended up together again. After Jensen had retired from the military with a stellar record, he'd joined the diplomatic service. After Bobby had been booted out of the Army on a trumped-up less-than-honorable discharge, his only opportunity to stay in the action had been with Fargis, the private military contractor he'd worked for in Afghanistan. Yet now he worked for an elite covert branch of the Department of Defense. How was that for irony?

A female voice from the hallway yanked him from his thoughts, and he snapped his head around. An ice-cold knot instantly tightened in his gut.

It *couldn't* be.

But it was. He'd recognize her voice from the grave—even though he hated to admit that.

Jensen confirmed Bobby's worst nightmare. "Ah,

here comes Talia. I can introduce you two right now, since you'll be working together."

"Talia . . . Levine?" The knot twisted.

Ted quirked a brow. "Yeah. You know her?"

Jesus Christ. "I didn't see her name on the TO."

"No," Ted said with a curious look. "My head security investigator just retired last month, so you'd have seen *his* name on the table of organization. Talia's on loan until I hire a replacement. I wish I could steal her from the embassy in Tel Aviv on a permanent basis. She's only been here a week, but it's clear that she's damn good."

Bobby stared at Ted blankly. *Talia. Here.*

Ted leaned back in his chair, clearly puzzled by Bobby's reaction. "I take it you know her?"

But he'd already tuned Ted out, his voice fading to background noise like a freighter sinking into a deep ocean fog.

Bobby stood slowly, walked to the door, and stepped out into the hall. And there she was, walking toward him, head down, concentrating on a sheaf of papers.

She hadn't spotted him yet, but she would if he didn't unglue his feet and get back into Jensen's office.

But there he stood, unable to move. Barely able to breathe, as anger and a treacherous rush of excitement seized his chest and ramped up his heartbeat.

She looked the same. Knockout gorgeous and kickass cool, still slim and sleek and in total control.

In Kabul, she'd worn camo or khakis, her hair woven into a thick black braid. Today she wore a white cotton suit with a snug skirt, and the blue top beneath her jacket looked soft and silky. Her heels were as black as her hair, which she'd pulled into an elegant and sexy knot at her nape.

Even before she looked up, he knew that the angles of her face, which he'd memorized by sight, by touch, and by taste, would be as golden and lovely as they'd been when she was his.

Except she'd never really *been* his. He'd been her target, her patsy. By all rights, he should hate her. And he *had* hated her, almost as much as he'd hated himself for falling into her trap. She'd been doing her job, and he'd been doing her.

That part was on him. He'd been a big boy, and he'd fucked up. Over the years, he'd found a way to live with himself, to keep fighting the good fight, to not allow even the hint of another mistake. It wasn't forgiveness; it was acceptance. The same thing he'd given her: acceptance of her skills of deception and seduction, of her loyalty to her country.

But forgiveness? Oh, no. That wasn't in the lineup, not for her, any more than it was for him.

Now here she was again. And for a moment, all he could remember was what it had been like to be her lover.

So much for being over her.

He hadn't thought that seeing her again would immobilize him; he felt like a turtle lumbering across a busy freeway. Nowhere to go to escape the inevitable collision. Unable to move fast enough to avoid certain disaster.

She'd almost reached him when she lifted her head to talk to an aide walking beside her. Her dark eyes landed briefly on his face as she walked past him, and his heart rate shot off the charts.

An instant later, she stopped, stood motionless for a long, pulsing second, then slowly turned around.

All the blood drained from her face when she realized it was him.

All the breath left his body.

After six years and countless regrets, he had the same reaction to her as he'd had the first time he'd seen her in the Mustafa Hotel bar. A searing connection, a sizzling electricity that was not only sexual but intensely soulful and deep.

Oh, God. Not again. He couldn't survive her again.

Their eyes were still locked—stunned, disbelieving— when a blast rocked the building like a magnitude-ten earthquake.

The jarring crash of shattering glass, falling concrete, and horrified screams joined with the acrid stench of billowing smoke and the hideous pain that consumed him. The concussion from the explosion knocked him off his feet, and he fell face-first to the floor, his vision blurred, his ears ringing above the pounding in his head.

He tried to get to his feet. Couldn't. Tried to focus. Couldn't do that, either. Thick, oily nausea roiled through his gut. And the last thing he saw before he passed out was a black high-heeled shoe flying across the shattered glass and plaster littering the embassy floor.

11

Heat above her. Cracked floor below. Ashes raining down.

Talia lay on her stomach, the side of her face pressed against the hard marble floor. Through the veil of her hair, all she could see was smoke. And ruin.

Afraid to move, she lay perfectly still, blanketed from reality by an eerie sensation that she was watching a scene from a newsreel. She closed her eyes. Shut it all out. Tried to convince herself it was a nightmare.

But deep inside, where the truth couldn't be denied, she knew she was in trouble. No nightmare smelled like this. No dream made the floor beneath her tremble. Or made her body weak.

She should get up. Knew on an instinctive level that she had to get out.

Gathering her strength, she pushed up to her knees and gasped when sharp pain ripped through her arm, ending her disconnect from reality.

Head spinning, she stayed motionless on her knees, covered in ash and plaster dust. Her arm burned and throbbed; blood dripped off the fingertips of her left hand; her ears rang as if a grenade had exploded right beside her.

But a grenade couldn't do this much damage.

Fire, smoke, and ash everywhere. Fallen walls, shattered glass, twisted steel, and crumbled piles of concrete.

Nothing but a bomb could have wreaked this kind of devastation.

The embassy had been bombed!

Self-preservation finally kicked in, and adrenaline surged through her blood, snapping her out of shock mode. And her heart ramped into overdrive as she realized another horrific truth: *she* had been the target of the bombing.

Hamas had found her. They'd somehow uncovered that she'd once been Mossad. This was the fear she'd lived with for six years. That somehow they'd discover her and dig through the cover she'd once used as a photojournalist, link her to Mossad, then tie her to her work against them.

And now it had happened.

They wanted her dead and wouldn't be satisfied until she was. Or until they destroyed everything she loved.

Everything she—

Meir!

She bit back a wild, primal cry. She had to get to her son! She should have gotten Meir out of harm's way yesterday, the moment she'd found out about the systematic assassinations of the rest of her old Mossad team. But she'd had to be careful to not make any moves to alert Hamas that she was on to them; even booking the flights for tonight had been risky.

And now it might be too late.

She automatically reached into her pocket for her phone. It wasn't there. It must have fallen out during the blast. She searched the floor on hands and knees, scrabbled through piles of debris, but couldn't find it. Not her phone. Not her attaché case. Nothing.

She had to get to a phone. She had to reach Meir's bodyguard and warn him. *Stop. Think.* She willed herself to calm down.

Meir got out of summer school at four. He'd asked her to let him spend time at a new friend's house for a couple of hours after school, and she'd agreed.

After all, Jonathan would be with him. And Jonathan must be taking him home right about now. If now was somewhere close to six p.m., which was when the bomb had detonated.

She knew the time because she'd left her office at six, walked down the hall, and then everything had gone black. Had she passed out for a while? There was no way to know how much time had passed; she only knew she had to get to Meir.

Scrambling to get her feet under her, she tried to stand—and went right back down. For several seconds, she sat with her head between bent knees and breathed deep until the light-headedness passed. *He'll be all right*, she told herself as she pulled off her single shoe. The other one was gone, lost with everything else.

She tried to stand again. Landed on her ass again and swore.

She didn't have time for this, but she had to wait for the dizziness to pass. And while it did, she assured herself again that Jonathan would never let anything happen to Meir. She'd fully vetted the bodyguard before she'd taken this post in Muscat a week ago, and she trusted him completely.

Surely he would hear about the bombing on TV or in the news feed on his phone. He'd know what to do, where to go. He'd keep Meir safe. And as long as Hamas thought she was dead, her son would stay safe. There was no reason to panic. But until she made contact with Jonathan, she couldn't completely believe Meir was okay.

She *had* to get to a phone.

On this attempt to stand, she took her time and stood slowly. Made it to her feet. Made herself breathe. For a dizzying moment, it was all she could do to maintain her balance and stare in horror.

Hell burned all around her. This end of the embassy complex had been reduced to blown-out walls, fractured glass, and piles of burning rubble. The roof gaped open through a jagged hole. Another alarm blasted in her head. The rest of the roof could fall anytime. She'd be damned if she survived the bombing only to die if the roof collapsed on top of her.

Have to get out of here.

She took an unsteady step, then another, and looked around for other survivors.

"Can anyone hear me?"

Her heart dropped when no one answered.

She called out again. Waited again.

Please. There must be more survivors.

But again, she heard nothing.

Then she spotted her aide. *Oh, please, God. Not Saul.*

A chunk of concrete the size of a desk had fallen on his back, pinning him to the floor. Blood pooled beneath his head. He wasn't moving.

She'd just met him this past week but already felt close to him. He was an amazing young man, smart, eager, and excited about the baby his wife was due to deliver in four months. Choking on the thick smoke glutting the air, she staggered over to him, dropped to her knees, and searched for a pulse.

He was gone. Fighting tears and now even more desperate to ensure that Jonathan got Meir to safety, she searched Saul's pockets, feeling like a ghoulish thief, and finally found his phone.

Torn between grief and hope, she punched in Jonathan's number—and got nothing. The phone was dead. The screen was black.

If she hadn't already been on her knees, despair would have taken her there. But then something clicked in her head. If she didn't get hold of herself right now, didn't shut out the grief, the survivor guilt, and the fear for her son, it would paralyze her. She'd die here, and she'd never see Meir again.

There was no shame in grieving. But there was no honor in giving up.

Above all else, the rigorous training she'd been subjected to as Mossad had instilled both physical and mental strength.

With renewed conviction, she rose to her feet again and searched for a way out. As she did, a sudden blast of memory hit that seemed as surreal as the devastation around her.

Right before the blast, she'd seen Bobby Taggart. Large and lean and as uncompromisingly male as she remembered. It made no sense, but he was here. In the building when the bomb detonated.

Propelled by renewed urgency, she started searching for him, shutting out the voices that reminded her that she'd betrayed him, that he must hate her. And if he didn't hate her now, if she found him alive, he'd soon have every reason to.

He couldn't be dead.

She couldn't accept that possibility. Couldn't accept that he'd shown up after six years, only to die right when she needed him most.

"Taggart, where are you?" she yelled into the smoking ruins.

She'd been within three yards of him at the time of the explosion, right outside Ted Jensen's office. She headed that way, stumbling over wedges of concrete, plowing through fragmented wreckage and broken glass as though rabid dogs nipped at her heels.

Shards of glass lay like booby traps, cutting her bare feet. She could deal with the pain later. She had to find—

Her breath caught when she spotted him, and she fought off a deeper kind of pain. He was lying beneath a metal door frame that miraculously stood while the walls around it were all caved in, burying Ted's office and Ted along with it in chunks of concrete. There was nothing she could do to help Ted, but Taggart might still be alive.

"Please, please, please," she whispered, choking on air thick with ash and smoke.

She crawled over and around more fallen concrete, skirting hanging electrical wires that sparked and sizzled when they hit the floor.

Winded, coughing from the smoke, and near collapse, she finally reached him. And, thank God, she found a pulse.

Cuts and bruises peppered his arms and the side of his face. There was blood everywhere, but she couldn't find any signs of major injuries other than a bleeding gash on his head.

Head wounds bled a lot, and she told herself staunchly that all this blood didn't mean he had a bad head injury. Didn't mean he was going to die.

He groaned. The sound amped up her heart rate and brought her a first glimpse of hope. "Taggart."

When he didn't respond, she pulled a ruined chair off of his legs.

"Taggart!" She shook him lightly as she tried to catch her breath.

He rewarded her with another groan and this time with a little movement. He lifted his head and promptly let it drop. "What . . . what happened?"

"Do you know where you are?"

"Embassy? Oman?" He lifted his head again and squinted at her. "Talia?"

"The embassy was bombed." She shrugged out of her ruined jacket and started ripping it apart. "We've got to get out of here."

She wiped blood from his face and away from his eyes. Then she tore strips of the lightweight cotton fabric, made a dressing, and tied it around his head.

"Sorry," she said when he winced. "It's got to be tight. The cut needs pressure to stop the bleeding."

"Bombed?" he repeated, his slowness to connect reflecting his confusion.

"Can you stand?" With no time to explain more or to wait for his answer, she helped him push up onto all fours. He was clearly weak and dizzy, so she let him rest for all of ten seconds. "Come on. All the way up."

Adrenaline could pull off miracles, and even though he outweighed her by a good hundred pounds, she managed to get him to his feet.

He swayed drunkenly.

She grabbed his arm, slung it over her shoulders,

and shored him up. Wrapping her other arm around his waist, she clutched his belt to help keep him upright.

Taggart wasn't in any shape to help her, and she could move much faster without him. But she didn't consider leaving him behind for one second. She needed him. She owed him for what she'd done to him. Owed him more than he'd ever know. And she would not leave him here to die.

"You've got to pull it together," she demanded. "We've got to move. Now, walk."

"Wait . . . just wait—"

"We can't wait." The building groaned and creaked, a precursor to imminent collapse.

"The roof could cave at any moment." Another electrical wire swung dangerously close. "There could be a secondary explosion. Now, move, damn it!"

He took one unsteady step and stumbled, nearly taking her down with him.

"Do *not* pass out on me." She strained against his weight. "Help me. Walk. Please, please, walk!"

Time was more than an enemy; time was death. For him. For her. And possibly for Meir.

12

Whether he fed off her determination or he'd shaken off the worst effects of his injuries, Bobby managed, with her help, to walk, stagger, and sometimes crawl painstakingly through the ruined building.

They didn't talk. She didn't have the strength or the breath, and clearly, he didn't, either. And then there was the possibility that his silence spoke more about his hatred.

She couldn't think about that now. But as they struggled and time passed like long shadows, she couldn't stop the memory of how it had been between them in Kabul. And she couldn't help but regret, as she had every day, that she'd had to leave him. That she'd had to betray him.

That she had, in fact, betrayed him twice.

Kabul felt like a lifetime ago, but it felt like ten lifetimes since they'd started clawing their way out of the building. The heat and dust and ash combined were suffocating. They were both drenched in sweat, rapidly losing critical fluids, and getting weaker with each step. It took forever to navigate as little as five feet. She had no idea how much time had passed when she finally spotted daylight, and on a renewed surge of adrenaline they crawled toward a break in the buckled wall.

Hell's own heat and the wails of emergency sirens met them as they stumbled out of the building and into their first breaths of fresh air.

Fire trucks, military vehicles, and ambulances had gathered in force. Long hoses shot plumes of water at a fire burning in the west end of the complex, where the worst of the damage had been done. That explained why she and Taggart were still alive; they'd been in the east end. Embassy security cordoned off the grounds from the public, and family members and friends of those who worked here begged from outside the gates for word of their loved ones.

"Over here!" someone called out.

Near collapse, Talia lifted her head to see one of the young Marines who provided embassy security rushing their way.

When he reached them, she let him relieve her of Taggart's weight and help them both to a hastily set-up triage station.

"Stay right here." The Marine headed off toward more victims, some walking, some being carried away from the ruined building. "The nurse will take care of you soon."

She didn't need someone to take care of her. She needed to get out of here.

The lone nurse spotted them, rushed over, and guided them under a tarp rigged between two emergency vehicles.

"Please, sit down over there." She nodded toward the makeshift benches made from long planks and packing crates. A woman sat on the bench crying, and others lay on tarps spread on the grass.

The nurse handed them each a bottle of water, and Talia gratefully accepted it and drank half of it down before she came up for air. Beside her, Taggart did the same. They both needed rehydrating badly.

"I need your phone," Talia told the nurse urgently.

"I'm sorry." The kind-eyed nurse exhibited amazing calm, considering the chaos and the cries of the wounded she was caring for. "I have to keep this line clear to consult with the embassy doctor in Kuwait."

Talia wanted to beg, but she knew all about protocol. "What time is it?" she asked, as the nurse quickly looked her over, then checked her vitals.

"Last time I looked, it was seven thirty."

An hour and a half since the explosion.

"Now, please, stay quiet so I can get a good look at you."

"I don't have time. I have to get to a phone. I have to get to my car."

"You need a hospital," the nurse insisted when coughs wracked Talia's body and made it impossible for her to speak. "We've engaged the Omani military to help. They'll get you to a medical facility for further evaluation. And you need to be fully debriefed—so you aren't going anywhere."

She moved on to Taggart, removed the makeshift dressing from his head, and quickly examined his wound. Then she checked his pupils.

"He needs further treatment, too. He may have a concussion or something worse." She efficiently cleaned the wound, then taped a sterile gauze dressing over it.

"Look," Talia insisted when she found her breath again. "I'll take care of him. I'll get us both to a hospital. The others need your help much more than we do. We'll be fine."

Now that he was off his feet and had downed his second bottle of water, Taggart had rallied. His strength was returning, and his eyes were clearer now. And they were full of contempt when he looked at her.

He could hate her all he wanted, but she wasn't letting him out of her sight. Every day for six long years, she'd regretted leaving him. Whether this chance meeting was God's will or an ironic twist of fate, she didn't care. Too many things had been left unsaid between them. Things she couldn't tell him when she had left him in Kabul.

Things he had a right to know.

And she needed him to help her save her son.

"Tell her you're okay." With a meaningful look, she begged Taggart not to fight her. "Tell her you're coming with me."

Sirens and shouted orders and the chaos all around them faded to the background before he finally turned to the nurse. "You heard her. I'm fine."

Relief and hope flooded Talia's chest. Then he crushed both when he told her, "But I'm not going anywhere with you. I'm going back in."

The nurse easily pushed him down with a hand on his shoulder when he tried to get up. "Sorry, sir, but—"

"My friend's in there!" His voice was scratchy and raw from the toxic air, but that didn't weaken his determination. "I've got to get him out."

Talia reached for his hand before she could stop herself. His hard glare made her pull it back. "You can't go back in there," she said.

"All I needed was fluids." Ignoring the desperation he must see on her face, he reached for another bottle of water. "Couple more of these, and I'm good to go."

"Look," the nurse said in a no-nonsense voice. "No one is to leave the triage area unless they're in critical need of a hospital. I'm to call a Marine to restrain anyone who tries to leave. I don't think you want that. And I don't think you want to take a Marine away from rescue and recovery to babysit you."

"She's right. Let them do their jobs," Talia said. "Please."

His eyes met hers, and for a moment, before they iced over, she saw them as she'd seen them when he hadn't hated her.

He looked toward the ruins of the embassy building. Let out a deep breath. "Fine," he said, finally backing down.

She'd seen the moment he'd accepted that in his current condition, he'd be more in the way than helpful.

Someone cried out, and the nurse looked back over her shoulder. "I've got to go. If you start feeling worse, call me."

As soon as she left, Talia moved in to help him up.

"You heard the lady. We're to stay put," he said.

"Yeah, I heard. Now, let's go before she gets back."

"You know that when our bodies aren't accounted for, we're both going to end up on a short list of suspects."

They kept a daily log of everyone who entered and left the embassy. She'd been here less than a week, and Taggart had arrived just today. So yes, she knew. But she couldn't let it matter.

She dragged his arm over her shoulder again. "Let's go," she repeated.

He muttered something under his breath and grabbed two more water bottles, and without a word, they started walking.

Fatigue started winning out over adrenaline; it no longer blocked the pain. Every bruise, every cut—especially the ones on her feet—stung like fire as they hurried across the lawn toward the parking lot.

She knew she had to keep moving. Anything inside the embassy compound was considered the sovereign territory of the United States government. If any of the Marines guarding the embassy caught them attempting to leave, they'd detain them for certain. They'd want to clear everyone before they were allowed to leave the bombing area.

She couldn't let that happen. Using the background pandemonium and the emergency vehicles as cover, she kept moving. Until Taggart stopped abruptly, and she almost took a tumble.

"What's going on?" he asked sharply. "What do you want with me?"

"Later. We need to get to my car and get out of here."

"You need keys for a car. I don't see any, and you sure as hell aren't carrying them on you."

He would know. There wasn't a part of her body that hadn't pushed, pulled, collapsed, or rubbed against his as they'd fought their way out of the building. Her ruined tank top and what was left of her skirt couldn't have concealed a breath mint.

"I've got it covered," she said, and pushed on until they finally reached the gate. Then she felt her heart stop when she realized it was locked.

"Now what?" Taggart asked.

She couldn't panic now. And when an ambulance rushed up to the gate from the bombed building moments later, siren screaming, she knew this was their chance.

"Be ready to move when I do," she said.

When the Marine walked to the driver's side of the ambulance, she hurried Taggart around to the opposite side. As soon as the gate swung open, Talia, pumped on her last burst of adrenaline, hurried alongside the vehicle, out of view of the guard, and slipped through the gate. Then she rushed into the thick knot of people standing outside the perimeter.

Once the Marine closed and locked the gate and returned to his post about ten yards from the perimeter fence, she took off toward the parking lot.

She didn't look back to see if they were being followed. Her car, while a good city block away, was in sight, which meant they were almost clear. They made it another ten yards before a moving wall of people stopped them. A dozen news crews swarmed around them like sharks around chum.

Everywhere she looked, a microphone or a camera appeared, snapping pictures, shooting video, as reporters shot questions at them like bullets.

"Were you in the building when it exploded?"

"Can you give us an account of what happened?" A camera zoomed in close on her face.

Oh, God, they had her on film now. Her face would appear on TV and the Internet, on news channels around the world via instant feed. The video was probably streaming live right now.

And her enemies could be watching right now, gloating over their victory—and suddenly discover that they'd failed when they saw she was alive.

There was no question now. They would immediately go after Meir. These vultures had just made certain that her son was now a target.

"Did you see who did this?"

"Was this the work of terrorists?"

"Get out of my way!" With Taggart's help, she pushed through the crowd, now frantic to get to a phone and warn Jonathan.

A balding man shoved a microphone in front of her. "Do you know if the American ambassador was in the building today? Can you give us your name and tell us how bad the casualties are?"

The large crowd felt like a pulsing wall of bodies, closing in and pushing against them. They leaned in and around her, pummeling her with questions.

When one of them stepped directly in their path, Taggart lost it. "Get out of our way, or I'll break your fucking face!"

As if he were Moses, the crowd fell silent and parted like the Red Sea.

13

Winded, head pounding, Bobby leaned against a light pole gathering strength, while Talia sprinted barefoot across ten yards of hot pavement to a white Ford Expedition. Heat waves shimmered over the parking lot. It had to be at least 110 degrees, even though the sun had dropped behind the nearby buildings.

The pavement would be even hotter and had to hurt like hell, especially on top of all the damage she'd done to her feet. When he pushed away from the pole and caught up with her, the pain etched on her face almost had him feeling sorry for her.

She hurriedly punched a code into a key panel on the driver's door, wrenched the door open, and dived inside, moaning in relief.

"I could have carried you." *Maybe*.

She just leaned over the wide front seat and unlocked the passenger door for him. Then she reached into the glove box, pulled out a single key hidden beneath the box's lining, and pushed it into his hand. "Behind the license plate. Hurry."

She'd stopped surprising and disappointing him six years ago. So it came as no shock that when he tugged on the plate, it dropped down and revealed a hidden lockbox.

If he hadn't been hurting so badly, he'd have laughed when he inserted the key and opened it up. Of course, she had a secret compartment with an extra set of car keys, a cell phone, and an automatic pistol with three extra magazines.

He quickly drew the Glock 26 out of its holster and pulled back the slide to make certain a round was chambered. Then he slapped the bottom of the magazine and slid it back into the holster, securing it before digging back into the lockbox.

And holy God, he spotted several passports. This time, he did laugh. What woman needed passports under multiple names?

He gathered everything but the passports, then stood up too fast. A wave of vertigo slammed him against the car. He closed his eyes. Breathed deep. Waited it out. And made an attempt to process every-thing about every single moment of this fucked-up day.

The bombing. Talia. Ted—possibly dead. He should be back there looking for him. The hell with Marines restraining him; they'd have to catch him first.

Which, he admitted as the dizziness slowly passed, wouldn't have taken much effort.

So he was with Talia instead. The one woman he'd promised himself he would never let affect him again.

There was no question she was balancing on an edge as sharp as a razor, and now that his mind was almost back to functioning at full capacity, it was clear that whatever drove her ran even deeper than surviving the bombing.

For some reason, she wanted him with her. He wanted to know why.

Steadier, he made it to the passenger door and climbed inside.

He held up the Glock. "I'm going to go out on a limb and assume we'll be needing this."

She ignored him and snatched the cell phone out of his hand. Her hands shook as she turned it on and then, with the impatience of a thoroughbred at the starting gate, waited for it to power up.

"You said to wait until we got to the car," he said. "We're here. So what's going on?"

"Not now." She shook her head sharply as the phone came to life.

They sat in the sweltering heat as she punched in a number. Closed her eyes. And, if he wasn't mistaken, held her breath.

Apparently, no one answered, because after several seconds, she ended the call. Her hand fell to her lap. The despair on her face hit him like a punch to the gut.

What the hell?

She'd hauled him step after painful step out of the blast site, her elbows and knees scraped raw, her arms and feet bleeding, and she'd never made a whimper.

Yet an unanswered phone sent a tear trickling down her ash-streaked face. *I. Do. Not. Cry.*

Her words came back as if she'd said them yesterday, not six years ago in her room at the Mustafa Hotel.

He had to look away, before he did or said something stupid. She didn't have the right to his sympathy. But he had rights. A whole shitload of them.

"What's going on, Talia?"

His voice seemed to snap her out of her momentary letdown, yet she ignored him, swiped away the tear, and reached for the keys.

This day just kept getting better. Bobby scrubbed around in the glove box, looking for something for his headache, as she fired up the Expedition and backed out of the parking space. He'd just found a bottle of painkillers and popped the lid when she slammed on the brakes.

Tylenol pills flew out of the bottle and up into the air like popcorn.

Fuck.

He looked around to see what was going on and swore again. The traffic—emergency, police, and military vehicles, news crews and lookie-loos— continued to rush to the bombing site. The congestion they'd created was so thick she couldn't get out of the lot.

"Looks like we're not going anywhere anytime soon," he said, and turned on the AC full blast.

He found three Tylenol on the seat, opened another bottle of water, and drank half of it down along with the pills.

He offered the other half and some pills to her.

She shook her head and glanced behind her. "Buckle up."

Executing a perfect bootlegger's turn, she swiftly jerked into reverse, smashed the gas, whipped the vehicle around in a one-eighty, then slammed into forward gear and put pedal to metal. They shot up over the curb and climbed up the grass berm that made a bowl around the parking lot.

"Chi-rist!" he swore, as they bumped to the top, then nose-dived down the other side, across a wide cement walk, and jumped another curb. They barely missed hitting a fire truck, and then she cut across the street sideways and barreled over a planted median separating four lanes of traffic.

The tires squealed on the hot pavement as she blasted off like a Formula One racer, finally going the right way.

When she rounded a corner on two screaming wheels, he braced his feet against the floor and got a grip on the door handle and console. "If you're going to roll this thing and kill me, I'd at least like to know what I'm dying for."

"You're not going to die. At least, not here."

That was reassuring.

She was all focus and purpose as they screamed through the city. She took her eyes off the street long enough to grab the phone from her lap and shove it into his chest. "Hit redial."

There was a lot he could have said right then, none of it nice. He just clenched his jaw, punched redial, and listened to the phone ring. And ring. No one answered. No voice message picked up to tell him to leave a number.

She shot him an anxious glance.

He shook his head.

That scared vulnerability surfaced again—just for an instant, before the tough girl was back—and left him wishing he could convince himself that he was immune to her pain and whatever was causing it.

"Keep trying."

He dragged a hand across his jaw and stared at the white stone buildings flashing by. Then he stared at her and wondered, again, why he was in this vehicle with her and her bleeding bare feet. It wasn't as if he couldn't outmuscle her—well, on any other day. It was more that she was a force of nature, and he'd had no choice but to bend to her will.

And, Jesus, look at her. Who wouldn't be compelled to find out what drove her?

Her hair tumbled wildly around her face where it wasn't plastered against her temples and neck with perspiration. Her ruined skirt had ripped well past her knee. Black ash and gray dust covered her everywhere—her clothes, her bare arms and bare legs, and that amazing face.

And blood was everywhere. Her blood. His blood, he reminded himself grimly, flashing back to the moment when she'd ripped her jacket apart, cleaned his face, and made a bandage to slow the bleeding while blood seeped from her own arm in a slow, steady stream.

He whipped his attention back to the street and hit redial again. She'd saved his life when she could have left him. The least he could do was dial the damn phone.

But why the urgency? They'd survived the bombing, so that left . . . what? Was she still running away from something? Or was she running toward it?

"Who am I calling?"

"Just keep redialing."

Short of jerking the wheel away from her and plowing into a palm tree to get her attention, there wasn't a damn thing he could do to make her talk if she didn't want to.

Brooding, he held the phone to his ear.

Did she think he didn't know she was Mossad? That he hadn't figured it out after she'd left him in Kabul? Only one country had wanted al-Attar more than the United States: Israel. They had sent Mossad to take care of al-Attar—and Talia to take care of him.

Maybe this was another top-secret mission, and she couldn't tell him anything. So why had she dragged his ass along with her?

He was up to his neck in questions and determined

to get some answers when she screeched to an abrupt stop in front of an affluent-looking house in a well-established neighborhood.

She kept the engine running and searched the street, then grabbed the Glock and jumped out of the Expedition. "Wait here."

Hobbled by her mutilated feet, she ran up ten wide steps and knocked on the front door, hiding the Glock alongside her leg and slightly behind it. He couldn't see who answered the door, but she talked with the person for a brief moment before running back to the Expedition.

Too late, she realized her mistake. He'd pulled the keys.

"Give them to me."

"Not a chance, *sweetheart*." His tone twisted the word into an unmistakable insult. "Tell me what's going on."

"Don't do this," she begged. "There's no time."

"Then quit wasting it. Talk to me." He met her pleading eyes with a stony stare.

She looked away, and it pissed him off.

"What do you want from me?" he roared, his throat tight, his patience long gone. "You do want something, or I wouldn't be here."

If she didn't tell him, he was bailing out. His head hurt, his ears were still ringing, and his body felt as if it had been slam-dunked by a Dumpster.

And she sat there looking tragic and not saying one damn word.

"You know I can't possibly be of any use to you if I don't know what the fuck's going on." The words were no sooner out of his mouth than he caught the idiocy of what he'd said. "Oh, wait. I didn't have a clue in Kabul, either, but it worked out real well for you, didn't it? You know all about using people while you keep them in the dark."

When a tear fell, he reached the proverbial end of his rope. It was either haul her into his arms and hold her or bully her. "Do you think it doesn't strike me as odd that a 'journalist' keeps several passports, a gun, ammo, a phone, and extra car keys hidden behind a license plate? Just in case—oh, I don't know—she has to run for her life?"

She gripped the steering wheel with both hands and lowered her forehead against it. "Give me the keys."

But he was on a roll. "I don't know what your game is or why you were coincidentally working for Ted just before I showed up. But I do know there's got to be a connection between you being at the embassy and—oh, wow, another coincidence—someone bombs it to kingdom fucking come!"

He had to look away then, because he was back to another impossible choice—kill her or kiss her—and it royally pissed him off that he liked the complicated option so much more than the easy one.

"Do you honestly think I don't know you're Mossad?" he finally asked, and got absolutely no reaction. "So why aren't you contacting your Mossad brothers to help you? Why me?"

"Because this is not Mossad's problem," she said abruptly.

He jerked his head around in surprise.

"And yes, you're right about the bomb, okay? It was meant to kill me."

Another shock that wasn't a shock. In his short experiences with Talia, she and trouble were equally predictable.

He'd decided a few blocks back that she wasn't running away; she was hunting. And if not for her Mossad contacts, then who?

"Who are you looking for, Talia?"

She lifted her head but wouldn't meet his eyes. "My son. I'm looking for my son."

14

I'm looking for my son.

The words replayed in Bobby's head in a slow loop, as if his mind needed time to process it over and over again.

She had a son.

"Taggart."

His name on her lips made his heart rate double. She said it with such intimacy, so much uncertainty and anguish, he had to look at her again. And saw the stark fear on her face.

"Taggart. I—"

He shook his head, silencing her. He didn't want to hear what she had to say. Didn't want to see the pain that came with the words. But he not only saw it, he felt it, as she held his gaze, clearly committed to telling him something he knew he didn't want to hear.

He jerked his gaze away. He wanted so badly to hate her with everything in him.

But he hated himself more, because her words had

just made him face an awful truth. He might still love her.

He was an even bigger fool now than he was back then, a fool for ever thinking he'd gotten her out of his system.

He hadn't written her off six years ago. He'd written off the idea of them being together by trying to convince himself that he hated her. Yet an idea that had lived for one week out of his life had somehow become a dream. A dream that her life would become a major part of his.

But it hadn't worked that way. She'd gone on without him.

It shouldn't hurt. And he was stupid and pathetic to let the thought of her with another man cut so deeply.

She had a son.

He breathed deep.

Well, hell, why not? He could fill a battleship with the things he didn't know about her.

He clenched his jaw and handed her the keys.

And he felt small suddenly, for holding on to so much anger over a weeklong affair and a bruised ego from six years ago. She had all the rights to pain in this scenario.

Neither of them said a word as she fired up the engine, shifted into gear, and took off.

Maybe she had a husband he didn't know about, too.

Maybe she'd already had both the hubby and the kid when they were in Kabul.

"Why did you make me bully that out of you?" He was surprised his voice didn't match his anger.

She hesitated. "It's . . . complicated."

No shit. He scrubbed a hand over his jaw. "Who have you been trying to call?"

She made a sharp left turn. "Meir's bodyguard."

Meir. The son now had a name. And yeah, a bodyguard made sense. Middle East. Mossad agent for a mother.

"He should have picked up right away," she said, talking more to herself than to him. "The lines are secure, so there's no reason for him not to."

Unless . . . aw, hell. "You think whoever targeted you is going after your son?"

"They *will* go after Meir."

"For God's sake, Talia. Why not just tell me that to begin with?"

"Because I've been hoping I'd reach Jonathan. That he'd tell me Meir was safe. And because telling you . . . saying the words out loud . . ."

Would make it all too real that her son was in danger, he concluded when she stopped and got hold of herself again.

Hate, love, anger, frustration—all of it had to take a backseat. If she was right, if the boy was in danger, they needed to find him. Fast.

"Let's back up," he said. "You're sure you were the target of the bombing? You, Talia Levine? Not you, the Mossad agent?"

"What does it matter now?" she snapped, then

settled herself down. "Because of those news crews, my face is all over TV and the Internet. They'll know that I'm still alive. And they'll go after Meir—if they haven't already."

"So why did we stop back there? How does that figure in?" He notched his head back over his shoulder.

"Meir had a play date with a friend after school."

"And?"

"According to the boy's mother, Jonathan waited outside in the car for him. They left at six o'clock as planned."

He glanced at the dash clock. Almost two hours ago.

And the bodyguard wasn't answering.

Whoever she was dealing with were real bad guys. So bad that they'd bombed a building, not caring how many people died as long as they achieved their goal. But they'd failed to kill her, so now it was on to plan B: rain down enough pain and suffering on her until she wished she was dead, until she prayed for death. All they had to do was take her son.

His gut filled with cold dread, his instincts telling him they'd accomplished their mission. It had been too long without a word from the boy's bodyguard, too many unanswered phone calls.

"Hamas did this," he said. It was the logical answer. The only illogical thing was Talia's insistence that Mossad wasn't involved. Why else would Hamas be after her, if it wasn't connected to her work for Mossad? Hamas's sole mission was to destroy Israel.

Mossad's mission was to stop them. The bombings and retaliations between them had played out for decades on the world stage.

When she didn't dispute his conclusion, he knew he was right. He also knew something was way off base.

"How good is this bodyguard?"

"The best I could find," she said. "But with Hamas after him, it would take a team to keep him safe. A team or a . . . a miracle." Her voice broke.

Damn it. He had to stop letting her pain get to him. Of course, he had sympathy for the boy. Of course, he would help her if that was what she wanted. But when this was over, one way or another, he was out of here.

"Where's your husband? Why isn't he here?" The instant the question popped out, he wished he hadn't asked.

"I'm . . . not married."

He felt something very close to relief. But that stupidity was soon eclipsed by a distant bell of alarm.

It's . . . complicated.

"Where is Meir's father?"

She stared straight ahead, her gaze locked on the street.

That was when a steel fist grabbed his heart. And squeezed. *Complicated.*

He stared at her long and hard, afraid to ask. Afraid not to. "How old is Meir?"

She flicked him a glance, then looked back through the windshield.

"How old?" he demanded, as the fist tightened.

"Five," she said quietly.

He closed his eyes. Felt the world shift beneath him. "His birth date?"

She told him, tears rimming her eyes.

Even though he knew the outcome, he did the math. Did it again, and felt a blow so crushing it sucked the air from his lungs.

But it couldn't be. He'd always used protection. The blood left his head in a rush. Not always. There'd been that one time. That one out-of-his-head-with-lust time.

He stared at nothing, barely breathing. Fought another urge to hit something. Needed to beat the ever-loving crap out of something.

"He's mine?" He barely whispered the words, too afraid to believe them, too rational not to.

Her hands clutched the steering wheel so tightly her fingers turned white.

"He's *mine*?" he yelled. *"That's* the complication?"

She bit her lower lip and nodded—and his world changed forever.

Shock and anger flooded his mind, until a primal rage, huge and raw and ugly, burst out of him. "Five *years*? *Five* goddamn *years*! You never thought to tell me?"

The Expedition swerved wildly, and he realized that he'd gripped her upper arm until he'd hurt her.

He let go. Couldn't stand to touch her.

He stared out the window as the streets rolled by, tenting his fingers on top of his head to keep it from blowing off. He'd never despised anyone as much as he despised her right now. And he'd never longed for something as much as he longed for those five lost years.

A child. A son. His own blood.

A weary resignation rode in on the heels of his anger.

"You hated me that much?" he asked into the tomb of silence filling the Expedition.

"I didn't hate you. I could never hate you. I—"

"Save it. Sorry I asked," he said wearily. "I don't want to hear anything out of your mouth that doesn't have to do with finding the boy."

The son he'd never known, who might already be lost to him.

15

"So what's your plan?" The question seemed as surreal as the conversation about the son whose existence he hadn't known about.

"Find Jonathan. He had to have heard the news about the bombing. He'd have taken Meir someplace safe."

"And that would be?"

"I . . . I hadn't been here long enough to set up a safe house for us. My best guess is his apartment."

"They'll be looking for your car. We could lead Hamas straight to him."

"What choice do I have?" Desperation overrode caution.

Unfortunately, he didn't have any other ideas. Just another hundred questions. "Tell me everything. Everything," he repeated, unable to look at her.

He'd lay odds that the bodyguard wasn't at his apartment. And if he was, he was probably dead. A chance still existed, however, that the boy—his son—

might be alive. He needed every piece of information she had if they were going to find him.

"Start with what you were doing at the embassy."

"I work . . . *worked* there," she said.

"Right. Undercover for Mossad."

"No. I'm not with Mossad now. I haven't been since . . . since before Meir was born."

A knifelike pain sliced him again at the mention of his son. Five years. He'd lost five years.

"I started working as a security investigator for the U.S. embassy in Israel after he was born." She glanced over her shoulder and made a quick lane change. "A couple of weeks ago, when the embassy SI here retired, I was temporarily reassigned here until they found a permanent replacement."

He remembered Ted telling him that before the bomb detonated. Ted. God, what if he was dead? Dead because Taggart had left him there.

"So you left Mossad," he said, shaking off the guilt by trying to piece everything together.

"I wanted out," she said, in a way that made him glance at her. She had that thousand-mile look in her eyes, telling him that her fear for the boy was getting the best of her again. "I wanted to provide Meir with a more stable life. I wanted him safe." She shook her head. "Look how great that worked out."

Yeah. Look how great it worked out. Bitterness tasted ugly. Uglier still if he'd let the words out of his mouth. They both knew that if he had been in his son's life, the boy would be safe now. He wouldn't be kidnapped and at the mercy of barbarians.

He swallowed back his frustration. "Did you know this was coming?"

"No. I sensed that something was going to happen. But not a bomb. Not at the embassy."

"But you suspected something? Why?"

"For the past several days, I've been fairly certain I was being followed. At first, I wanted to write it off as paranoia. You were a special operative; you know what it does to you. You never stop looking for threats, even ones that don't exist."

Yeah, he knew about paranoia. Now he knew a helluva lot more about blindsides. "So what was different this time?"

"I just . . . I couldn't shake it off. So I went with my gut and tried to reach out to one of my old teammates last week. To see if he'd heard any rumblings. Anything in the wind."

"And?"

"And I found out he was dead." She stopped, swallowed, and tore away from a stoplight. "But no one wanted to talk about it. I knew then that something was wrong. I was finally able to get hold of another friend there—I'd been her trainer when she was first drafted. She quietly did some digging for me and found out that over the past five years, my entire team had been killed." Her voice broke again. "One by one."

"Christ. Mossad couldn't have given you a heads-up? They had to know you were on the list."

"The team split up shortly after I left. It's possible that no one put it together that the specific operatives they'd lost had all been part of the same team at one time."

"So why target your old team specifically?"

She let out a deep breath. "Because we took out al-Attar."

Jesus. Talk about the past coming back to haunt him. It was because of al-Attar that Talia had targeted *him*.

It was because of Talia's part in the Mossad op that he'd ended a mission in disgrace. And with a son he didn't know.

Anger boiled up again. Again, he tamped it down. It wouldn't help the boy. "Why was al-Attar so important to Mossad?"

Unspoken was, *Why was al-Attar so important that you had to screw me over to get him?*

"Because he was a monster," she said without apology. "His specialty was killing children. Attacking schools, buses. Anything to get to them. The Mossad director lost his grandchild in a school-bus bombing orchestrated by al-Attar. He hit number one on Mossad's wanted list that day. Things are never supposed to get personal. But they do. They did. And that's why we went after him."

"And I ended up as collateral damage? Is that how you wrote me off?" Fuck. So much for controlling his anger.

"Taggart—"

"Forget it. Forget I said it. Just . . . forget it all."

Except he couldn't forget anything. He had a child. *They* had a child—a child who could end up as more collateral damage if they didn't get on top of this.

"Is it safe, then, to say that our working theory is that al-Attar's followers considered his death personal, too? That's why they went after you and your old team?"

"It's as good a motive as any. Al-Attar is a legend in Hamas. The most vicious yet charismatic of their war chiefs. His followers are devout. They'd want retribution for his death, no matter how long it took to get it."

"Why a bomb?" This had been bugging him since al-Attar's name had come up. "And why inside the U.S. embassy? Why not just get you in your car on the way to work?"

She shook her head. "I'm not an easy target. I've always been hypervigilant. And since I found out about the deaths of my team, I've taken even greater countermeasures."

"So they risked the wrath of the United States government by bombing our embassy?"

"Hamas has no love for the United States, you know that. Al-Attar's followers subscribe to the same doctrine he did. No risk is too great. No blood spared. If they had killed me, they would have managed to hit two birds with one stone and gain a lot of attention for their cause. And the al-Attar Hamas followers wouldn't stop to care whether the majority of Hamas leaders would approve or disapprove of their actions. They've almost become an entity unto themselves."

She could be right. Hell, Hamas couldn't even get along with their Palestinian brethren.

In the meantime, Bobby had no doubt that all hell had broken loose at the Pentagon as they tried to determine who was responsible. As soon as he got the boy to safety, he'd make sure they knew what he knew. For now, he didn't want any D.C. desk warriors interfering.

"Another thing," Talia continued, breaking into his thoughts. "Maybe they got desperate. Maybe they had a timeline. Maybe since I'm the last one on their list, they were impatient to tie it all up. Anyway, as soon as I found this out yesterday, I tried to get Meir out of Muscat. The earliest available flight was tonight at nine o'clock."

"I don't think you're going to make it." He didn't mean to sound flippant, but it came out that way. He didn't bother to apologize. "Does anyone else know about this?"

"About Hamas? No. I didn't dare talk to anyone. I didn't know if they might have had a mole inside the embassy."

Something else had been bothering him. "Why didn't you make sure that Meir—"

"Was safe until we left?" she interrupted, her voice glutted with guilt. "I should have. I should have pulled him out of school. I should have had Jonathan get him out of the city. But he'd had such a dif-

ficult time adjusting to his first week here. That's why
I enrolled him in summer-school classes. So he'd
meet children his age. He was so . . . sad. Missing his
friends. Missing everything that was familiar. When
he came home from school yesterday, he was excited
and happy for the first time. He'd made a new friend.
He'd been asked over for a play date today. I didn't
want to alarm him. I didn't want to disappoint him.
So I made a decision to keep today—this one single
day—as normal as possible. And he had Jonathan . . ."
She trailed off, so clearly miserable with guilt and regret that he was in danger of empathizing.

She slammed on the brakes, shifted into reverse,
and backed up past the last intersection.

"What?"

"Jonathan's car. I think I just saw it."

She made a tight right turn and sped down a street
toward a black Lincoln Town Car parked crookedly
by the curb. The driver's-side door hung open.

Talia stepped on the brakes, pulled up nose-to-
nose with the Lincoln, and slammed the Expedition
into park.

"Talia, wait."

There was no slowing her down; she'd already
wrenched open the door and rushed outside.

Swearing under his breath, he unholstered the
Glock, then followed her into the sweltering heat.

The Lincoln's engine still ran. Bullet holes riddled
the dark, tinted windshield, the glossy black paint on
the hood, the doors, and even the roof.

Overkill.

Vendetta.

He caught up with her, stopped her before she reached the driver's door, and pushed her behind him. "Stay back."

The windows were darkly tinted, and he couldn't see inside. Approaching warily, two-handing the Glock, he walked around the open door, then slowly lowered the gun.

A big, burly guy with personal security written all over him was slumped back against the seat. One bullet hole pierced his forehead; he'd taken several more rounds in his arms, in his thighs, and above the neck of his body armor. Blood ran everywhere.

Talia pushed around him before he could stop her. "Jonathan!"

He caught her when she swayed. Somehow she pulled herself together, wrenched away from him, and jerked open the back door.

"He's not here," she said, faltering somewhere between relief and alarm after searching inside. "Meir's not here."

Bobby reached around the steering wheel and pulled the keys. Pulse hammering, he walked to the back of the car and pushed the button on the remote.

Then he waited for the trunk to open, with a crushing mix of hope and dread. And for a moment, his heart stopped beating.

"Empty."

Talia spun around so her back was to him. She

hugged her arms around herself and let her head fall
back.

Bad news and more bad news. They could have
killed the boy here, but they hadn't, which meant
they wouldn't—yet. First, they wanted to make her
suffer. The look on her face more than proved they
had succeeded.

She was doubtless aware of every possibility, as he
was. They could still kill the boy; they could ransom
him to get to her; they could send him back to her
one piece at a time. Or they could make him disap-
pear and keep her in torturous limbo for the rest of
her life.

He quickly searched the town car, looking for any
clues or cryptic messages they might have left behind.
Nothing. Not even the bodyguard's cell phone.

"We've got to get out of here, Talia." When she
stood there nonresponsive, he grasped her arm and
led her back to the Expedition. "They may be watching, and if they are, you can be damn sure they'll
come for you."

He recognized shock when he saw it, and right
now, she was frozen with it. And with grief. He wasn't
in the best shape to drive, but he was a damn sight
better than she was. He guided her into the passenger
seat, then got behind the wheel.

16

Sometimes he trickin' hated being right. They'd barely pulled away from the Lincoln when a white Volkswagen Golf ripped around a corner behind them and sped toward them.

Bobby had spent enough time undercover in Palestine to know that VWs, particularly Golfs, were popular there. And while that didn't guarantee that it was Hamas on their tail, it fell back to basic math again. The sun was about to set, and the traffic in this part of the city was slim to none. Add the VW Golf to the mix, and it was more than coincidence.

"We've got a tail," he said, his eyes fixed on the rearview mirror.

The Golf picked up speed, and he hit the gas.

It took a moment before Talia snapped out of her shock and twisted around to get a look. "Hang a quick left at the next intersection," she said, buckling her seat belt. She knew the city. He figured she'd know how to lose them.

"Shit," he swore when he felt blood drip into his eye. He'd started bleeding again.

"Don't." She grabbed his hand to keep him from rubbing blood into his eye and making it worse. She found a tissue in the glove box and cleaned him up. Then she dug a first-aid kit out from under the seat and quickly taped a thick gauze patch over the bandage. All the while, she fed him directions as he zipped down the streets, trying to shake the Golf.

"How many?"

She twisted around and took a head count. "Four."

Any other time, he'd have stopped and squared off against them. But one Glock between the two of them wasn't enough of an arsenal, not in the shape they were in.

"This Expedition modified at all?" he asked, taking a corner on two squealing wheels, before slamming down a straightaway.

"If you're asking if it's armored, no."

"Then let's hope it's got a damn solid frame. Hang on. I'm tired of playing mouse to their cat."

He tromped on the gas, led the Golf through several intersections, and managed to put some distance between them when traffic kept the Golf at a red light. When he was ahead by two blocks, he hooked a sharp right-hand turn, then another and yet another, until he'd doubled back to a street where he'd spotted a narrow alley.

Two tall buildings flanked the alley's entrance. Heavy shadows fell across the yawning opening. He

hung a hard left and drove straight in, then stood on
the brakes, pulling the Expedition into the mouth of
the alley, hiding from the view of any passing cars. He
knew the Golf would be stalking them. Just like he
knew they'd soon be sorry.

"Get to the corner of the building. Tell me when
you see them coming. Then shoot me a countdown."

She was a soldier, so he knew he could count on
her to follow an order. She didn't let him down. She
climbed out of the vehicle and trotted to the edge of
the building. He winced for her with every step.

Face grim, he kept the Expedition revved, his
eyes locked on Talia in the side-view mirror. She'd
flattened herself against the wall at the corner of the
building, just out of view of the street but able to peek
around the wall to see if the Golf approached.

When she held up her hand, fingers splayed, he
knew it wouldn't be long.

Five fingers switched to four.

He tightened his grip on the steering wheel.

A long wait between four and three told him the
Golf was creeping as the occupants searched up and
down the street for the Expedition.

Two fingers.

Wait, wait, wait . . .One!

Slamming the Expedition into reverse, he jammed
the accelerator to the floor, and rocketed backward
out of the alley. He T-boned the Golf with his rear
bumper, crashing into the driver's door like a semi
on steroids.

Metal screamed against metal, rubber squealed against road, as the big Expedition propelled the smaller vehicle sideways along the street.

He didn't let up on the gas until he'd driven the Golf onto the far sidewalk and pinned it against a wall of concrete and steel. The Golf collapsed in on itself like an accordion. The plate-glass storefront shattered and rained down like jagged knives.

He jammed the Expedition into park, jumped out, and, with the Glock in hand, sprinted up to the wrecked vehicle.

Not the best move he'd ever made. Pain blasted inside his head, and he felt himself going down when Talia ran up beside him and shored him back up. She wrenched the Glock out of his hand and shoved it into the driver's face.

"Where is Meir? Where is my son?"

But she was talking to a dead man; he had likely died on impact. The guy in the passenger seat was also dead, crushed by the force of the impact. So was the man behind him; a shard of glass pierced his neck, apparently hitting an artery given the amount of blood.

Only one man remained alive and conscious.

"Where's the boy?" Bobby grabbed him by the throat and dragged him half out of the car through the shattered window. "Where is the boy?" he repeated, as the man's blood ran across his hand and down his arm.

Mortally wounded, he gasped for breath. Bobby

loosened his hold on his throat. "She . . . should have died . . . today," he croaked, his words faint and gurgling with blood. "Now her child . . . will take her place."

"Where is he?" Talia pressed the Glock against his temple.

The glazed eyes of a religious zealot stared back at her. "You should . . . have died. Now you will suffer . . . worse than death."

"Where is he?" Talia screamed, as the man's eyes drifted shut. "Where is he?" she shrieked desperately, until Bobby gripped her shoulders and shook her.

"Stop. Stop it. He's gone."

The raw anguish on her face matched his own. The only regret he felt was that they hadn't been able to get any information out of these monsters before they died. Not that they would have talked anyway.

Careful not to cut himself on the broken glass and twisted metal, he searched the bodies as best he could, hoping for some clue about where their buddies might be keeping Meir.

"Nothing?" Talia asked after Bobby had used the Expedition's tire iron to pry open the ruined trunk.

Grim-faced, he shook his head. "Do you recognize any of them?"

"No."

"Give me your phone."

When she handed it to him, he quickly snapped pictures of each dead man and then the license plate.

"Text these to your Mossad buddy. See if she can

find out if any of these guys are part of al-Attar's old group."

"I can try. But I don't think I'll hear from her. She made it clear that she couldn't risk any more contact with me."

"Because you're no longer in the loop," he concluded. Even when she nodded, something didn't feel right.

He'd figure it out later. Right now, they had to scramble.

"We've got to get out of here before someone calls this in and the local police show up, see four dead men, and draw some pretty obvious conclusions."

The last thing they needed was to get arrested. Talk about your international incident.

Suspected U.S. covert operative and former Mossad agent involved with the brutal killing of four in downtown Muscat.

No, thank you.

If he thought the local PD would help, he'd risk it, but it would be pointless. He and Talia would end up in interrogation, then detained while spools of red tape raveled and unraveled—and in the meantime, Meir remained in danger. They were going to have to go rogue, because neither the United States nor Israel would support an unsanctioned operation to save the child.

So right now, they needed to get the hell away from here.

Even more, he needed to shake off the overwhelming protective mode that had washed over him as the news that he was a father continued to sink in. He needed to shift into full-fledged operative mode. Needed to divorce himself from all emotion and function as he'd been trained to do.

The first item on the to-do list: get someplace safe, where they could regroup and come up with a plan.

17

Any covert operative worth his salt had *Cover Your Ass* tattooed on his brain. So before leaving U.S. soil, all team members were briefed on exactly where they could find safe haven if the need arose.

While the ITAP team was unofficially under the Department of Defense umbrella, no one there would acknowledge their existence if any team member was compromised on a mission. That meant there was always a safe house in place, to avoid any events that could jeopardize the tenuous relations between the United States and any nation harboring terrorists but claiming not to.

So an hour after leaving four dead terrorists in the Golf and taking a rambling route through the city to make certain they didn't pick up another tail, Talia directed Bobby to the address he'd given her. An address he'd committed to memory—along with two sets of combinations, one of which he assumed was to a keypad entry code on the safe house—before he'd left the States for Oman.

"There. On the right," Talia said, as Bobby cruised up the street about thirty minutes after sundown and the Muslim call to prayer.

He spotted the house number, searched through the dark for any signs of trouble, then drove on by. All in all, he made three drive-bys, coming from a different direction each time, before he was satisfied that he could take a chance and approach the building.

"We've got to get this vehicle out of sight. If your Hamas friends have been in Muscat for a while and you had the twitches, it's most likely because they've been following you. So they'll be looking for the Expedition. Also, we can't count on zero witnesses seeing us destroy the Golf."

He drove a little farther, found a shadowed alley, cut the lights, and parked. Talia had already turned off the interior lights, so he pulled the keys and handed them to her, along with the holstered Glock. "If I'm not back in ten minutes, you need to be gone."

And *bam*, there it was. An instant and undeniable feeling of loss—like the loss he'd felt when he'd returned to her hotel room that night in Kabul and found her gone. A gut-wrenching feeling of hating her for what she'd done to him and recognizing how closely hate and love intertwined.

Now here he was again, possibly seeing her for the last time. And all he could think about was that he'd lost her once and could lose her again in a matter of seconds if things went wrong. He could lose their son—and God help him, an impossible picture of the three of them together had already implanted itself in his brain.

How damn hard did you hit your head, fool?

Hard enough to kill a few brain cells that dealt with self-preservation, apparently.

Shoving everything but the immediate moment out of his mind, he slipped out of the vehicle. After a quick look around, he took off through the shadows and doubled back the four blocks to the safe house.

The neighborhood was upscale and quiet. He'd learned long ago never to be surprised by Middle Eastern cities. Before his first deployment, he'd had a preconceived idea that the countries surrounding the "cradle of civilization" would consist of ancient dwellings and run-down conditions. Sometimes that was true. But Muscat, Oman, didn't fit that mold. The city was modern, clean, and quite beautiful.

As he approached the safe house, he could see why it had been chosen. Like the rest of the buildings in this part of the city, it was constructed of sleek white stone to deflect the daytime heat that often reached 120 degrees. The safe house blended in with every other dwelling around it. Even better, the house was built on a slight incline, and a single-car garage, hidden from view in the dark during their drive-bys, had been dug out beneath it.

Huge score. They could not only hide the Expedition inside but enter the house through the garage and not be spotted.

Relieved, he trotted back to the SUV.

"We're good," he said, and she handed him the keys.

Five minutes and two more drive-bys later, he cut the Expedition's lights and pulled up in front of the garage. He hopped out and keyed one of the combinations he'd committed to memory into the lock pad on the driver's side of the garage door. The door opened quietly, and Talia slipped over to the driver's seat and pulled inside.

Only after the door was shut behind them did he turn on a light so he could find his way into the house and breathe a long breath of relief.

And only after they were safely inside, with all the blinds pulled down and a single light burning in the small kitchen, did he let the ringing in his ears and the pounding in his head take him down. He'd taken a beating in the bombing, and adrenaline could only power him up for so long.

He needed to call Nate Black, the leader of both the Black Ops Inc. team and the ITAP team, and fill him in. See what resources he could offer. But first, he needed five minutes of being horizontal.

He dropped to the long tan sofa, covered his eyes with a forearm, and let the fatigue and the pain consume him.

Five minutes—to take a breath, to get ahead of the fatigue, to come to terms with everything about this day that had started with a handshake from an old friend and ended up a living hell.

Five minutes. Then he'd figure out how to find his boy.

Talia stood just inside the door, exhausted, raw, and terrified for Meir. She watched Taggart collapse on the sofa. She knew he hated her, and she couldn't blame him. And she envied his ability to let go of the horrors of the day and fall immediately asleep.

Envied that he could compartmentalize everything that had happened—including finding out that he had a son—and then lock it away so he could rest.

It wasn't fair that she also resented him for it, but she did. Meir was out there. Afraid. He'd seen Jonathan brutally murdered. She couldn't stop thinking about Jonathan, either, although there was nothing she could do for him.

She had to think about Meir. Had they hurt him? Was he even alive? Was he crying for her? Wondering why she hadn't come for him?

Helplessness and fear for him clutched her chest, tightened her throat until it ached. A fear she hadn't let herself completely bend to until now. Now, knowing they had him, not knowing if he was alive or suffering, it finally broke her.

Her heart felt as though it had splintered into a million pieces, as horrific images of what they could be doing to her sweet little boy sped through her mind.

A sob welled up in her chest, painful and huge. She fought to hold it in, but it was too strong. Too raw. And she was too weary. In too much pain.

Drowning in utter despair, she covered her mouth to muffle a sound that soon became a keening cry. Her knees folded, and she dropped to the floor, no longer recognizing the sounds pouring out of her, not knowing how to stop them.

Then she felt him there. Taggart.

On his knees beside her. Pulling her into his arms, then holding her as she clung to him and let the anguish consume her.

"I'm his . . . mother," she cried. "I should have protected him. Now he's . . . now he's . . ."

"We'll get him back," he whispered against her hair as sobs wracked her body. "We *will* get him back."

18

Déjà vu all over again.

Here he was, exactly where he should *not* fucking be after picking her up, carrying her into the bedroom, and laying her down.

He'd had no intention of staying with her. But she'd clung to him, her body shaking so violently he was afraid she'd come apart if he let her go.

So he stayed. Held her. Remembered another time. Another place. Another moment when she'd cried and he'd kissed her for the first time. When he'd been blissfully unaware that what he felt for her and what he thought she'd felt for him was all a lie.

But the longer he lay there, the softness of her body nestled against him, her bare arms and legs locked around him as though gravity had pulled her in and held her tethered to him, the easier it was to think about forgiveness. And forgiveness made him feel weak. And ashamed that she could so easily bring him to his knees. Again.

Steeling himself against emotions she didn't deserve, he pried himself away as soon as she fell asleep. Then he left her there, his gut knotted with emotions that ran the gamut from anger to empathy to self-disgust.

He walked through the small house and collapsed back down on the sofa, knowing he was in danger of getting in way too deep with this woman again.

Horizontal lasted all of a minute. Suddenly, he was too tired even to sleep. Restless, he rose stiffly to his feet again and started searching the house. There had to be a phone—a *secure* phone, and he wasn't certain that hers was. There also had to be weapons. Clothes. Food.

In the small kitchen, he hit the jackpot. He snagged an energy drink from the fridge and downed half of it while he snooped through the cabinets. Military-issued Meals Ready to Eat, dried fruits, and nuts. All the essentials to refuel and power back up.

He'd tear into one of the prepacked MREs later. Right now, he needed to find that phone. And since he still had another combination of numbers in his memory, he figured there must be a safe tucked away in the house somewhere.

Because he knew how some of the top minds in U.S. covert ops worked, he found it a few minutes later. The planked bamboo floors in the living room were highly polished. He moved the low, wide coffee table off the area rug that lay in front of the sofa, then flipped back the rug to expose the floor. Then he lay down on his stomach, his cheek pressed to the wood, and searched the boards not only by sight but with his fingertips, until he found the slightest gap between the seams.

After that, it was a matter of carefully prying up one section of board at a time, and *bam*. There was the safe, sandwiched between the floor joists.

He made quick work of the combination lock, whipped it open, and *hoo-ah!* Inside, along with a satellite phone, were enough weapons and ammo to level the playing field.

Every member of ITAP knew the number to call when the shit hit the fan and they were out of options. Satellite phone in hand, Taggart closed the bedroom door so he wouldn't wake Talia, then, to be doubly safe, opened the sliders at the back of the house and stepped out onto a small, secluded deck.

Although the sun had set an hour ago, the desert heat hit him like a tank. The weight of it made it difficult to breathe—as did the smell of burnt gasoline in the air.

In the distance, he heard the muffled sound of traffic, but here, in this residential neighborhood, the night was quiet.

He punched in the number and hit send, then waited for Nate Black to pick up.

Black was smart, tough as gravel, and he had been there, done that, with the scars and nightmares to prove it. There were very few people who could rattle Taggart, but Black was one of them. Black subscribed to General James Mattis's axiom: "Be polite, be professional, but have a plan to kill everybody you meet."

Like Mattis, Black didn't have a problem stacking bodies high and deep if he thought it was necessary.

He finally picked up on the third ring. "Black."

"It's Taggart."

"About damn time," Black said, covering what Bobby knew was concern with a clipped reprimand.

"Sorry. Been a little busy."

"So it would seem." Black would have kept himself well apprised of the embassy bombing. "Good thing you called," he went on. "Since we hadn't seen your name on a survivor list, the boys were setting up a lottery to see who got your new desk chair."

A laugh burst out, the first honest relief Bobby had felt since he'd come to in that bombed-out building. "You tell my 'buddies' to keep their mitts off my chair. I waited six months for that bad boy."

"Bound to be disappointment all around."

"I'm sure they'll recover," he said, feeling the same affection for his teammates that he knew they felt for him.

"So . . . you okay?" The flat-out concern was back in Black's voice.

"Yeah. Fit and fine," he lied, then asked the big question. "Any news on Ted Jensen?" He held his breath and, in the background, heard the familiar squeak of Nate's desk chair.

"He's alive."

The relief he felt could have filled a football stadium.

"In serious but stable condition. Barring any complications, they say he'll pull through."

Thank God. "That's good. That's very good."

"What've you got going, Bobby?"

"A fucking nightmare, that's what I've got." Where did he start? "I need help, sir. Assets. Intel. A team on the ground. Infrared cameras. Hell, a drone if you can make it happen. Whatever you've got, I need it. Yesterday. Only there's one catch."

"Hold on while I get hold of Rhonda. Sounds like she needs to be patched in on this."

Taggart had a special friendship with Rhonda, the wife of his friend Jamie Cooper. Like Coop, she was also a member of the ITAP team, one of their go-to girls when it came to intelligence gathering and organization. As a field operative, she'd take a pass. But in truth, the blond bomber could hold her own with any of the guys. More important, she could work spooky magic with a keyboard. And the fact that Black was willing to bring her on board immediately told Bobby he'd bring the full weight of both his BOI team and the ITAP team to the table.

He only hoped he'd get the same response when Black knew the whole story.

"Sir. Um . . . hold on before you connect Rhonda." He stopped, swallowed.

He hadn't yet fully processed the implications of Meir's existence in his life; he wasn't even close to being ready to share it with others. But he *was* fully invested in his son's safety. "There's something I'd like kept between the two of us for the time being, if you don't mind, sir. The team doesn't need to know. Not yet."

"That would be the catch, I take it?"

A smart man, Nate Black. "Yeah. This is . . . this is personal, sir. One hundred percent. DOD would never sanction what I'm about to ask of you."

The silence on the other end of the line was so thick he figured it was all over but the apologetic refusal. And he respected Nate Black too much to make him say the words. "Look. It's okay. I know you can't—"

"Taggart." Black cut him off. "What did I tell you and Brown and Cooper when you agreed to come on board with me? We have complete autonomy over what we choose to do and not do. Now, tell me what I can do to help you, son."

19

Fifteen minutes later, Bobby had filled Nate in on the bombing and Talia's and Meir's connection to it, as well as their certainty that al-Attar Hamas followers were behind it all. After a quick search of the Expedition, he found Talia's cell phone and fired off the photos he'd taken of the Golf's license plate and the four dead men. Rhonda would make short work of pinning them down. He hoped.

When he disconnected, he felt as though the weight of the bombed-out building had been lifted from his shoulders. Nate hadn't browbeaten him about his involvement with Talia six years ago; he hadn't heaped on guilt about being so irresponsible that he'd fathered a child. Most of all, Nate had assured Bobby that he'd dump everything—maybe even with DOD's approval—into a transport plane that would arrive within twenty-four hours with as many team members as he could gather.

"What's the situation with the boy's mother?" Nate

had asked with straightforward concern after Bobby had explained about Talia and Meir.

"It's complicated," Bobby told him, echoing Talia's words.

"Yeah. That much I'd figured out."

Ordinarily, Bobby would have smiled.

"Can you work with her?"

"Yes," he'd said without hesitation. "If she can pull herself together. You can imagine, she's terrified for the boy."

"And you?"

"I'm going to find him. I *need* to find him. Alive. But I need something to go on. Someplace to start looking while I wait for you to get here."

"I'll get Rhonda right on it. Stay by the phone," Nate said, and disconnected.

Feeling his first glimmer of hope, Bobby headed for the bathroom and a shower. They'd sketched out a strategy, and Nate had assured him that they'd go all in on Meir's rescue.

Energized, he rummaged around in the hall closet and found T-shirts, jeans, dress pants, shoes, underwear—all kinds and sizes.

He also found traditional Omani attire. The dishdasha was a white, ankle-length, collarless, long-sleeved gown. He considered slipping one on; it would feel a helluva lot better on his nicks and bruises than street clothes.

In the end, he grabbed a black T-shirt and jeans.

After downing a couple of painkillers and applying some antiseptic salve and a fresh bandage to his head, he felt like a new man.

Almost.

He peeked in on Talia and found her tossing the covers back, about to get up.

"You're awake." He'd thought she'd sleep for some time yet.

"How long was I out?" She sat up stiffly, blinking the sleep from her eyes.

"Less than an hour."

Plenty of time for him to contemplate, again, that this had been the second time he'd taken Talia Levine to bed and held her while she'd cried herself to sleep. Her grief tonight, however, had gone beyond anything he'd ever experienced.

What's the situation with the boy's mother?

Bobby still didn't have a clue. She looked pretty fragile—not a word he'd ever associated with her before.

A vindictive man would say she'd brought this all down on herself. He'd thought he was that man, but it turned out he wasn't. He didn't know what he was or what he felt for her, either.

But more important right now was how *she* felt. Could she come back from a breakdown that brutal? Her heart and her soul both seemed as shredded as her feet.

"You should get cleaned up, take care of your feet before the cuts get infected," he said, schooling himself, for God's sake, not to let her affect him again like she had when she'd clung to him, her body trembling and convulsing with anguish. "There's a first-aid kit in the bathroom medicine cabinet." He cleared his throat of his suddenly scratchy voice.

"I don't have time to shower. We have to—"

He held up a hand and cut her off. "What we have to do is regroup and recover. And wait—for now," he said quickly when she opened her mouth to object. "Then we have to discuss our next moves. I'm already working on a plan, okay?"

She dragged the wild mass of her hair away from her face. "What kind of plan?"

"I found a floor safe with a SAT phone, weapons, ammo." He looked down at his jeans. "I also found clothes. The kitchen's stocked with food. More important, I spoke to my team leader in the States. I'll fill you in later, but for now, just know that they're using every resource they have available to help find Meir."

"They? Who are *they*?"

"The good guys, Talia." Both Nate's direct team and the ITAP team were highly covert units. Only a handful of people in the Pentagon were on the need-to-know list, so he sure as hell wasn't going to tell her. "That's as much as I can give you."

She didn't look convinced. But the soldier slowly surfaced, and she apparently accepted him at his word.

Then she eased unsteadily to her feet.

And damn, what a striking, wretched mess she was. Her skirt had ripped all the way to the top of her thigh. Her silk top was filthy and torn. Her eyes were red and swollen from crying. She was bandaged and bruised and covered in ash and blood. And yet she was still the most beautiful woman he'd ever—

Fuck. Do not *go there again.*

"Do you need help?" He hoped she could make it on her own, because if she was so physically and mentally beaten that she'd accept his offer of help, he was afraid she wouldn't rally at all. And she needed to. Just like he needed to keep his damn distance.

"I'm fine." She wasn't, but she wanted him to think so, as she took step after careful step toward the bedroom door, her jaw clenched in pain.

That was the best reaction he could have hoped for. She was tough.

Still, he had to stuff his hands into his pockets to keep from picking her up and carrying her into the bathroom to get her off those feet.

He sorted through the stack of dishdashas and found a small one he thought might work for her. Then he grabbed the smallest pair of boxers he could find and rapped a knuckle on the bathroom door.

"Found something clean for you to wear. I'll leave it on the floor outside the door."

It wasn't long after that she stepped out of the bathroom, scrubbed clean, her long, wet hair falling around her face. Her feet were still bare. Her face hadn't been spared, either. Here and there, he spotted nicks and bruises that had been hidden beneath the grime.

She looked lost in even the smallest dishdasha. The loose-fitting garment was made of soft white muslin and designed to mitigate the burn of the Omani heat. It made her look tiny, even waiflike, and he felt that catch in his chest that came at the oddest times.

"Eat while we can," he said, his mouth suddenly dry. Sitting down on a stool at the kitchen counter, he tore into his second energy drink and an MRE—and damn near burned his tongue.

A hundred thoughts raced through his mind while she sat down beside him, silent, still a little shocky, suffering but dealing.

He forced his thoughts to Ted, relieved to know he'd gotten out of the building and was expected to be okay.

Now they needed a miracle to help the boy.

He glanced at Talia, who'd grown gut-wrenchingly quiet. And though he'd fought it for six years, he finally came to terms with another truth he'd managed to suppress. Okay, refused to acknowledge. Today wasn't the first time she'd saved his life.

"In Kabul," he said. "When your boys took down al-Attar and his crew, they could have killed me. Instead, they tossed me into the street and turned me loose."

She turned to him, and he knew she'd grasped where he was going.

"How much did it cost you to make that happen?"

Her gaze wavered, then lowered. With an unsteady hand, she reached for the energy drink he'd set out for her.

She had to have pulled in major favors to get him out of there alive. Navy SEALs, Special Forces, MI-6, or Mossad agents—operatives all went by the book. They'd minimize collateral damage if they could, but he hadn't fallen into that category. He'd fallen squarely into the "loose ends" category that night. By rights, they should have killed him along with al-Attar and his men.

"What was the price of my life?" he asked again, softly this time.

She didn't answer, so he said it for her.

"They booted you out, didn't they? Suddenly, their hotshot operator had a weakness—me—so they cut you loose."

She propped an elbow on the counter and lowered her head into her hand, as if she couldn't bear the weight of it. "It doesn't matter." Her voice was ragged, weary. "Saving Meir is what matters."

Yes, Meir was what mattered now. But for all these years, he'd refused to acknowledge that he must have mattered to *her*, too, back then. He must have mattered very much. And he couldn't help but wonder if maybe he mattered even now.

I don't hate you. I could never hate you.

He studied her profile and felt a swell of emotion he didn't want to own. He fought to resist everything that made him want to react to her as a man who had once thought they had a future.

"Your team leader," she said, abruptly changing the subject. "You said you talked to him. Said he's a good guy. What kind of resources does he have or have access to?"

He felt relief that she'd waylaid his thoughts. He didn't understand where this sudden bending of his defenses came from. It wasn't that he could ever forgive her. It wasn't as if what she'd done *for* him could ever compensate for what she'd done *to* him.

"Eat while it's still hot," he said gruffly. "And I'll tell you what I know."

She looked at the MRE he'd set in front of her. Then she shoved her damp hair over her shoulder and, on a resigned breath, picked up a fork. He watched while she took a bite. Knowing all that she'd been through today, the helplessness and loss she felt for Meir, he almost reached for her. Almost drew her into his arms again.

"Do you know anything about what I've been doing since you left Kabul?"

He wasn't sure why he'd asked or why her answer should matter. Yet the longer her silence went on, the more it did matter. It was stupid to feel so tense, but it felt as if something important depended on her reply.

Something other than the pathetic hope that possibly, she had cared enough to keep track of him. A hope that he just now realized had always been with him.

20

Talia set down her fork. She wished she could tell him that she knew everything about him. She had wanted to know where he was, what he was doing, if he was well and even alive after all this time. She'd had sources with access to information, but she hadn't let herself ask. Somehow it had seemed less painful that way.

"No," she said honestly. "I don't know what you've been doing."

She wasn't sure what to draw from his silence, but she imagined he felt the same blow she had felt upon discovering he'd had no idea she was no longer with Mossad. It hurt to know he hadn't cared enough to keep track of her. And based on the little he'd told her about his team, it seemed he also had access to resources that could have helped him find out if he'd wanted to know.

More likely, he'd been so angry he'd simply written her off.

"So you're not still with Fargis?"

He grunted, as if he found some cynical amusement in her question. "No. Not for several years. Seems we've both made some big changes."

"But you're still in the same line of work." She was counting on that—desperately. She needed the Taggart she'd known in Kabul, the whip-smart, tough soldier she'd seduced. Meir's life depended on him still being a warrior.

"If you tell me who you're with, maybe I can network them into resources here in Oman, maybe even into the city, where we need help *now*. Right now. There's no time for—" She heard the hysteria leaking into her voice and stopped herself cold. She couldn't fall apart again. She needed to be the agent she'd once been.

"This team is deep-sixed into an abyss, Talia," he said, picking up the conversation. "They're the best at what they do. You're going to have to trust me on this."

"We're talking about my son," she said, fighting the anguish threatening to drown her. "I have a right to know everything. I *have* to know everything, and I don't want to play twenty questions to get one simple damn answer. My son's—*your* son's—life depends on us. Depends on whoever you just called. I need to know we can count on them to be—"

"Count on them to be what?" he interrupted, his voice taking a hard edge. "To be who *I* say they are?"

"Yes." She clenched her hands in her lap. "I need something to hang on to, someone to believe in." *I need hope.*

"Do you know how rich that is? Coming from you?" His tone was as sharp as a razor. "This is different from Kabul, Talia. In case you hadn't noticed, I'm not playing you. I don't *want* anything from you. I'm trying to find the boy. That's all."

She hung her head, fighting for control. *Please, help me, God. We don't have time for rehashing the past. But I need Taggart.* She drew a shaky breath, forced herself to look up and meet his gaze. "I'm sorry. I didn't mean to—"

"What if I hadn't been here?" he bit out, interrupting her again. "What if you were on your own? Would you question an offer of help then?" He stood unexpectedly and stalked across the room. "I can't believe this. I can't fricking believe I was actually starting to . . ." He trailed off, shaking his head as if he felt like a fool.

"Starting to what?" She had to ask. Forgive her? Understand what she'd gone through?

"Never mind. What I can't believe is that you have the nerve to question me. After what *you* did to *me*."

Anger. He was so filled with it. She'd done that to him. And she deserved every bit of it. Yet suddenly, she needed him to understand. "Did I set out to betray you?" She shifted her gaze to the kitchen, away from him. "Yes. You were my mission. You were my avenue to get to al-Attar. So yes. I used you. I seduced you. I betrayed you, because the American government wanted him alive, and he needed to die for all the Israeli lives he'd taken."

Feeling stronger now that the words were out, she turned around to face him. He stood with his back to her, fists clenched at his sides.

"I was Mossad," she reminded him forcefully. "I volunteered for the mission, prepared to do anything necessary—including seducing you—to get the information on al-Attar."

"Mission fucking accomplished." Sarcasm dripped from each word.

She couldn't let his bitterness stop her now. "But you . . . you were not what I expected. And I—" She stopped herself short of saying *I fell in love with you*. He wouldn't want to hear it. "I never planned on caring about you."

"As you're so fond of saying, what does it matter now?"

Oh, it mattered. It mattered to her. And although he wouldn't admit it, she was certain it mattered to him. He wouldn't be this angry if it didn't.

Most of all, it mattered to Meir.

"You were right about the reason I'm no longer Mossad. I broke the code. I got personally involved with an assignment. And before I went into the operation, that's all you were. You understand that, right? You of all people? You were a name in an action plan. An individual to target to accomplish a goal."

She stopped again and composed herself. "After we became . . . close . . . I begged for your life. I pleaded with Mossad to spare you. And yes, it cost me."

He turned around and glared at her. "We both paid a price, then, didn't we?"

"I didn't keep track of you after Kabul," she went on, holding his flat gaze, "because I knew you would hate me. You had every right to. And I knew there would be no purpose, no good to come from attempting to contact you. So I did the only thing I could do. I forgot about you. At least, I tried."

"Right," he said after a long moment. "Must have been a little tough, what with you carrying my kid and all. A real bitchin' bad place to be."

Bitterness and vitriol. He was entitled to both. And she was entitled to get this all out in the open. "What would you have done? Ask yourself that. I didn't plan to get pregnant." She rushed on. "But it wasn't long after I left Kabul that I realized I was. Did I have choices? Yes. I could have had an abortion. But I didn't. I could have told you. But I didn't do that, either.

"Think about it," she demanded after a brief silence. "What would you have done if you'd known? What *could* you have done? You hated me. You hate me now. How could I bring a child into this world and introduce him to a man who hated his mother?"

He'd grown very quiet, his entire body tense.

"After . . . right after he was born, I came very close to looking for you. To telling you. But I was afraid you would try to take him from me."

She dragged the hair away from her face, exhausted by the slow pulse of fear washing through her body. *My son . . . my son . . .*

"You were a soldier for hire," she went on wearily. "Undoubtedly, you still are. How could I have risked losing him to you? If I'd told you and you'd wanted him, you would have taken him. I know you well enough to know that. To hell with a courtroom and the law. You'd have taken him in the night and made sure I never found you. And how could a child have possibly fit into your world?"

He turned around, his expression a flat plane of anger. "So because *you* couldn't see a child in my life, *you* decided he was better off without me." He tapped his chest with a tight fist. "When did *I* ever get to weigh in on that decision? Jesus, Talia. Did you ever even *once* think that I might have liked to have known about him? That I had a *right* to know about him? That I had a right to decide what my role in his life would be?"

She had no more tears to shed. "I've thought about it every single day. Questioned every day if I'd made the right decision. And now that I see you, now that I see the angry man you've become—"

"I am *not* an angry man!" he roared. "I am angry with *you*! And by God, I have every right to that anger."

She lowered her head, because she couldn't bear to see his rage and pain.

He was right. And she accepted now, as she should have all along, that he was still as lost to her as the day she'd betrayed him. "Please tell me the plan," she said, ending not only their conversation but any hope that they could ever bridge the distance between them. "How are we going to get him back?"

A phone rang then, adding new anxiety to the brittle tension.

21

"Rhonda," he said, his voice still light, as he answered the SAT phone. "What have you got for me?"

Talia watched and listened, not wanting to, unable to help herself, as his features and his voice slowly softened. An instant ago, his jaw had been clenched, his brows rigid with rage. Yet this woman—Rhonda—had wiped out his anger with "hello."

Was she someone on his team? Someone in his life? Both? It would be naive to assume he wasn't involved with someone. A man like him, a man who looked like him, who loved like him.

Even though Taggart mostly listened and paced, head down, phone close to his ear, the conversation was clearly about Meir. For that she was beyond thankful.

His major contributions to the conversation were short and clipped words between long pauses. "Got it . . . Yeah . . . Copy that . . . Yes . . . Understood."

Not knowing what was being said made her crazy, so she eased off the counter stool and limped into the bathroom in search of the first-aid supplies. She'd cleaned and bandaged her arm, but she hadn't yet taken care of her feet. The pain she could take. An infection that might put her down she couldn't. She had to be able to find Meir.

Taggart's team might be on the way, but she couldn't wait. It was close to nine thirty; those barbarians had had her baby for three and a half hours.

She fought anxiety and shaking hands as she gathered peroxide, cotton balls, antiseptic cream, and bandages, then carried them to the living room, where she had more room and more light to work on her feet.

"Yes, babe. I'm okay," Taggart said, actually smiling into the phone, and God, it hurt to remember that he'd smiled that way once for her.

It also hurt that he had the nerve to flirt with Rhonda when her child—*their* child—was in unimaginable danger.

"I've got a little bump on my head. Other than that, I'm good. I promise. Look. I need you to get on that for me ASAP. Call me back when you've got things arranged, okay? Yeah. Love you, too."

Talia tightened her jaw.

"Make sure you tell your husband I said you're way too good for him."

If it wasn't one kind of guilt she felt, it was another. How petty. How outrageously unacceptable for her to feel relief that Rhonda wasn't a lover but the wife of a friend.

She set out the medical supplies. Nothing about her feelings for Taggart should be in play here. It shamed her that even for a moment, she thought about herself, not about Meir.

"Part of your team?" She started folding squares of gauze, then ripping lengths of tape.

"Rhonda's our computer hacker techno wizard. And she already has information for us to go on."

Every cell in her body shot to attention. "A lead?"

He continued to pace the room. "When I called Nate earlier, I filled him in on what we knew. That Hamas was responsible for the bombing, that you were their target, and that when they realized you were still alive, they kidnapped Meir."

It all sounded so surreal, as if it were happening to someone else, when he said the words out loud in such a detached, matter-of-fact way. But it jolted her back to reality. She had to start functioning as if this was a mission happening to someone else.

She needed to divorce herself from her fear and love for her son and attack the problem as an operative would. As she'd been trained to do. Logically and systematically. If she kept letting her emotions come into play, she wouldn't be any good to Meir.

"Back up a second, please. Nate—he's your boss?" she asked as calm settled over her.

"Yes. Earlier, I sent him the pictures of our four dead terrorists. He forwarded them to Rhonda. She's in the process of running the photos through our

database. While she's waiting for results, she went
ahead and accessed NSA files."

"NSA?" That stopped her in the middle of applying the antiseptic cream to a nasty cut on her heel.
"You have access to the NSA's digital files?"

"Sort of," he said, heightening her curiosity about
his organization. "Rhonda ran a check on al-Attar's
background. Family. Friends. Partners in terror.
Whatever. Al-Attar has a son, Hakeem. Did you know
about him?"

"He was in his teens, I think, when . . ." She trailed
off and went back to work on the bandages.

"When Mossad killed his father," he said, finishing
the thought for her. "He's twenty-something now, and
he's on a terrorist watch list along with al-Attar's older
brother, Amir. While no ironclad cases have been
made against them, in addition to numerous bombings and attacks, both are suspected to be connected
to the Mossad agents' deaths."

She let out a long breath. "That pretty much con-
firms that this *is* about retribution. If I'd known about
the deaths earlier, Meir and I would have been gone
before this ever happened."

"But you didn't know. And all the self-recrimination
in the world isn't going to change that."

Her head came up. She was surprised to see that
the anger in his eyes had been replaced by a look of
purpose. He, too, had shifted into operative mode. His
focus, his intensity, all geared toward finding Meir.

"I wonder how they found you out," he said

pensively, and she could tell it had been bothering him.

"That makes two of us. No one outside of Mossad knew the photojournalist job was a cover. They never would have leaked it."

"I knew," he said, watching her face intently. "What makes you think I didn't leak it?"

Probably a good question. He'd figured out she was Mossad immediately after she'd betrayed and left him. But she knew it wasn't him. "There's a difference between anger and evil. You're not evil."

The set of his mouth told her he wanted to be indifferent to her trust. His eyes told a different story. "I'll probably never know how they connected me with Mossad. I saw no need to change my identity when I went to work for the State Department. It was a natural transition."

He pinched his lower lip between his thumb and finger, still not satisfied. But it didn't matter how they'd found out; the damage had been done.

"Do they know anything about Ted Jensen? About casualties in general?" she asked.

"Ted's going to be okay. The death toll is much less than I expected, considering there were around two hundred people inside. Seven dead at last count. Many more hospitalized, some in critical condition."

And she wasn't supposed to feel guilty. She closed her eyes, saw her dead aide. Wondered how many others might still die. She'd thought she heard a voice at one point during their struggle to get out of the building, but her ears had been ringing so loudly she couldn't tell what direction it came from. Even if she could have found them, what could she have done? "They might still be alive if—"

He cut her off again. "You aren't responsible."

"But if I hadn't come to Muscat—"

"Hakeem, Amir, and the rest of their al-Attar Hamas brothers are the bad guys here. So stop with the guilt trip. It won't do Meir any good. We need to look forward, not back."

He was right. "So what else?" she asked, and returned to bandaging her feet.

"The word on Hakeem is that he's hotheaded. Very radical. Very devoted to his unholy cause and the memory of his father. And he's out for vengeance. Clearly, he didn't think about the fallout of bombing a U.S. embassy. Both the Pentagon and DOD are in a tailspin, trying to figure out a strategic and diplomatic plan for addressing the bombing. So requests are apt to get knotted up in the red tape. Which is actually good for us. It means we may not have to dodge a U.S. military operation that could screw up our search—at least, not right away."

"What about Amir?"

"A false religious zealot. The worst kind. He spouts all the 'Hamas versus infidel' propaganda, but he likes his alcohol and women. He might be the weak link that leads us to Meir. Rhonda will text us pictures of both Amir and Hakeem."

The SAT phone rang just as he said it. But it wasn't

photos of Hakeem and Amir. It was another call from Rhonda.

"I'm going to put you on speakerphone so Talia can hear the conversation, okay, babe?" Taggart hit the speaker icon and set the phone on the coffee table in front of them. "All right. Shoot."

"Talia. Hello." A strong woman's voice came over the line. "I'm sorry we're meeting under these conditions. But we're going to get your son back, okay? You've got the best people possible working on it."

"Thank you. Thank you for helping," Talia said, suddenly overwhelmed by the idea that someone she didn't know was doing so much for Meir.

"Talk to me, sweetheart," Bobby said.

"Okay. I've got a lot of info, so I'm starting from the top, and it's coming fast, so hang on. First, we got an FRS match" —

"Facial recognition software," Taggart mouthed to Talia.

— "on one of the dead men. Known associate of Hakeem al-Attar, so they were definitely his men. I suspect we'll get a match on the other three soon, but we're not waiting around for confirmation. We're moving on this.

"Next, I believe I already told you that Hakeem and Amir are on the terrorist watch list. We got real lucky. Hakeem was last spotted five days ago at a rental-car desk at the Muscat International Airport. So he's definitely in Muscat, because there've been zero sightings of him anywhere else since. And now we know that in addition to a white VW Golf—that was the vehicle, right?"

"Right," Taggart said.

"In addition to the white Golf, they rented two more vehicles: a light blue four-door Golf and a cream-colored Toyota Highlander. I'll text you the plate numbers after we hang up."

"So we're looking at four more men fitting inside the blue Golf and five in the Toyota?" Talia asked.

"Sounds right. They could maybe squeeze another into the Toyota, but why? We're thinking they'd want cargo space for weapons and supplies."

Nine, Talia thought, as a sickening knot formed in her stomach. Nine more men had her baby.

"We've also put a watch on the airport for Meir or any child with an Israeli or American passport attempting to leave the city," Rhonda continued, helping Talia to focus on what they had, not what they didn't have. "We don't think they'd have had the foresight to prepare false papers for Meir, but just in case, we've got that area covered. I hacked the school's database and found a picture of Meir that's been sent out over the wire. No one's getting that boy out of Muscat by air without someone in security recognizing him. So far, no children have been flagged."

"They could transport him on the ground," Talia said, and Taggart nodded in accord.

"They could," Rhonda agreed. "But why move him out of Muscat? You're their target, not the boy.

He's their ticket to get to you. We think they'll want to use him as bait to draw you out. And as frightening as that sounds, we think that's a good thing, Talia."

"How can that be good?" She couldn't help it; fear for Meir got the best of her.

"The general consensus is they're not taking him anywhere. The odds are they'll attempt to ransom him—for you. We feel this very strongly. And when they finally make that call, you're going to ask for proof of life. You're going to demand that they let you talk to him. And they are going to anticipate that. For that reason alone, we're sure Meir is alive."

Talia let that settle, then looked to Taggart for some indication that he agreed with Rhonda. He nodded, looking confident.

"Talia, do they have any way of getting in touch with you?" Rhonda asked.

"Yes," Taggart answered for her. "I think they do. I searched the dead bodyguard's car and didn't find his cell phone. Makes sense that if they plan to ransom the boy, they'd need that phone to contact Talia. Her number would be stored on it."

"That does make sense," Talia agreed. "We attempted to reach Jonathan several times. My name would have shown up on his missed-call log."

"Good. That's good," Rhonda said. "Then we wait for the call. But we're going to find Meir long before you have to worry about meeting any ransom demands. Right now, there's a 737 cargo jet filled with equipment fueled up and ready to go at Dulles Airport. And guess who Nate persuaded the Pentagon to send over to investigate the bombing?"

A smile bloomed on Taggart's face. "I knew he'd figure out a way."

"We're just waiting for the guys to touch down at Dulles, then they'll be wheels up."

"Wait?" Talia asked as alarm shot through her. "Why do they have to wait?"

"Rather than tie up the line, I'll let Bobby fill you in. I've still got a lot of info to feed you."

Something wasn't as it should be; she could feel it. Why weren't they already on their way?

"Okay." Rhonda drew a deep breath. "Bobby, after we disconnect, watch for my texts with those plate numbers and the photos of Hakeem and Amir to come through—I'll send to both the SAT phone and Talia's cell. You're going to need them to start your search tonight, even though I still think you should both get some rest and start looking tomorrow."

"Noted. But we're going out tonight. What about transpo?"

He'd surprised Talia again; she hadn't been sure he'd be on board with her plan to search tonight. She was beyond relieved that he was. It had been a long time since someone had had her back.

"Get a pen and paper," Rhonda said.

"Just shoot it to me."

"All right, Memory Man. I knew you wouldn't take my advice and start tomorrow. So in forty-five minutes, you're to walk to the following intersection." She very precisely gave him the street names. "That location should be exactly six blocks from the safe house. I don't have to tell you to take measures to make sure you aren't followed. There'll be a city taxi, number 393, waiting for you. That's 393," she repeated.

"Copy that," he said firmly.

"Don't get into any cab but that one. If another cab shows up, leave, call me, and we'll regroup. You'll find what you asked me for in the backseat. Should be enough money to get you in and out of where you need to go. And Talia, if the clothes don't fit, blame Bobby, not me."

Talia was impressed that Taggart had thought of that very important detail. They needed to blend in. And she wondered again what kind of organization he worked for that had assets here capable of arranging the things Rhonda had managed on this very short notice.

"One final thing," Rhonda added. "Unfortunately, you two made quite a stir with the media. And you look like hell, Bobby. Talia, you look a little rough, too, sweetie. Are you sure you're both up to going out tonight?"

"Your point?" Bobby said, rolling past Rhonda's concern.

"My point is, you have to be very careful out there. There's a 'be on the lookout' for both of you. Not only the embassy staff but the local police and the military want you for questioning about the bombing."

"I figured that would happen when we didn't show

up among the living or the dead at the compound. The news coverage didn't help any." Bobby sounded disgusted. "Isn't there anything you can do to squash that BOLO?"

"I'm working on it, but these things take time."

"Don't worry about it, babe. We'll be careful."

"All right, then, chickies." Rhonda's voice was soft with concern and affection. "Keep your eyes open, and watch each other's back, okay?"

"We'll be fine," Taggart assured her.

"You'd better be. And Talia, you have every reason to hope for the very best outcome. We're going to get him out. If you two get lucky on your search tonight, we'll have him back even sooner."

Talia closed her eyes and nodded, unable to speak. She wanted to be hopeful. She needed to be hopeful.

"I'll be back in touch with an ETA for the team's arrival. Keep the phone charged, and keep it close. And for God's sake, Bobby—"

"I know," he cut in. "Don't do anything stupid."

22

"Who are we waiting for?" Talia looked up from the sofa. "I thought they'd already be on their way."

Bobby had known this was coming. "Some of the guys were doing drills in the field, down in Central America. The good news is they weren't running black, so Nate was able to call them back."

All the blood drained from her face.

"Don't. Just don't," he said, seeing her panic set in. If this was a flat-out op where her child wasn't involved, she'd be icy cool. So he cut her a little slack. "They're already on a charter flight back to Virginia. Should touch down within three hours."

"And you know this how?"

"Because I've done those same drills. I know how quickly they can gear up and get home. That 737 in Dulles will be wheels up shortly after midnight Oman time."

"So we're looking at what? Another twenty-four hours?"

"Unfortunately, yes. The miles are there, they have to fly them."

"And then what? How do they clear their landing with the Omani government? It's not as though the United States has a military base here."

"They'll make it happen. They'll be cleared, okay?"

She still looked skeptical. "It's too long."

"It's not too long. And it's the time frame we've got to work with, so you need to accept it. With a little luck, by the time they arrive, we'll have something for them to go on."

She lowered her head, clearly frustrated and attempting to control it. "We're looking for a sand pebble on a beach. How can we possibly—"

"You're not thinking like an operative," he snapped. "You have to get your mind-set right."

She gathered herself. Drew a deep breath. "You're right. I'm sorry. I will."

Her phone rang.

She grabbed it, checked the screen. "Text from Rhonda."

"I'm going to change into a dishdasha," he said. "No one's going to be looking for a local."

"No," she said, glancing up from the phone. "They're going to be looking for a Caucasian with a huge bandage on his head."

"Got it covered." He headed for the bedroom.

"Virginia?"

He looked over his shoulder, one hand on the door frame. "What about it?"

"You said the charter flight from Central America

was on its way back to Virginia. And Rhonda said the Pentagon approved your 'team' to investigate. CIA? Is that who you're with now?"

She didn't miss much. The ITAP team *was* stationed out of CIA headquarters in Langley, and Nate *had* worked his magic and gotten the Pentagon to sanction this op. But that was where the connection ended. "No. Not CIA. Look, don't sweat the small stuff. We've got you covered. All you have to do is keep it together."

Along with the dishdashas, he'd found a few pieces of traditional men's headwear. He was pretty sure that here in Oman, they called the white cap he put on first to hold his hair in place—no biggie for him—a thagiyah. The gutrah, a scarflike white head covering, fell a little past his shoulders in back and almost to his brows in front.

Someone would have to be looking really hard to pick up on the bandage on his forehead. Both the thagiyah and the gutrah were held in place by an ogal, a black band that surrounded the top of his head. Too bad he couldn't figure out how to get the damn thing to stay put.

He walked out of the bedroom dressed in the dishdasha, the ogal in his hand. "I need some help with this."

Talia looked up at him, her expression wild.

"What?" he asked.

She held up the phone, screen toward him so he could see Rhonda's text. A head shot of a young Arab man filled the screen.

"Hakeem?"

She became a warrior before his eyes. "If he hurts my child, I'll kill him."

He stared into the face of a dead man walking. "You're going to have to stand in line. She send a pic of Amir?"

She nodded, found the other text, and brought Amir al-Attar's head shot up to view. A shiver ran through her body as she held up the phone for him to see again.

Jesus. Straight out of Ali Baba and the Forty Degenerates. Amir had a mean, crazed look in his eyes, and for the first time, Bobby gave in to a stark, gut-clenching fear for Meir. If that bastard touched him —

He stopped. Shut off his thoughts. He couldn't think of the possibility of the child being hurt by this man, or he wouldn't be able to function.

"Those license-plate numbers come through?" he asked, taking the phone from her hand.

She nodded and looked away, but not before he saw the haunted look in her eyes. He understood, but it wouldn't do either of them any good to live in that mind frame.

He walked to the kitchen, opened a drawer where he'd spotted a charger cord earlier, and plugged in her phone. Then he returned to the living area and held up the ogal. "I can't get it fastened."

She rose from the sofa and took it from him. "Clothes may make the man, but they can't make you into an Arab man. Your skin is too light."

"It'll be fine. The places we're going will be dark. No one's going to notice."

"And where exactly are we going?"

"To hunt for Amir in his playground."

She studied the ogal and then his head. "Back up to the coffee table so I can reach you." Then she stepped up onto the low table.

He should have thought about proximity, his to her, before he gave up on the ogal. Too late now. He backed up to the table, and she looped the cord around his forehead, then brought the ends to the back of his head.

"Hold still." He sensed her unease at being this close to him again as she pulled the band tight.

"Easy."

"Sorry. Um . . . can you move the cord so it hits someplace where it doesn't bother you? Then I'll tie it."

He reached across his body with his right hand to position the ogal and the gutrah over the bandage on the left side of his forehead, and his fingers touched hers. Touched and, after a moment's hesitation, covered. Large over small. Rough over smooth.

It would have been a forgotten moment if he'd merely moved his hand away. But he didn't. For some reason, it felt as if he couldn't. The unexpected physical contact seemed to tether them in an unbreakable hold. And for long, tentative moments, they both stood frozen, neither of them capable of moving.

Only the tips of their fingers touched, one soul reaching out to another and hanging on, because both needed something to hang on to so badly.

She slowly turned her hand into his, and nothing in the world could have kept him from lacing their fingers together and holding on.

Just holding on.

"We're going to get him back," he whispered, as much for his sake as for hers.

"I know." Her voice was thick with emotion. "I know."

For another long moment, they stood that way. And then her fingers tightened in his, tugging on strings attached to memories of how good they'd been together and to thoughts of what could have been, what should have been, and to a very big piece of his heart. He turned and faced her.

"You . . . you could have walked away," she whispered, her eyes glistening as she searched his. "You could have—"

"I couldn't," he interrupted. "I wouldn't," he assured her. And because he couldn't tell which one of them had started to tremble, he slid his arms around her and pulled her close.

She leaned into him, laid her head against his shoulder, and drew him tighter. And there they stood, locked in an embrace of emotions that bound them together with a common history, a common fear, and one common goal.

He didn't want to be on the attack with her anymore. He couldn't continue to let his thoughts lead with anger. In this one thing, they must be united. They'd both lost something. And the only thing that mattered was getting Meir back.

What would you have done? How could I bring a child into this world and introduce him to a man who hated his mother? And how could a child have possibly fit into your world?

She'd been right to be afraid of what he would have done.

But not any longer.

"I don't want to fight with you anymore," he whispered into her hair, as her remembered words brought not only understanding but an aching need for peace between them.

She made a sound, part sob, part relief, all gratitude. And she clung even tighter.

23

A white taxi with orange markings and the number 393 on the roof waited for them exactly where it should be and exactly on time. The driver was a local, and Bobby had expected to haggle over the price of the fare, but the man—Sanju, according to the placard mounted on the dash—said in English, "All is taken care of, sir. I have been provided with a list of places where you may wish to go."

"Thank you," Bobby said. Sanju nodded and closed the glass divider between the front and rear seats, giving them privacy. He pulled away from the curb, headed toward the heart of the city, and not long after switched the radio station from Arabic pop to American pop.

It made Bobby wonder just how much Sanju knew. He had no choice but to trust the man.

"Sounds like Rhonda came through," Talia whispered.

"She always does." Bobby turned toward her in the dark backseat. He'd been more than grateful that

Rhonda had called just before they'd left the safe house, telling them the driver would know where to take them. He would drive them to hotels, clubs, and bars where a man like Amir al-Attar might go to satisfy his appetites for partying and women.

"I take it you found the package," he said, hearing the rustle of paper. The backseat was fairly dark, and there was only a sprinkling of streetlights in this part of the city, but he'd spotted the promised package when he'd gotten inside.

"She seems to have thought of everything. I think this is for you." She handed him a packet that could only be currency: Omani rial.

He unwrapped the packet, gave it a quick count, then whistled low. Inside was a stack of notes worth fifty rial each. They shouldn't run out of cash anytime soon. "Looks like my bonus came early this year." He tucked the money into one of the dishdasha's deep pockets, right next to the 9mm Beretta and an extra clip he'd taken from the floor safe. Then he glanced at Talia. "You have everything you need?"

"Looks like more than enough."

She'd already hiked the dishdasha above her knees and was in the process of tugging off the white socks she'd worn in lieu of shoes for the six-block walk to the rendezvous point. Short of going barefoot again, it was the best she'd been able to come up with. In the dark, with little foot or car traffic in the neighborhood, if anyone had seen them, they'd assume they were a father and son out on the streets together.

"Are those going to work?" he asked, as she slipped on low-heeled sandals with straps covered in gold beading.

"Better than the socks." She glanced his way as she started tugging the dishdasha up her thighs. "You might want to look to the left."

He whipped his head toward the passenger window as the sounds of crinkling paper, swishing silk, and delicately jangling glass beads filled the backseat. Then he tried to ignore the bouncing of the seat springs as she shifted and started to remove the dishdasha.

Okay. He'd once been an altar boy—his mother had insisted—but he was no monk. And when a streetlight illuminated her reflection in the window glass, he couldn't resist looking as she lifted the dishdasha over her head and bared all that golden skin. Her graceful neck. Her slim shoulders. Those incredible breasts, which he knew by touch and taste. Her dark brown nipples pebbled tight against the air-conditioned cold, the way they used to peak for him when he touched her.

He closed his eyes too late; the picture would be burned into his mind forever. Just like memories of them together, skin on skin, remained branded in his psyche for what he was beginning to think would be forever.

Despite the air-conditioned chill in the taxi, a line of perspiration beaded on his upper lip. He'd done his damnedest not to think about how good they'd been together. But here, in the shadowed intimacy of the taxi's backseat, with only inches and a newly minted peace separating them, it wasn't working.

"How are you doing over there?" he made himself ask, because he needed to get grounded again.

"Okay, I think. It's not one size fits all, but the loose construction makes everything wearable."

When he turned to her, she was covered from neck to wrist to ankle in delicately embroidered and beaded silk. They'd reached a more central part of the city, which meant more streetlights and more light in the taxi.

Rhonda had managed to acquire a woman's dishdasha for Talia, made of multicolored silk in a swirling pattern of blues and greens and golds, coming just below her knees instead of to the floor.

Beneath the dishdasha, she wore sarwal—trousers—drawn snug and embroidered at her ankles, then loose to the waist.

She'd wrapped a soft blue waqaya around her head and neck, and over that a scarf—a lahaf—fell like a shawl to her shoulders. With her complexion and dark eyes, no one would question whether she belonged here.

She motioned toward her traditional clothes. "This could go either way tonight. These clothes will conceal our identity, but they may bring more attention if we end up being the only ones in the crowd dressed this way. A lot of the young people here wear Western clothes."

"We'll be fine," Bobby assured her. "Rhonda wouldn't let us go out like this if she thought it would increase our profile."

The center window slid open, and Sanju caught Bobby's eye in the rearview mirror. "Excuse me, please. We are about to arrive at your first destination."

Talia's body tensed beside him. It was showtime, with no dress rehearsal. This could be an exercise in futility, or they could get lucky and find a lead. Either way, they were walking straight into the fire and stood a very good chance of getting burned.

"You're probably aware of this, but remember," she said, looking across the seat at him, "we're 'locals,' so we can't slip up. Keep your left hand in your pocket. Don't shake hands with it; don't accept food with it. Use your right hand only. A tourist could be excused for making that blunder, but a local would immediately become highly suspect."

He knew the drill, but he let her talk. She was focused, and they both needed to be that way.

"And no PDA, even if the situation seems to call for it. No holding hands, no hugging, no kissing. No public displays of affection of any kind. We'd draw the wrong kind of attention."

"Got it." He watched her draw her Glock from the folds of the discarded men's dishdasha and tuck it into a roomy pocket.

He'd debated the wisdom of carrying tonight. If either of them was caught with concealed weapons, they'd be marched straight to jail, where they'd be no good to Meir. They'd lived through a bombing, a high-speed chase, and a forced car crash today, but they couldn't depend on luck getting them out of another scrape. So they'd weaponed up.

"You ready for this?" he asked.

"Let's go find him." A renewed strength seemed to have come over her. Her short nap and the food and energy drinks must have helped recharge her batteries, but her tipping point had come afterward.

I don't want to fight with you anymore.

Everything had changed for both of them in that moment. He'd felt a weight lift from his shoulders and from his soul. And she'd apparently felt something similar.

He leaned toward Sanju. "Wait for us."

"I will be right here, sir."

Armed with a single-minded purpose, they slipped out of the taxi and into the nightlife.

24

A few hours later, Taggart said, "We'll hit it hard again tomorrow."

They hadn't found Amir. So they hadn't found Meir. They'd spent five hours pounding the pavement, checking out bars, flashing Amir's and Hakeem's photos, questioning bartenders, and approaching working girls to see if Amir had been a customer. And they'd turned up nothing.

When they'd narrowly escaped a confrontation with the local police, they decided fatigue was making them careless and called it a night.

Sanju had dropped them off where he'd picked them up, with the promise to meet them again in the morning. They'd hoofed it back to the safe house, and Taggart had collapsed on the sofa.

Talia watched him from across the room as he removed the headwear, laid his Beretta and his phone on the coffee table, then slumped back, legs spread wide. He pinched his nose between his fingers.

"We'll get the break we need." He looked exhausted and battered, and although he put on a brave front, Talia suspected he felt as disheartened as she did.

It was nearing three in the morning. She was too weary even to talk; exhaustion had sunk into her bones like a deep ache. Her arm throbbed. Her feet burned. Her entire body felt like one big bruise. But nothing hurt as bad as her heart; fear for Meir had beaten her down to rock bottom.

"Get some sleep," Taggart said. Not bothering to undress, he stretched out on the sofa. "Sanju will be waiting for us at nine."

He appeared to be asleep already when she limped past him into the bedroom. Dejected and disappointed, she undressed, found a small men's T-shirt, and pulled it on over the boxers.

Then she pulled back the covers and fell into bed.

The last thing she thought of before her sleep-deprived and wounded body demanded that she get some rest was her son, alone and afraid but, please, God, unharmed.

Bobby bolted straight up on the sofa. For a moment, he sat in the dark, sleep-dazed, wondering what had woken him. Both phones lay on the coffee table beside him. Talia's was lit up, telling him it was four a.m. Barely an hour since he'd dropped like a stone. When it vibrated and rang, he wiped a hand over his face, then reached across the sofa and turned on a light. Figuring it was Nate or Rhonda, he picked up the phone and was about to answer when he saw the caller's name.

Jonathan.

Shit!

Someone was calling from Meir's bodyguard's phone. It could only be the kidnappers.

He sprinted into the bedroom and flipped the switch for the overhead light.

"Talia! Wake up."

She shot straight up in the bed, squinting against the sudden brightness. "Wha—what's happening?"

"It's them."

She was still half asleep, but when he handed her the phone, and she saw Jonathan's name on the screen, she woke up as if she'd been hit with ice water.

"Put it on speaker," he said before she punched the answer button. "Make sure they let you talk to Meir."

She shook her head to clear the cobwebs, turned on the speaker, and, after a slight hesitation, pushed answer. "What have you done with my son?" she demanded.

"Excellent," a man replied in English. "So you know why I am calling."

"I know that whoever stole this phone killed a good man to get it," she said, her voice strong. "And I know you also stole my son."

Bobby lay a supportive hand on her shoulder.

"Do you not wonder why I took him?"

"Because you're a coward."

A long, ominous silence followed.

"Take care with your words, Talia Levine," he warned. "It would not do to anger me or to forget who is in control here."

"Please," she said, gripping the phone tightly, clearly struggling to maintain control. "Please tell me you haven't hurt him."

"The boy is unharmed. For now. He is a brave little man. And yet sometimes I can see he wants to cry for his mother."

She squeezed her eyes shut. "What do you want?"

"Surely you must know by now. I want retribution. My father is dead because of you. Now do you know precisely who you are dealing with?"

"Hakeem al-Attar," she said numbly.

"Very good. Now tell me this. I lost my father. Should the boy not also lose his mother?"

"Please, Hakeem," she said quickly. "It's me you want. He's an innocent. Let him go and you can do whatever you want to me."

"Oh, I have many plans for you. You will wish you were dead long before I am through with you. And I may consider a trade for the boy. Your life, however, is no longer enough. The American who helped you kill four of my men must also die. Yes. I know about him. My men radioed me that you were not alone before they died. And I now also require money to avenge their deaths as well as my father's life and blood."

What the hell? Bobby knew the way these guys thought. Revenge, exploitation, and death—those were terrorist motives. That's why they wanted him as well as Talia. They didn't give a shit about money. They had money. They'd added that for just one reason: to increase Talia's torment.

"Anything," Talia said. "Just don't hurt him. Please don't hurt him."

"Your life for the boy's then. Your life, the American's life, and three million American dollars."

Bobby gripped her shoulders tighter when she gasped. "I . . . it will take some time to . . . to come up with that much money."

"For the boy's sake, do not take too long."

"Let me talk to him. Please. I need to talk to him."

"He is sleeping. If I wake him, he may cry and rouse Zaire—which would not be good for your son."

"Oh, God."

She almost broke then but somehow pulled it back together. "Please. Don't hurt him."

"Then do not make me wait."

Bobby lifted her face with a finger under her chin. It killed him to see the tears tracking down her cheeks. "You have to talk to Meir," he whispered. "Hakeem knows this. Tell him no deal if you don't talk to him."

"I need to talk to my son," she told Hakeem firmly. "I need to know he's alive or we don't have a deal."

The line went silent before Hakeem came back. "Wait."

Bobby sat down on the bed beside her, wrapped his arm around her shoulders, and pulled her against him. "Stay strong," he whispered into her hair.

She drew a quivering breath, then pulled herself together.

His heart slammed against his ribs as he waited, and waited, and then, for the first time in his life, he heard his son's voice.

"Momma?"

"Oh, baby!" Talia cried, and Bobby hugged her tighter. "Yes. It's Momma."

"I want to come h-home."

A knot of emotion crowded his chest, making it impossible to breathe.

"I know, sweetheart. I know you do," Talia said, working to keep her voice soothing. "And you're going to come home real soon, okay?"

"I want to come home now."

Bobby hung his head, pinching his eyes shut to stall the burn welling up behind his eyelids.

"I know, baby. But you're going to have to be brave for a little longer, okay? Momma's doing everything she can to get you back home. Don't cry, little man," she pleaded. "You must be brave for me. You must do what the man says and not cry, and he'll take care of you until I find you, okay? Everything's going to be fine. I promise. You must believe me." The line stayed silent.

"Meir?" she cried.

But it was Hakeem who answered. "As you can see, he is fine. You get the money, and he will stay that way."

Bobby had killed to defend himself. He'd killed

to save his buddies. He'd killed for his country. But he'd never felt the urge to tear another human being to pieces with his bare hands. Now he understood bloodlust.

"How . . . how long do I have?"

Talia's voice broke through the haze of a rage so black it shaded his vision.

"I am not an unreasonable man," the bastard said. "You have two days. Forty-eight hours. I will call again tomorrow to check on your progress."

25

When the phone went dead, so did Talia's eyes. "Promise me they won't hurt him," she begged.

Bobby held her tighter, tucking her head beneath his chin. "They won't hurt him," he said, because she needed to hear it. And so did he. He needed to hear a voice other than Hakeem al-Attar's. He needed to hear himself say they would not hurt the boy. And then he needed to believe it.

The arrogant fucking pigs. They'd just pulled off the bombing of a U.S. embassy and kidnapped the child of a former Mossad agent. They should have beat feet and already been so far down a hidey-hole no one would have a clue where to look for them.

So why weren't they? Maybe it wasn't a case of arrogance. Maybe it was flat-out stupidity that they were still within a thousand miles of Oman. Because if they really wanted to torture Talia, really wanted to make her pay, they'd have left her hanging. She'd die a thousand deaths, not knowing what they'd done to her son. To his son.

For the first time in a long time, he second-guessed himself. Maybe he should have talked to them. Told them to cut the bullshit. Told them he knew what they really wanted. To kill Talia and kill him and the boy.

Money? Hell. That didn't fit. Hamas had money even God didn't know about.

So maybe the money wasn't even for Hamas. Maybe Hakeem and dear old Uncle Amir were getting greedy and wanted it for themselves. Amir was a degenerate. Maybe Hakeem had decided to follow in his uncle's footsteps.

Either way, they were playing with her.

And it was working.

This new wrinkle made the situation even more dodgy. The world knew that these assholes were loose cannons. Their interpretation of their religion was corrupted, and that made them not only unpredictable but more dangerous.

It had been five minutes since the phone call that had created both hope and renewed fear for Meir.

I want to come home.

Taggart's eyes filled and burned as the voice of innocence played over and over in his mind.

He had to get out of here. "We should try to get some sleep." He started to rise.

Her arms tightened around him. "Stay with me. At least for a little while."

As much as he needed some time and space, he couldn't make himself leave her. "If you're not able to sleep, at least lie down," he said, and when she did and then made room for him, he ignored the urgent need for solitude and stretched out by her side.

For long moments, they lay that way. Talia in her men's T-shirt and boxers, he in the bulky dishdasha. Inches of physical space between them, miles apart in every way except for the fear for their son.

She badly needed sleep. So did he. Yet he was suddenly desperate for information about Meir. Something he hadn't let himself ask for before.

"Tell me about him."

The dark bedroom swelled with the absence of sound for several moments before she gathered herself and started talking. "In Hebrew, Meir means 'giving light.'" Her voice grew tender with love. "He brought so much light into my life after . . . well, after a very dark period. He still—" She stopped, swallowed, and continued resolutely. "He still does."

Bobby had yet to see a picture of his son. He could have asked Rhonda to text the photo she'd hacked from Meir's school records. Something held him back. Fear, he imagined. Fear that the only image he'd ever see of Meir was a photograph.

"He's always been a very inquisitive, intelligent child. And kind. I love that most of all about him."

The love in her voice said so much about her. Opened doors that led to thoughts of forgiveness, to wanting to reevaluate the reasons she'd done what she had, to believe she regretted not telling him about the baby.

You were a soldier for hire.

That truth cut close to the bone. She'd been right. Even now, he was still basically that same man.

"What does he like to do? Like to eat?"

"What most five-year-olds like. Pizza is his favorite, next to ice cream. He loves to watch and play American football. In Tel Aviv, he organized football games during recess." She stopped, and he could see her mind framing a picture of Meir that was at once painful and sweet.

"Was he . . . was his birth . . . ?"

"He was six pounds, nine ounces, eighteen inches long," she supplied, apparently sensing his hesitation and understanding what he couldn't quite bring himself to ask.

Look at all the lucky number threes he could make out of those stats, Bobby thought with a bittersweet smile.

"And no, his birth didn't cause me problems. He was eager to be born. Three hours, and it was all over. I barely made it to the hospital because I couldn't believe things were going so quickly."

At the oddest times, during these desperate hours, he had pictured her in labor. The images would just appear. Her hair drenched in perspiration. Her body wracked in pain. His son arriving into the world with a lusty cry and ten beautiful fingers and toes.

He felt a deep pang of loss that he hadn't been there to witness the birth and to help her through it.

"I bet you were a real warrior," he said before thinking.

She turned her head and gave him a small smile. "Didn't have time to find out. Three hours? I hardly needed to channel my inner warrior for that."

Maybe he'd been wrong. Maybe as he lay here beside the mother of his son, as their hands brushed against each other, then entwined, maybe this was where he needed to be. Not alone, mourning for a child he might never know, but in this bed, in this tenuous reunion with her, getting to know his son.

He turned to his side so he could fully see her face. "According to my mother, I was bald and fat and happy."

"Meir had a head of thick black hair, a wiry little body, and a cry as strong as his father's."

Pride, loss, yearning. This time, he couldn't stop the tears. He lifted a hand to wipe them away; she stopped him.

"I'm so sorry," she whispered, and pressed her lips against his cheek to catch them. "I am so, so sorry."

He'd tried to hold on to the anger that had been his companion since she'd left him in Kabul, but he couldn't. He knew she was sorry. Sorry she'd deceived him. Sorry she'd kept his son from him. Sorry that everything they could have been together had been stolen by circumstance, duty, and war. Too much had happened between them to be forgotten. Too much to be forgiven. And he knew she was as sorry as he was that nothing they did in this bed tonight would change things between them come morning.

Yet when she kissed her way to his mouth, he didn't stop her. He opened to receive her tongue, the sudden hitch of her sob, her almost frantic need for connection.

"I loved you," she whispered against his lips, then spread tender, desperate kisses across his jaw and along his throat with a hunger that swelled with regret. "I loved you."

He shouldn't let her say that. He shouldn't let her do this. But they both needed something other than pain and fear to rule, if only in this moment. Needed release from the darkness shadowing their past together.

He arched his back on a groan and tangled his hands in her hair as she unbuttoned the dishdasha and bared his shoulder. He gasped when the backs of her fingers fluttered down each inch of his body that she laid bare, then brushed against his growing erection as she trailed hot butterfly kisses down his chest and into the hollow of his belly.

"I still love you," she whispered, as she stood up on her knees, tugged the T-shirt up and over her head, then shimmied out of the boxers. She moved over him, gloriously naked and yearning, and pressed hot, wet kisses down his cock before taking him into her mouth.

He gasped as she sucked him, arched his hips to match her rhythm, and held on to control by an unraveling thread. This was physical union at its most primitive, primal level. But even more, it was an offering. An appeal for forgiveness and an acknowledgment of shared grief.

He couldn't hate her here. He couldn't hate her now. He could only feel how deeply she cared and the honesty of her passion. And over it all, he could sense that she needed the physical release from all those crosses she'd carried, even more than he did.

With his last ounce of control, he lifted her up, set her over his lap, and gripped her hips in both hands. "I need to be inside you."

She rose to her knees, straddled him, then surrounded him with her small hands and guided him home.

And it did feel like home. God help him, it felt like the most natural and nurturing place he could possibly be, as she planted her palms against his shoulders and he lifted her up and down on his swollen cock.

His rhythm grew faster, harder, then harder still, as emotion swamped him. She'd left him. Used him. She'd kept his child from him. And her apologies were too late and not enough.

Suddenly, he realized that he was pounding out his anger and humiliation, wanting, in the wounded corner of his mind, to repay her for all the hurt she'd made him feel—and he stopped.

God, oh, God, what was he doing?

He drew her down so they were breast to breast, her head on his shoulder, her wild black hair falling across his face.

"I'm sorry," he whispered, ashamed for being rough with her.

That was when he knew he had to let it all go. Not just give lip service but let go of the anger, the pain, his soul's demand for retribution.

"I'm sorry," he whispered again, as he brushed the hair back from her face.

"That makes two very sorry people," she murmured, and this time he wiped away *her* tears.

He loved her slowly then. Eased in and out of her sweet, wet heat, healing two wounds, rekindling the fires, until her breath rushed out in soft, catchy gasps, and his heart beat so wildly he thought it would explode.

He came with a guttural groan just as she cried out in release. Then he clung to her, feeling a tentative sense of peace for the first time in six years.

For long, floating moments, they lay together, she sprawled on top of him, he still inside her. Hearts beating wildly, breath hard to catch, bodies worn and wet and spent.

When he drifted off to sleep, the words *I loved you . . . I still love you* whispered through his mind like a dream. But as with the echoes of a storm that pummeled and destroyed, then moved slowly off toward the horizon, the damage could never be forgotten.

26

Rami Yahya sat cross-legged against the wall and glared at the child. Thank Allah he was finally asleep again. Sleeping meant he was no longer asking for his mother, and Amir and Hakeem were no longer yelling at Rami to shut him up.

He was not a babysitter. He was a believer. Yes, he was only sixteen, much younger than most of the men in Amir and Hakeem's group. Yes, he was small for his age, but he was no less devout. No less of a man. He was a better soldier for Allah. He had the discipline. And he was no longer certain that Amir and Hakeem and their men were what he'd thought them to be.

Across the large room, Amir sat at a table in deep conversation with Hakeem. He dared not say it aloud, but he'd figured out some time ago that Amir was not a true believer. Amir was the kind of Hamas man who made it difficult for the world to see the true cause. The world hated men like Amir, who professed his work was for Allah when, in truth, his work was for himself. Amir killed because he liked to kill, not to further the cause of Allah and of Palestine.

Earlier today, he'd heard Amir and Hakeem argue. Amir wanted to make money off the boy. To ransom him for a profit, then kill him and the mother when she came for him.

He still couldn't believe that Hakeem, whom Rami had once admired, had given in. Hakeem had even telephoned the infidel's mother, the woman they said had been responsible for the annihilation of the great Mohammed al-Attar in Afghanistan six years ago. She had not pulled the trigger, they said, but she had been responsible for leading a Mossad hit squad to Hakeem's father and his men.

They had been martyrs for the cause, and this operation in Oman was to serve justice. They said.

Yet the woman still lived. And now they chose to seek justice against this little boy.

He stared at the sleeping child, at the dried tears on his face and the way he curled into a tight little ball, as though making himself small would make him invisible. And he tried not to think about his own little brother. Or his mother.

He dropped his head back against the wall and closed his eyes. He saw his mother's face. Heard her comforting voice.

"You are a good boy, Rami. Be a good boy now, and take your little brother outside for a while. The two of you, you are always underfoot," she'd said with a smile.

It was her way of letting him know she was not afraid for them to go outside. That she knew the streets were sometimes dangerous, but they should not live their lives in fear.

"Life is to be lived," his mother had told him often. "Do not be afraid to be a part of it. Do not live it looking from the outside in."

So he hadn't. He'd gone to school. He'd learned his lessons. He'd said his prayers. He'd heard the call to arms. The call to rise up against the infidel dogs and fight for Palestine.

"Let's do it." His friend Ehab's eyes had been wide with excitement. "Let's quit school and join Hamas. We will be heroes."

That was nine months ago. Now Ehab was dead. Martyred for the cause only six days ago, when he had strapped a bomb vest to his chest and walked into an Israeli deli.

Rami felt tears well up in his eyes when he thought of his friend, and he questioned the need for him to die. As he questioned the need for all those other people to die. The mother and her baby daughter? Their only "sin" had been walking by the deli at the wrong time. *The Koran does not preach war, Rami.* His mother's voice came to him again as he sat in the dark, wanting to sleep, but his mind wouldn't stop working. *What these men do, these Hamas outlaws, in the name of Allah? It is not what he asks. He does not ask them to kill.*

At fifteen, he could not see it her way. He'd seen

the many online videos and calls to arms. He had thought they proved his mother was wrong, and he had become Hamas.

Now he was here, his mother's words in his head, Ehab's death in his heart.

This small boy's life in his hands. This small boy, who had never done anything to anyone.

27

"Can you tell me, please. Have you seen this man?" Talia asked the waitress in Arabic.

"Can you not see that I am busy?" She was very young and very pretty and *very* irritated, but she managed a tight smile.

"Only a moment," Talia insisted, and held up the phone with the picture of Amir al-Attar for her to see.

The girl balanced her tray of empty drink glasses on her hip and, with an impatient scowl, looked at the photo. "No. I do not know this man." Then she rushed off toward the bar to fill another order.

Talia slumped back in the booth, her strength and her optimism wavering.

She and Taggart had left the safe house a little before nine a.m., walked to the street where Sanju and his taxi waited for them, and, once again, started the long and tedious process of searching for a sighting of Amir.

Throughout the day, Taggart had been in contact with Rhonda, who had steered them to restaurants and tea shops, then on to the bars tonight. It was closing in on midnight now, and they had stopped in at least ten clubs. Still no sign of Amir. Still no sighting of a light blue VW Golf or a cream-colored Toyota Highlander with the license-plate numbers Rhonda had texted to them.

"Maybe we're not looking at the right kinds of clubs," Taggart said into Talia's phone as they walked out of a bar in a lower-rent part of the city, where the blast of Arabic rock music followed them out the door. "Maybe Amir has a taste for more expensive booze and a higher class of working girl."

Talia walked straight to the waiting taxi and collapsed into the backseat, while Taggart stayed outside, talking to Rhonda.

She'd held it together between six and seven p.m., the window of time when Meir had been taken by Hakeem. The twenty-four-hour mark. Now thirty-two hours had passed. And each hour drove her deeper into a despair that manifested as a numbing fog. Like she was sleepwalking but awake.

But she'd die before she gave up on finding her son.

She glanced out the window and watched Taggart, the lights from the bar and the darkness of night casting shadow and gold across his face. And for a moment, she let herself think about last night. Those moments in his arms were the one place she could go to escape the pain, hopelessness, and despair. In those moments, he had been his true self with her. He had hated her. He had loved her.

And she had hoped.

But in the stark sun of the brutally hot morning, it was clear that he couldn't give her the one thing she needed from him: forgiveness.

Everything about the way he acted told her she'd be foolish to think he ever would.

"Last night," he'd said when they'd met in the living area after dressing for the day. "It shouldn't have happened. I'm sorry . . . if I hurt you."

She'd nodded. "I understand."

And just that quickly, he'd closed the door. All day, he'd been kind and polite and encouraging and relentless in his search. But the man who had held her, who had kissed her, who had filled her in the darkest part of need, was as gone from her as Meir.

She startled when the door opened on a hot rush of air and he slipped inside the air-conditioned taxi.

"We're going to try another section of town." He leaned forward and gave Sanju an address.

Then he slumped back against the seat and closed his eyes. "Rhonda found another resource who says the chances are good there will be both 'regular girls' and freelancers at the Muscat Holiday Inn."

"The Holiday Inn?"

He shrugged. "So she said. Also Trader Vic's, a club called the Left Bank, and another one called Rock Bottom. The Golden Tulip supposedly also has 'temporary companionship' hanging out at the bar. Apparently, prostitution is rampant in Muscat; there's even a high-end prostitution racket in the classy hotels. There are no Omani women in the business but a lot of foreign women willing to make money from the oil boom."

She looked straight ahead and prayed he was right.

The woman sitting at the bar, smoking and looking watchful, was blond and slim and dressed for sex. She was on the north side of forty but still attractive enough to draw business—until she opened her mouth and the *attractive* wore off real quick.

Bobby introduced himself and Talia.

"Lauren. From London," the woman said, tamping out her cigarette and giving them a long onceover. "Lookin' for a party, luv?"

Bobby glanced at Talia, and Lauren laughed. "No need to be shy. Three works for me. And I'll say this, the two of you, yer both crackin' good to look at, but it'll still cost double. I'll show ya a real bang of a good time, though."

"Actually, we'd like you to take a look at something." Bobby pulled up Amir's photo on Talia's phone.

Lauren looked a little disappointed but got over it quickly. "Give it over, then. Let's 'ave a look-see."

She studied the picture so long Bobby decided they'd hit another dead end.

"Yeah . . . yeah. I know that arsehole." She handed back the phone.

Talia clutched his arm, and he felt her excitement like electricity. At last, they'd hit pay dirt.

Adrenaline zipped through his blood. "When was the last time you saw him?"

Lauren lit another cigarette, then squinted against the smoke. "Information'll still cost ya double. Time's money, ya know."

Bobby knew, and he wasn't about to blow this. He fished into his dishdasha and pulled out a stack of rial notes guaranteed to make her eyes pop and her jaw loosen.

She smiled and tucked the notes into her cleavage. "First time I seen 'im, 'e come in 'ere, 'e took a shine to Peggy." Lauren took another drag on her cigarette. "I told 'er, 'e looks a bit dodgy to me. Had a mean look about 'is eyes, ya know? Just like in that picture.

"You sure you want to go with 'im, I ask 'er," Lauren continued, apparently determined to give them their money's worth. "And oh, she was sure—Peggy's always so bloody sure—so she takes 'im up to 'er room."

"When was this?" Talia demanded.

Bobby covered the hand that gripped his arm, squeezed, urging her to tamp down her impatience. But he could feel her shaking beside him. At least, he thought it was her.

"I'm gettin' there, luv. So Peg takes 'im up to 'er room, right? Three hours later, 'e comes waltzing outta the lift and 'eads out the door. I'm still worried about Peg, so I goes up to 'er room—I was 'avin' a slow night."

Lauren lifted a highball glass to her lips, and Bobby gave Talia a warning look when she almost flew around him to get in the woman's face.

"Easy," he whispered.

"Takes 'er a long time to answer," Lauren said after a deep swallow. "And when she did, I almost 'ad a bloody 'eart attack. 'E'd bloodied 'er face. Split 'er lip wide open. And she said the bastard rogered 'er till she bled. When she told 'im to stop, 'e had another go at 'er till 'e'd done all the damage 'e wanted."

"When was this?" Bobby repeated Talia's question.

"Two nights back. But 'e came back again the next night. Tonight, too."

"He's here now?" It was all he could do to keep his adrenaline in check. He wanted this bastard. He wanted him now.

Lauren shook her head. "No. Come and gone. And good riddance."

Bobby closed his eyes and swore.

"How long ago?" Talia's voice was taut with tension. "How long since he left?"

Lauren shrugged. "Fifteen, twenty minutes, maybe. Oh, no need for the mad face, now, luvs. 'E'll be back. A mean bugger like 'im? When a woman is willin' to take the snoggin' from the likes of 'im, they always come back fer more. Peggy's pretty, but she's young. And a fool. I told 'er, tell 'im to bugger off. But no. 'E.'s got money and heaps of it. 'E pays 'er triple 'er price."

She leaned in close then. "Ain't no one's to know that but us," she said in a warning voice. "No one deserves an extra cut of what Peg's worked for."

"What time does he usually show up?" Bobby asked stiffly.

"'Round nine. Leaves a little after midnight. 'E's a bastard, but 'e's as regular as my nanna's prunes. I give up on Peggy. If she wants to let 'im bugger 'er up that way, I got no more to say about it."

She lifted her hands, her story finished. "That's what I know. What do you need with 'im, anyway?"

"We just need to talk to him," Bobby said.

Lauren laughed. "You want to 'urt 'im, don't ya? You'll get no squabble from me."

"Tell you what." Bobby reached back into his pocket, then offered her several more notes. "This is for your trouble and for not mentioning to anyone that we were looking for him, okay?"

Smiling, Lauren nipped the money out of his hand and tucked it into her cleavage with the rest. "I'da kept me mouth shut for free, luv, if it meant someone was going to 'urt 'im the way 'e 'urt poor Peg. So don't you worry. I ain't never seen nobody askin' about the bloody bastard, no matter who wants to know.

"Sure you don't want a little rumpy-pumpy just to take yer edge off?" she added with an inviting smile. "Might come up with a better rate, bein' as 'ow we're mates and all now, right?"

"Appreciate it," Bobby said. "I really do. But we're in a bit of a time crunch."

"Offer's open anytime, luv."

"Fifteen minutes." Talia's expression was tortured as they left the lounge and headed across the tiled hotel lobby. "We missed that monster by *fifteen minutes*."

Bobby hated the rotten timing, too, but he had to put things in perspective, or he'd end up pounding his fist through a wall. "It sucks, I agree, but glass half full, okay? We found Amir, and we know he's coming back. So tomorrow night, we'll be waiting. The team will be here, and we'll follow him to whatever rock he crawled out from under. And that's where we'll find Meir."

"I know," she said. "I know this is huge. But . . ."

"But it's another twenty-four hours. I get it. They're not going to hurt him," Bobby assured her. "They don't only want you and me, now they want the money, too."

"So why hasn't Hakeem called again?"

"Because he knows it makes you crazy with worry. He'll call. And you'll ask to speak with Meir again. And then you'll tell Hakeem that you must speak with him every hour prior to the exchange, or the deal is off. That's our guarantee that he's alive. And here's my promise," he added. "We'll have Meir back long before the time they set for the exchange."

"And if we don't?"

"We will," he said firmly.

"But if we don't," she repeated, just as resolute. She stopped in the middle of the large lobby and faced him. "I *will* exchange my life for his. Promise me, if it comes to that, you won't do anything to stop me."

"It's not going to come to—"

"Promise me," she demanded, her eyes dark and tortured.

"I promise," he said, cupping her shoulders and looking her square in the eye.

She held his gaze for a searching moment, then nodded and started walking again.

And he found himself wondering if he really could honor his word. If he could let her sacrifice her life. He was still contemplating the thought as they maneuvered the large revolving door and stepped out of the air-conditioned coolness of the hotel and into the oppressive Omani night.

They hadn't taken two steps out from under the three-story portico when Talia stopped abruptly. Her hand dropped into the pocket that held her gun.

Instantly alert, Bobby reached for his Beretta. "What?"

"Someone's out there."

28

Gun in a two-handed grip, Bobby searched the parking lot and moved with Talia behind the protection of a stone column supporting the portico. It would be easy for someone to hide out there in the acres of asphalt interspersed with palm trees and dim lights.

"I don't see anyone," he whispered close to her ear. "Not even Sanju."

"Stand down. It's me." A voice came out of the dark beside them.

Talia swung around, aiming at the source.

Bobby pivoted with her, then grabbed her hands and jerked her Glock skyward. Surprised by her strength, he spun her around and immobilized her by trapping her arms between them.

"What are you doing?" she cried when he wrestled the gun away from her.

"He's trying to keep you from killing me." Nate Black stepped out of the shadows.

"It's okay, Talia. It's Nate." When Bobby was certain she'd gotten the message, he released her. "You've made better entrances, boss."

"Yeah," Black said, and for the first time ever, Bobby thought he looked a little sheepish. "Bad timing. I thought I'd catch you in the lobby. Thank God you make one pale, tall Arab and I recognized you, or this could have gotten ugly," he added, giving Bobby's native garb a once-over. "Great reflexes—both of you."

Bobby pocketed his Beretta and handed Talia her Glock. "Talia Levine. Nate Black."

"Miss Levine."

Talia's small frame was still coiled tight with tension. "Mr. Black."

"We need to move out. There's an Omani military patrol about two blocks behind us, and you two share the number one slot on their most wanted list."

"How did they find us?" Talia sounded alarmed.

"How did *you* find us?" Bobby wanted to know. "And when did you get here?"

"Let's get into the car. Then I'll explain everything."

Tucked into the shadows behind the hotel, a black Land Cruiser idled quietly. Black settled into the shotgun seat. Taggart opened the back door, urged Talia inside, then climbed into the backseat beside her.

The interior was dark—no light came on when the doors opened—so it took Talia a moment to recoup her night vision. Only when he spoke did she realize another man shared the backseat with them.

"It's always gotta be high drama with you, huh, Boom?"

"Coop." Taggart tugged off his headwear and reached across in front of her to shake Coop's extended hand. "Glad to see you, man. Damn glad."

"Thank *you* for getting us out of Honduras. Always did prefer a dry hell to a wet one. And you know how Carlyle is." Coop notched his chin toward the man behind the wheel. "Grumpy as a swamp rat when his golden locks get all curly from the humidity."

"Hey. At least I've *got* hair." This protest came from the driver—Carlyle, apparently—as he shifted into reverse and backed away from the hotel.

"Carlyle." Affection filled Taggart's voice. "I appreciate it, bud. Anybody else in here?"

"The rest of the team is setting up shop." Black checked his watch. "We should be there within twenty minutes."

Just as they swung around the side of the hotel and headed out through the service entrance, three Omani military vehicles roared up the front drive toward the portico.

"Now, I'd say that's good timing," Carlyle said, driving past them.

Black glanced over his shoulder. "Are we going to need to worry about anyone in the hotel ID'ing you?"

"I think we're good." Taggart glanced at her, and she nodded in agreement. "Place was dark, and we were well concealed in these clothes. And the bar was packed. We spoke to one person, and she's just as eager for Amir al-Attar to get his as we are."

His statement had Black wrenching around in his seat. "You got a lead?"

"Yeah," Taggart said, sounding relieved. "We got a lead."

"Nose like a hound dog," the man called Coop said with a grin.

"Okay, before the shit gets too deep in here," Taggart cut in, "Talia Levine, meet Brett Carlyle, our wheel man tonight."

"Pleased to meet you, ma'am." Carlyle met her gaze in the rearview mirror.

Warm from not only the Omani heat but also the close quarters in the vehicle, Talia removed her headwear and indulged in the cool blast from the air-conditioner. "Thank you for coming."

"Happy to help."

She couldn't see much of Carlyle's face in the dark, but she sensed the same qualities in him that Taggart and Black possessed: integrity, determination, and confidence. She wondered how much they knew about Meir. Were they here helping to find her lost child, or did they know Taggart was Meir's father?

"This guy and I go way back," Taggart said, leaning around her again to get a look at the man beside her. "He knows what he's doing. What Rhonda sees in him, however, is lost on me. Talia, meet Jamie Cooper."

"Ma'am," Cooper said with a nod. "I'm sorry for your trouble."

"Thank you." So this handsome man was Rhonda's husband.

"So what's with the hair?" Taggart asked him.

Cooper smoothed a hand over his bald head. "Learned my lesson the last time we drilled in Central America. Too damn hot. Much cooler without it."

"And how does Rhonda feel about it?"

"She's got a thing for Vin Diesel so it's working for her. At least, for the time being."

She wasn't sure why Taggart found that funny, but he actually laughed. Something Talia hadn't heard him do since Kabul, and she'd missed it.

It was a release for him. His team was here; the two of them weren't in this alone now. Needling, joking, trash talking—it was how warriors let off steam. It was how they stayed sane.

"Don't mind these idiots," Black said from his shotgun seat. "They'll level off soon enough."

"It's all right." And it was. She was so thankful they'd actually arrived. It wasn't that she'd doubted Taggart; it was just that so much could have gone wrong and kept them from getting here.

"I know you want information," Black continued, "but if you can hold off a little longer, we'll arrive at our temporary HQ. You'll meet the rest of the team then, and we'll read everyone in at the same time."

"That's fine. And thank you again. I can't tell you how much—"

"No need," Black interrupted kindly. "I hope you don't take this the wrong way, ma'am—"

"Talia." She interrupted this time. "Please call me Talia, all of you."

"All right, Talia." Black began again. "You two look exactly like you've been through a bombing and are running on little sleep. You sure you're okay?" Concern darkened his expression as he took in Taggart's head wound and the bruises on her face.

"I'm fine," they both said in unison, and got a *sure you are* look from Black.

"Just the same," he said, "if you boys can keep the reunion jabs down to a dull roar, maybe Talia can catch a much-needed combat nap."

She didn't get her nap, but she did close her eyes and rest for several minutes. When she opened them again, they'd neared the waterfront and the beginning of a major industrial area, where the buildings appeared to house administrative offices. They passed several blocks of both old and new construction. The scent of the sea and crude oil hung thick in the air, even in the air-conditioned interior of the SUV.

Carlyle bypassed several complexes and finally stopped in front of a gated, chain-linked lot that enclosed a newer three-story cement-block building. *Royal Brit Petroleum* was painted in red block letters across the front of the building. Cooper jumped out and unlocked the padlocked gate, then locked it behind them after Carlyle drove the Land Cruiser through.

He pulled around to the back of the building, hit a remote entry clipped to the visor, and waited until an overhead garage door opened. Then he pulled inside and closed the door behind them.

Talia stepped out of the SUV with the others and found herself in a cavernous parking garage housing two similar SUVs and a large white utility van. Otherwise, the garage was empty.

"Presents?" Taggart asked, walking toward the van.

"Take a look," Black said.

Taggart opened the van's double back doors. "Holy shit."

Talia couldn't help gaping at what was inside. She was looking at a rolling armory: 1911A1 pistols and sound suppressors to fit them, M4 carbine rifles also equipped with sound suppressors, FAST helmets with top-of-the-line night-vision/thermal-imaging goggles fixed to them.

There was body armor, boxes of thirty-round magazines, and the ammo to fill them. She spotted flashbangs and smoke grenades and radios for communication that, given the high-tech quality of everything else, probably had voice-activated throat mikes and earpieces that fit under sound-deadening hearing protection.

These guys didn't kid around. They could lay siege to the entire city with this much firepower.

"No shit?" Taggart said, smiling. "You brought the drone?"

"Said I would."

Taggart laughed. "Yeah, but I didn't think you could pull it off. So where's the Abrams tank?"

Black almost grinned. "Requisition didn't come through." He closed the van's doors. "Let's go hook up with the rest of the team."

He punched a series of numbers into a keypad by a thick steel door. "Since Muscat is pretty much locked down because of the embassy bombing, Rhonda was able to secure this building on short notice. It helped that our British friends play well with others."

Yeah, and for a lot of money, Talia thought. Whoever these guys worked for, it was obvious they had the resources to back up the operation. And while she was still consumed with fear for Meir, she also felt energized with a new sense of hope.

Once the door opened, Black led them down a long concrete and steel corridor. Their footsteps echoed hollowly in the dimly lit hallway; the air-conditioning made a soft, shushing sound as it traveled through silver ducts running along the tall ceilings. They reached another door that opened to a set of stairs and walked down them to a basement-level conference room.

Black rapped twice on the door and waited. When the door opened, he urged her and Taggart into the room ahead of him. A huge table filled the center of the room, surrounded by cushy leather chairs. Plastic plants were arranged in the corners, and pictures from ads showing Royal Brit Petroleum company workers giving ice cream and school supplies to impoverished children filled the walls. She was stunned to see the level and complexity of activity already taking place.

Four men and one woman, all dressed similarly in dark T-shirts and pants, occupied the large room that now also held her, Taggart, Black, Carlyle, and Cooper. The scent of freshly brewed coffee perked her up a bit, and she spotted a Bunn coffeemaker on a side table. A screen and a projector were set up at the front of the room. Several laptops were booted up and filled with data and photographs.

When the door closed behind them, the room grew quiet, and all eyes turned to her and Taggart.

"Boom!" They all greeted him in unison.

Taggart grinned and lifted his hand. "Man, am I glad to see you all."

"Talia Levine," Nate Black said, "meet the rest of the team. Sound off, people."

"Enrique Santos." A short, solidly built Latino with a soul patch and soft brown eyes smiled at her. "Pleasure to meet you, ma'am."

"Mike Brown." The movie-star-gorgeous operative had the tall, dark, and handsome thing down to an art form. "Sorry you got stuck with one of the ugly ones," he added, with a grinning nod toward Taggart.

Beside her, Taggart snorted a laugh. "Stick it where the sun don't shine, Primetime.

"He's pretty," he told Talia, "and he's vain, but as you can see, he comes through in a pinch."

The woman in the group, a stunning brunette with kind eyes and a warm smile, walked forward and extended her hand. "I'm Stephanie Green. I'll be working with Rhonda, who will be handling things back in the States. We're going to get your son back," she said, with a conviction that had Talia gripping her hand like a lifeline.

"Thank you," she whispered.

"The quiet one back there"—Stephanie nodded toward another tall, lean warrior type—"is my husband, Joe."

Talia returned Joe Green's somber nod. His confident manner told her all she needed to know about him.

She swallowed a gasp when a man stepped out of the shadows and introduced himself as Gabe Jones. He had a poet's face and a soldier's bearing, and the combination was breathtaking.

"We're missing a few." Taggart turned to Black.

"They all wanted to come, but DOD does have its limits."

"Hey, you've got the cream here, man. Let's get this done." Cooper clasped Taggart's shoulder in encouragement.

"Thank you," Taggart said, his eyes suspiciously moist as his gaze swept the room, landing on each member of the team. "You're a bunch of knot-heads for volunteering, but I'm damn glad you're here."

That was when Talia understood the depth of Taggart's feelings for them. They were his family. His brothers, his sisters. And just as they'd followed him into a situation that could threaten their lives, he'd follow them down the same path without a moment's hesitation.

29

"Need your attention, people." Nate took charge when everyone was settled around the table. "Officially, we're here searching for the perpetrators of the embassy bombing. Unofficially, we know—thanks to Talia and Taggart—who the perps are but not where to find them. More on that later.

"Primarily, however, we're launching this op to rescue Talia's son, Meir, who was abducted by a Hamas group led by Hakeem al-Attar and his uncle Amir al-Attar."

Stephanie pressed a remote control, and Hakeem's and Amir's photographs appeared side-by-side on the projector screen.

"Hakeem and Amir are also responsible for the bombing," Nate added.

"Why take the boy?" Santos asked. "And does his abduction tie into the bombing in any way?"

Nate glanced at Bobby. "Want to field this one?"

Talia's admiration for this team grew tenfold. They'd come to help just because Taggart had asked, not knowing any of the details.

"I'll make it as short as possible," Taggart said, standing. "Talia is former Mossad."

Talia felt the sudden uptick of interest directed her way. Mossad agents earned every bit of their reputation as elite and courageous international special operators. In the eyes of Taggart's team, she had just been elevated from a potential liability to an asset.

"Six years ago in Kabul," Taggart went on, "she was instrumental in leading a Mossad hit squad to Hamas leader Mohammed al-Attar, the father of Hakeem and brother of Amir. Al-Attar was responsible for countless civilian deaths in Israel, mostly children. Talia's team took him out of the picture, along with twenty of his lieutenants. It was a devastating blow to Hamas."

He glanced at Talia, and she waited for the other shoe to fall. The one that told of her betrayal. But he moved past it.

"Since then, Hakeem and Amir have quietly and systematically hunted down and executed every member of the Mossad team responsible for al-Attar's death," he continued. "With Rhonda's help, we tracked them in Muscat and ascertained that the bombing was their attempt to assassinate Talia—with the bonus of wreaking a little international havoc with U.S. relations in Oman. When Hakeem and Amir discovered that Talia had survived the bombing, they abducted Meir and killed his bodyguard. They still want Talia and plan to use the boy to get to her."

"Why now? Why go after you after all this time?" Green's question was direct and spot-on.

"Because they couldn't find me," Talia explained. She'd given this a lot of thought during the past several hours. "At least, that's what I'm assuming. My cover as a war correspondent and photographer had never been blown. It must have taken them this long to realize that whenever a Hamas leader was taken out by Mossad, there was generally a story with my byline about some other event in the area."

Bobby gave her a nod of approval, then told them how they'd discovered Jonathan's body, then encountered and killed four of Hakeem's men before making it to the safe house.

"Give us a time frame," Jones said.

"Sure. I arrived at the embassy around five forty-five p.m. Blast detonated around six p.m. I hooked up with Talia shortly after and discovered around seven thirty that Meir had been abducted. With Rhonda's intel and going on info that Amir likes the ladies and the booze, we hit the streets the same night looking for some sign of him. Had to give it up around two a.m. and head back to the safe house."

He paused for a second, then went on. "Somewhere around four a.m., Talia received a call from Hakeem via the bodyguard's cell phone. They'd decided to add a demand for money to the ransom as part of their scheme. They want Talia and three million U.S. in exchange for the boy. Oh, and they want me, too. Seems they're a bit upset because I offed their four friends in the VW Golf."

"So we're now approximately thirty-six hours into this," Stephanie stated.

Talia glanced at the wall clock. Almost midnight.

"Yes," Taggart said. "Thirty-six."

"When do they want to make the exchange?" Jones asked.

"We're still waiting for the call," Talia said. "And I have no illusions about an exchange. They'll kill Meir no matter what, if we don't get him away from them first."

"Have you talked to the boy?" Black asked.

"Yes," Taggart said, apparently sensing that she was experiencing difficulty with the memory. "And Amir knows we'll require proof of life right up to the time of the 'exchange.'"

"You said you got a lead tonight." This from Cooper, who'd filled a coffee mug and rejoined them at the table.

Bobby nodded. "Right. After canvassing for hours, we finally connected with a hooker at the hotel where you picked us up. She says Amir is 'dating' one of her friends. He roughs her up bad but pays her well, so she lets him. Lauren, our hooker, says Amir's been there several nights in a row, always around the same time. Says she's certain he'll be back again. Talia and I missed him by fifteen minutes tonight."

She still got a knot in her chest when she thought about how close they'd been.

"We've also got the makes and models of the rental cars they're driving and the plate numbers. Based on the sizes of the cars, we're figuring we're dealing with at least nine fighters. Possibly a couple more but doubtful."

All this time, Stephanie wrote notes on a whiteboard, which Talia suspected would end up being the blueprint for their plan of action.

"What can you tell us about Meir?" Black asked her gently.

"He's five," she said, working to keep her voice steady. "He's a smart little boy, but he's scared. From what I could tell when I talked to him, he hadn't been hurt."

Stephanie hit a button, and Meir's picture popped up on the large projection screen. "Is this his most current photo?"

Talia felt herself go pale, and somehow she managed to nod. It was Meir's school photo, the one Rhonda had hacked. In it, Meir's smile was a little tentative. His bright white shirt and red tie that made up his school uniform were crisp and clean. The cowlick at the crown of his black hair was stubborn as always. He looked young and innocent and . . . she had to look away to keep the tears inside.

She glanced at Taggart, who had dropped heavily into the chair beside hers, and her breath caught. She wasn't the only one struggling. A huge, encompassing empathy swamped her, and she reached out and covered his hand with hers under the table.

This was the first time he'd ever seen his son. His big body had grown statue still. Only his eyes moved as he stared at Meir's photo on that very large screen, taking in every detail. Committing his face to memory. Undoubtedly seeing the likeness to her but, without question, recognizing the physical traits he and Meir shared.

Even at five years old, Meir had Taggart's strong nose, his full lips, and a definition to his eyes and brow that no one could dispute came straight from his father.

"I know this is hard, Talia." Nate Black addressed her, but his concerned gaze swung to Taggart before he turned back to her. "Are there any medical issues we need to be aware of? Any medications he takes? Any allergies? Physical disabilities?"

"No," she said quietly. "He's perfectly healthy."

"And I hate to ask, but what's his blood type?"

Her heart lurched. Of course, they needed his blood type. It was necessary information for the rescue team. "O positive."

Taggart turned his hand into hers and squeezed.

"Noted. And we're good to go," Carlyle said. Apparently, he would act as team medic.

"Anything else we need to know?" Black asked. "Okay, then," he said when no one spoke. "Let's get this hammered out."

Bobby stood with the rest of the team when Nate called a five-minute break. He needed a bottle of Tylenol, and he needed sleep. But mostly, he needed to find his son.

Seeing that Stephanie had taken Talia under her wing, he left the women together and headed to the Bunn for a moment alone, to get himself back together.

His son. *My God.* An emotion he could barely handle had ripped through his body when Meir's picture came up on the screen.

"You look like you need to be in a hospital," Coop said, walking up beside him.

Bobby pulled himself together. "I'll settle for coffee." And because he knew it was expected, he managed to come up with an insult. "And man, I cannot take you seriously with that damn bald head."

Coop laughed. "It's kind of growing on me."

"You realize how stupid that sounds, right?"

"Okay, so it's not *growing*, but I could get into this low-maintenance gig."

"Said the man who's as high-maintenance as his wife."

"Pretty has a price," Coop said, straight-faced. Bobby shook his head, filled a cup, then closed his eyes and leaned a shoulder against the wall.

"What aren't you telling me, brother?"

He knew that tone but chose to ignore it. He and Coop and Brown went way back. And when Brown walked up and closed in on him, too, he knew he was in for the equivalent of the Spanish Inquisition.

"So . . . you just happened to 'hook up' with Talia,"

Brown said speculatively as he refilled his mug. "After the bombing. A woman you didn't know. Even though she *happened* to be in Kabul when you were there six years ago. Wild coincidence, huh?"

Coop looked from Brown to Bobby. "Nicely done, Primetime. But you left out the part about the boy being five years old and having the same damn smile as Boom here. Anything you want to tell us?"

Bobby looked from one friend to another. He'd known it wouldn't take long for them to figure out that Meir was his son, but he wasn't ready to talk about it yet. "Just help me get him back. There'll be time enough to hash this out later."

Then he pushed away from the wall and walked back to his chair.

30

⟍

Two hours later, after a strong debate about whether they should return to the safe house or stay with the team at Royal Brit, Carlyle dropped them off at the house and headed back to HQ at the petroleum building.

"I don't feel right about this." Talia walked past Bobby into the living room. She set the duffel with Bobby's clothes—the guys had raided his locker back at ITAP—and some clothes Stephanie had brought for her on the kitchen bar.

Bobby tossed his headwear onto the coffee table. "That makes two of us. But when Nate issues an order, I damn well better obey it."

"Well, he's not *my* boss," she said, but without much punch.

He got it. She was exhausted, she was worried, and if she felt anything like he did, there weren't enough painkillers in the world to take the edge off.

And Nate wanted them rested. If they'd stayed with the team, they wouldn't have gotten any sleep, something Talia needed badly. They would have worked right alongside the rest of them.

"What if something time-sensitive comes up?" Talia had argued. "We'd be right there. Ready to act. If we're at the safe house, it'll be at least thirty minutes before we can get back here."

"We'll take that chance," had been Nate's final word.

"For the sake of this op," Bobby said now, after collapsing on the sofa, "I'd say Nate is your boss. And our best hope. I have to agree with him on this front. You do need sleep. Apparently, I'm guilty by association." He rubbed his painfully stiff neck. "So let's roll with it, okay? The team's got things well in hand, and we'll be in better shape to help if we catch a few."

It was already past two a.m. Neither of them had had more than four hours of sleep in the last forty-eight, and they planned to be up and at it again by six a.m.

"Where are they sleeping?"

He glanced up at her, seeing her exhaustion in the slump of her shoulders and her slow movements as she plugged her phone into the charger. "The team? They're not. I know Nate. He made sure they all got some solid shut-eye on the flight. Don't worry about them. They'll be fine. And they'll be busy. Black and Stephanie are already checking out areas of the city where the al-Attars might be holing up. They'll plan potential infiltration and escape routes, figure out probable traffic issues, and lock in GPS coordinates on the off chance they can get ahead of the game."

"Someone should be watching the hotel," she said. her look dark as she slumped onto a stool at the counter. "What if Amir comes back early?"

"Cooper and Santos are on it, okay? They left for the hotel where Lauren ID'd Amir about the same time we left to come back here. On the off chance that he does come back early, they'll be there. And then we'll move in."

When she didn't look convinced, he turned to her. "Look, there is no way Amir is slipping past us. When we get him in our sights, we'll let him lead us straight back to the hideout where they're keeping Meir."

"And then what?"

"And then, once we have them pinpointed, we'll refine the details of the rescue plan."

She chewed on her lower lip. "What if Lauren is wrong? What if Amir doesn't show up again?"

"You've got to stop this, Talia," he said wearily. "All this 'what if' and second-guessing isn't helping anyone. Especially you."

She glared at him.

"Fine. Brown, Jones, Carlyle, and Green were heading out to look for the two rental cars. Yes, it's a long shot that they'll spot them, but big cases have been broken on long shots. And you heard Stephanie. She and Rhonda are busy tapping assets and calling in favors, hoping to find an in with an undercover CIA operative rumored to be in Muscat."

"Key word: rumored."

"Even so. If he is here and if they can make the connection, the CIA operative might have heard about the al-Attar Hamas group. Might even know where they're lying low. Supposedly, he's deeply infiltrated in the Islamic Militants from Uzbekistan terrorist group, which is closely affiliated with Al-Qaeda. If—and yes, it's a big if—they can find him, it's very possible the IMU group has knowledge of Hakeem's and Amir's Hamas hideout. They might even be helping them."

"Now who's talking about ifs?"

Bobby scrubbed his hands over his face, weary beyond words. "Go take your shower. Then get some sleep. You're going to need it."

She hesitated, looked as though she wanted to say something more, but headed for the bathroom.

He understood the look in her eyes. Besides her fear for Meir, everything had changed between them last night in that bed—and yet nothing had changed. Meir was still at risk. They were still who they were and had still done what they'd done. And as much as he would always desire her, as much as he would always care for her on some level, he could never get past her betrayal.

He scrubbed his hands over his eyes again. He couldn't even think about it right now. He collapsed on the sofa, covering his eyes with a forearm. All he could think about was Meir. Getting him back safe and sound. No matter how they managed to do it, everything depended on finding the Hamas stronghold before the imposed deadline.

Why haven't those fuckers called?

He both dreaded the call yet hated Hakeem ten times more for keeping them on tenterhooks this way. The animal was a true terrorist. And the true definition of terror was not facing down the enemy. The true definition of terror was feeling helpless to protect or save those who were most important to you.

A tear trickled out of the corner of his eye and ran down the side of his temple, completely blindsiding him. He wiped it away. Blinked away the burning behind his eyelids. Understanding, for the first time, what a parent went through every time a child was deployed. What a wife went through every time a cop took to the streets. Every time they received word that someone they loved had been injured or had been declared MIA or, worse, KIA.

His situation was different. Yet so much the same. And as he lay here, his gut knotted with this horrible feeling of helplessness and impending loss, he swore that no matter the outcome, he would somehow make it up to his own mother for all the hell he'd put her through over the years.

His subconscious must have been waiting for Hakeem's call, because when the phone rang at four o'clock, Bobby woke up fully alert. He'd never gotten around to a shower. He'd more or less passed out. Still dressed in the dishdasha and barely able to move because of all his aches and pains, he muscled his way upright. Rising stiffly, he hobbled over to the kitchen counter, where Talia had left the phone plugged in and charging.

She almost beat him to it. She came flying out of the bedroom, barefoot, sleep-mussed, wearing boxers and a T-shirt again. Her eyes met his, frightened but resolved.

"You can do this," he said.

With a nod, she picked up the phone and switched it to speaker before answering. "Hello."

"Do you have the money?"

"I . . . I have half of it," she lied, carrying out their plan to stall until they found the hideout. "I can have the rest by tomorrow."

"Tomorrow?" It was more of a snarl than a question. "You want your son released alive? You will have the money today."

This was what they'd been afraid of. That Hakeem would renege on his two-day time frame. And this was where Talia had to be particularly careful.

"You said two days. That was only twenty-four hours ago."

"I grow impatient."

"I want my son released alive. I'm doing everything I can as fast as I can to get the money. I'm not a rich woman. I have to reach out to family and friends. The time difference between Oman and the States is complicating things. International banking laws, everything is taking additional time."

Bobby nodded in encouragement. She was doing fine. Even though it killed them both to stall, killed them to leave Meir in Hakeem's and Amir's blood-thirsty hands for another second, they had to draw this out long enough for the team to find the Hamas hide-out. Everything hinged on finding them before the ransom deadline.

"Please," she added, her voice trembling when Hakeem didn't respond. "I have to be careful, or I'll raise alarms and draw the wrong kind of attention. The U.S. NSA will be all over money transfers of any sizable amount. Israeli intelligence also. Then we both lose."

"How much time?" he asked, finally accepting that he was beaten in this one thing.

"I need that other twenty-four hours."

Another long silence. "Twenty-four hours. No more," he said, his tone grudging but conceding. "I don't have to tell you what will happen to your son if you attempt to delay."

"I won't. I'll have the money. Where do I meet you?"

"You do not yet need to know. I will call again with the time and the address."

"I need to talk to Meir," Talia said quickly, before Hakeem could disconnect.

"As before, the boy is sleeping."

"I must talk with him. I must know he's alive. That he's unharmed—not one bruise on his body, do you understand? Or not only will this deal not happen, but I'll track you down and kill you myself."

Bobby cupped her shoulder, steadying her. The tension, the lack of sleep—it was all crashing down on her.

"Brave talk from a dead woman."

"Let me talk to my son!" she demanded, her small body shaking with rage. "And I will talk to him again tomorrow when you call, or there will be no exchange."

Hakeem didn't respond. Finally, they heard his voice in the background yelling at someone to bring the boy.

"Keep it together," Bobby whispered when her trembling became so violent he was afraid she'd pass out.

"Momma." Tears and sleep filled the little boy's voice, and a strength that Bobby hadn't thought Talia capable of at this juncture washed over her.

"Hi, baby."

"You said I could come home soon. You promised. I want to come home."

"I know, baby. I know you do. And I did promise. Don't I always keep my promises? You *are* coming home," she assured him, with an excitement that the boy could translate into trust.

"When?"

"Very soon now. Tomorrow. If I could come for you sooner, you know I would. But these . . . men. These men have promised to take care of you until I get there. Do they take care of you, baby? Are you hurt in any way?"

"I'm okay. Rami takes care of me."

"Rami?" Her clear relief at Meir's quick *okay* was evident in her deep breath.

"Rami stays with me. He brings me food. And he sleeps beside me so I don't get scared."

Her face drained of blood. "S-sleeps beside you?"

"On the floor, yes. Rami likes American football, too."

"Oh . . . oh, good. He sounds like a g-good friend," she choked out, her shoulders sagging with relief.

Bobby knew she was doing everything in her power to keep him on the line for as long as possible.

"And don't be afraid, Meir. Everything is fine. I will see you tomorrow, okay? You stay close to Rami until then."

A small silence on Meir's end told them both that tomorrow was not soon enough. "I have to go," the boy said in a whisper.

"No, not yet." She gripped the phone tighter. "Meir!"

But he was already gone, the connection broken.

She stood so silent, for so long, that he finally had to pry the phone out of her hand.

"You did fine. He sounded fine."

And his words sounded empty. Felt empty. As empty as her reserve of strength. She'd had to tap into it too many times.

She turned tear-filled eyes to his. "I can't do this anymore. I . . . I need him back with me. I n-need my son. I need him back. I need him back. I . . . need . . . him."

He didn't think about his needs when she leaned numbly against him. He didn't think about past or present or promises broken. He walked her back to the bedroom.

But he didn't stay. He couldn't. Not again.

He covered her up, told her to get some sleep. Knew she probably wouldn't.

Then he walked back to the living room, sank down on the sofa, and lay awake in the predawn darkness for a long, long time before he finally fell asleep.

31

Amir al-Attar stumbled out of the elevator and into the hotel lobby.

"Got eyes on," Bobby whispered into his collar mike as he sat in a corner at the back of the bar, with Lauren from London snuggled up beside him like a proper date.

From his vantage point, Bobby could see Amir walk across the lobby toward the entrance doors. He moved too carefully to be sober as he tossed his keys to the valet.

"Target's at the front door; valet's getting his car."

"Roger that." Coop's voice sounded hollow through his earpiece. "Took his damn sweet time."

Coop and Brown had taken first watch starting around two o'clock this morning. They were relieved by Jones and Green around two p.m., and now both pairs were double-teaming Amir. As Lauren had promised, the man was as regular as clockwork.

He'd shown up at the bar around nine; Bobby had made certain to be in place by seven. After what had been one of the longest days of his life waiting for Amir to show, he wouldn't risk losing him after all this trouble.

"Run, you rat bastard," he muttered. "Run back to your sewer, and I'll bring you some rotten cheese. Better yet, a nice shiny bullet."

He waited until the valet brought Amir's blue Golf around, then unwrapped himself from Lauren's arms. "Thanks, Lauren." He handed her a bundle of rial notes.

"My pleasure, love. Easiest money this bird's ever made. 'Urt 'im once for Peg, would ya? Then 'urt 'im again for me."

Bobby dropped a kiss on her forehead, then headed for the door and watched the Golf pull away. A few seconds later, Green and Jones pulled out of the parking lot in a newly rented white Honda and eased into traffic behind Amir. When Coop and Brown pulled up under the portico in a four-door silver Camry, Bobby jumped into the backseat. The two black Land Cruisers were parked tonight. Both would be too conspicuous, and they didn't want to give Amir an opportunity to make them as tails.

"Do not lose that car," he said, sitting forward on the middle of the backseat with his head between Coop and Brown.

"Always with the backseat driving," Coop sputtered, and fell in a block behind Green and Jones, who were three car lengths behind Amir.

For the next fifteen minutes, they took turns peel-

ing on and off Amir's tail, sometimes even passing
him so as not to raise any suspicion.

"Anyone up for a quick game of I Spy?" Coop
wanted to know, and he looked at Bobby in the rearview mirror. "I'll start. I spy someone who needs a
hug."

"I'd be up for a game of Stuff a Sock in the Bald
Guy's Mouth," Bobby muttered.

Coop grinned at him. "Chill already, okay, bud?
Sit back. Enjoy the ride. There's not a damn thing
you can do that we aren't already doing."

Okay, fine. Coop was attempting to dull the razor-
sharp tension. And he was right. Alert, prepared, in
control—all made for successful ops. But there was
such a thing as being too pumped, too wired, too
ready. Bobby had passed that point the second he'd
seen Amir stagger out of the elevator.

On a deep breath, he sat back and slouched against
the seat. And thought about Talia.

He'd finally fallen asleep sometime after five a.m.
When he'd come around, she was up and had already
brewed coffee.

"Thanks," she'd said, pouring him a mug.

"For?"

"Last night. For not judging."

Judging? Hell, he couldn't judge her for wanting
her son back. Not for that. And he couldn't judge her
for falling apart. He'd been damn close himself. So
close he'd almost caved. Almost let himself crawl into
bed with her again and respond to her soft hands and

willing body. It would have been easy. So easy to lose himself again in her. To give them both escape.

I loved you . . . I still love you,

Her words lingered. Long after they should have. Maybe she did love him. Maybe she just thought she did. Either way. It didn't matter. He couldn't let it matter. Because he couldn't forget. Maybe that made him an ass. Probably, yeah, it did. But for six years, her betrayal had eaten at him like poison in his blood. The taste wasn't going away in a matter of hours. Dangerous, stressful, revelation-filled hours.

Maybe when this was over and they got Meir back—and they *would* get him back—maybe then he could look back and think about forgiving.

But not now. Not after he'd seen her face this morning, the moment it had registered in her eyes that everything was the same between them.

By the time Carlyle had picked them up and driven them back to Royal Brit, they'd both shaken it off, and Talia was back in operator mode. She'd not only recovered, but she'd been royally pissed when she'd found out he was leaving her with Nate, Steph, Carlyle, and Santos while he joined the hunt for Amir.

"I want to be in on this," she'd said, her dark eyes flaring with fire.

"Not a chance," he'd said.

Nate had been more diplomatic. "I'm sorry, Talia. We can't afford to have you anywhere near Amir until we're ready to breach the hideout. They might make you. And then it's all over."

She'd settled down but still hadn't been happy.

"You know we can use you here," Nate continued. "And I know it's been a drag because you've been at it all morning, but we need to keep digging for the blueprints on this warehouse our CIA asset pointed us toward."

Earlier this morning, the guys had been able to make brief contact with the undercover CIA agent. He was aware that a Hamas cell had recently arrived in the city. Had gathered that they were holed up somewhere in the warehouse district, but other than that, he didn't have anything concrete.

Still, the team had run with it. Because the warehouse district was so huge, they'd worked all day doing title searches and locating the names of owners who might have ties to the al-Attars or Hamas.

Just before Bobby had left for the hotel to help with surveillance on Amir, Stephanie had hit pay dirt.

"I've got something." Her fingers had flown across the keyboard. "Look at this. I've found a company—Mideast Blades—that provides site security for various petroleum companies in the Mideast. One of those companies is Ultramar PLC. And Ultramar happens to own a warehouse-slash-office complex here in Muscat. Guess who owns Mideast Blades?"

"Hakeem would be too easy," Jones had said.

"Yeah, it would. But Hakeem has a cousin who's married to a guy named Qasim Nagi. Nagi owns Mideast Blades. He also happens to be on a terrorist watch list. His specialty? Money laundering for Hamas."

"So most likely, Mideast Blades is actually a shell company?" Black had concluded.

"I'd bet on it. Bet real big that Nagi's company allows him to move people and money around in ways that can't be traced by international security analysts, and that's why he hasn't been picked up or charged yet. I've uncovered patterns of money transfers that make it obvious to me that Ultramar is paying protection money so they'll leave the company and its people alone.

"Like they always say," Stephanie had added, "follow the money. And in this case, the money points to payoffs funneled directly into Hamas bank accounts."

"Of more immediate importance, following the money may have found Meir." Black had smiled. "It's a damn big coincidence that Hakeem has a cousin who provides security for Ultramar. I say we look at this warehouse really hard. Nice work, Steph."

"NSA's going to love me when I get back and play show-and-tell with them. They've been after this guy for a long time."

"Wish I could tell you your work was done," Black had added. "But now I need you to see what you can do about finding the blueprints for this warehouse and whether it's currently operating as an active business. If it turns out to be our Hamas hideout, we're going to need that info ASAP to plan the rescue. And Talia, we can use you to help us set up our driving route and action plan. If Ultramar turns out to be our target, we'll be one step ahead of those bastards."

They all knew that time was running out. Anything they could do to speed up the prep process went in the win column for Meir.

"And if it doesn't?" Talia had asked. "If Ultramar turns out to be a near miss?"

"Then we keep looking."

At that point, Bobby had to get out of there. He'd felt Talia's frustration as keenly as if it was his own. And if he'd hung around much longer, he might have caved and tried to talk Nate into letting her come along on surveillance duty.

"Hold on, ladies and gents."

The veiled excitement in Coop's voice snapped Bobby back to the moment. He sat forward in the backseat again. "What? What's happening?"

"Amir just turned into that lot up there." Coop drove on by so as not to draw any attention.

Bobby craned his neck around as they passed the security gate. Spotted the sign identifying the company on the tall chain-link fence that surrounded a warehouse roughly the size of a football field.

Sonofabitch. We got him!

His hand was unsteady when he reached into his pocket for his phone. "We've found them, Talia." He wished he could be there to see her face. "Amir led us to the hideout. It's Ultramar."

He barely heard her whispered, "Thank God."

"It's almost over," he promised. "We're getting him back. Make no mistake, we are bringing him back to you."

32

As much as Taggart wanted to follow Amir straight into that warehouse, put a bullet in his head, and fight his way to Meir, he knew he had to keep himself reeled in. If there had been any chance that he could have taken on the terrorists by himself, he wouldn't have needed the team.

Wired and impatient, he sank into the backseat, prepared for another wait, as Coop headed back to Royal Brit. Jones and Green stayed behind and set up surveillance on the Ultramar warehouse. Finding the hideout was only the first phase. It would take the entire team and careful planning to pull off Meir's rescue—and even then, it was going to be dicey.

Complex snatch-and-grab ops were generally preceded by days, sometimes weeks, of precision training drills. Hours and hours of running and rerunning the infiltration and extraction plan until each operative had their individual and their team members' tasks embedded in their psyches. Until muscle memory took over and they could run the routes in their sleep.

They didn't have weeks or months. He checked the time on his phone. Felt a double tap from his heart. One forty-five a.m. They had mere hours. Two hours and fifteen minutes exactly if Hakeem stayed true to form and called at four a.m. to give Talia the time and place where she was to give herself up to them in exchange for Meir. Only everyone knew there would be no exchange.

Meir's life wasn't the only one on the line in this op. They were all gearing up to stop bullets if they had to, to save the boy.

Another rolling rush of emotions swamped him. The boy who was his son. Every time the reality of it hit him, he felt a rush.

He clenched his jaw so tightly his teeth ached. He could not, he *would* not, let his son die.

"You're right," he said.

Coop shifted his gaze to the rearview mirror, and Brown turned around in his seat.

"Meir is my son."

"We'd figured that out," Brown said softly. "We're going to get him back, Boom. No doubts."

His eyes burned with emotion, and he swallowed it back, too overcome to speak.

Except for the constant grinding of the Bunn making yet another pot of coffee, the conference room in the basement of Royal Brit was church-quiet. All eyes were on Stephanie, who stood at the front of the conference table, entering key strokes on her

Toughbook while a tense Nate Black watched over her shoulder.

The tension in the room was familiar to Talia. Her years with Mossad had been filled with similar briefings. Everyone wanted success. Everyone wanted to come back alive. And everyone knew the odds were stacked against them.

Not this time, she repeated over and over in her mind. This time, her son's life was on the line. He was an innocent. He didn't deserve to be part of Hamas's bloody games.

And neither did the people at the table with her.

When this was over, she would find a way to repay them. She only hoped they would all be alive for her to thank.

"Okay!" Stephanie said, sounding excited. "We've got eyes in the sky on the Ultramar warehouse. Thank you, technology gods!"

Everyone expelled a breath of relief, and Coop let go of a "Hoo-ah!"

Five minutes ago, Stephanie and Black had returned from carrying the dismantled ultralight surveillance drone up to the roof, reassembling it, and hand-launching it. Since the launch, Stephanie had been remotely guiding the drone using software loaded on her Toughbook.

"You can call Green and Jones in now," Stephanie told Black, who immediately picked up his phone and dialed. "I've got the coordinates for Ultramar locked in, and the Puma will circle the building at around five hundred feet until I change the command or until it runs out of battery power, whichever is first. If anyone leaves or arrives at that warehouse, I'll know within seconds."

The Israeli military and Mossad had been the first to employ drones to locate targets as far back as the 1970s, so Talia was very familiar with the technology. The Puma was an excellent choice. It had a two- to three-hour loiter time and was equipped with onboard sensors, a thermal imaging camera, and nearly silent electric motors so it wouldn't be heard from the ground.

"What's the resolution on that?" she asked, wanting to know just how good the thermal-imaging camera was.

"We swapped out the basic sensor package for top-of-the-line," Stephanie told her, "so we should even be able to see if they have a mouse problem. We'll know pretty soon."

"Okay," Black said after hanging up. "It'll take Green and Jones what? Around twenty minutes to get here?"

Coop nodded. "This time of night, traffic's light. Twenty minutes should do it."

"While we're waiting for them, bring the drone in closer, Steph. See if you can pick up some heat signatures inside the building."

This was the part they'd all been waiting for. The test to see if the drone and the thermal-imaging equipment could lock onto the heat signatures each human body created and tell them how many people were inside the Ultramar warehouse and where they were. More specifically, where Meir was.

The room grew silent as Stephanie shifted the images the drone sent from the Toughbook screen to the wall screen so they could all see them.

All eyes strained to see the details in the photos that arrived, one after another after another. For several long frames and multiple shots, they saw nothing but dark, nothing but gray. Nothing that indicated there was a single sign of life in the building. Finally, when the drone reached the east side of the warehouse, there they were. Fuzzy red horizontal blobs.

"Got 'em," Brown said. "Way to go, Steph."

A few heat signatures indicated people at ground level. Others were at a higher level and others even higher than that.

Stephanie said, "Inside this warehouse, there's a four-story building that houses administrative offices and more. As you can see by the various heights, our terrorists are spread out from the first to the fourth floors, sleeping."

Suddenly, the images were blank again.

"Give it a few minutes," Stephanie said. "The drone moved out of range. It'll circle back, and we'll have another look."

Talia made herself breathe as she waited for the drone to fly back into thermal-image range. She couldn't be sure, but she thought she'd seen a smaller image among the other red lumps, another larger one close beside it.

"Here we go again," Stephanie said. "Sharp eyes, everyone, so we can pin this down."

Talia watched closely, then made a quick diagram with pencil and paper. "I think I've got them."

When the drone went out of range again, they all compared notes.

"So we're in agreement?" Black asked after they'd conferred. "Meir and . . ." He trailed off and glanced at Talia. "What was his name, the one Meir told you looked out for him?"

"Rami," she supplied quickly.

"Right. Meir and Rami appear to be sleeping side-by-side in a room in the middle of the fourth floor. Then we've got eight other signatures which we're tagging as tangos. Two on the ground floor guarding the entrance door, two on the second floor, two on the third, and two outside the room we've designated as Meir's and this Rami guy inside with him."

Everyone nodded.

The conference-room door opened, and Green and Jones walked in.

"Gentlemen," Black said. "Good timing. Let me bring you up to speed."

33

"But he's my son." Talia tried to stay calm. She knew this battle wouldn't be won by out-of-check emotions. But her heart pounded, heat enveloped her, and if she hadn't clasped her hands together beneath the table, they'd be shaking with rage.

"With all due respect, Talia, you haven't worked with us before," Black pointed out. "You know the value of team synergy. Especially in this situation, where we haven't had the chance to fine-tune the plan. One move out of sync with our usual rhythm could jeopardize everything. And frankly, you're too emotionally involved."

"I'm the only one he'll recognize," she protested. "He'll be frightened. I need to be there when we find him."

"You're going to be there, but in a backup role. Use your head, not your heart, and you'll realize we'll all be much safer—Meir included—if you fill the support role where I need you. Taggart will be there with you."

She looked over at Taggart, who nodded. She knew he wasn't happy about being assigned to a support role, too. And Black was right. He was handling this exactly the way she would if she were team leader.

"Fine," she said reluctantly, and let it go.

They were moving out at three thirty a.m., a little less than an hour from now. Her heart leaped at the thought. If all went as planned, she would have Meir safely back with her very, very soon. She had to believe that.

"Steph." Black's voice brought Talia's attention back to the front of the room. "Pull up the blueprint."

A digitized blueprint of the Ultramar warehouse filled the large projector screen.

"Talia, you were the one who finally located the blueprints online. Do the honors, would you?"

She nodded stiffly and rose. The moment she started talking, she felt herself shift into operative mode. Comfortable, filled with purpose, and in control. "The warehouse is around the size of a football field. One hundred yards long, half as wide. Inside the warehouse, they've constructed another building."

Stephanie handed her a laser pointer, and she used it to indicate the location of the building inside the warehouse.

"For the sake of clarity, we'll refer to this interior building as the Bunker. As you saw on the drone shots, it's four stories tall, is situated inside the east corner of the warehouse, and was designed not only to house administrative offices but also as a stronghold in the event there was ever a security threat.

"It has showers," she continued, pointing them out, "a stockpile of food, beds, a kitchen, and so on. The bad news is, the Bunker is built like a fortress. After the Arab Spring, they upgraded the security so that if something like that happened in Oman, key players from the warehouse could hide in the Bunker until they could be extracted or until the battle died down."

"So," Black added, assessing the somber faces around the table, "think of the Bunker as a safe room on steroids. If we don't take advantage of the element of surprise, they may have the capability to seal themselves up tight and hold off our siege."

Or—and Talia had tried desperately not to think it, but there was no getting past it—they could martyr themselves in the name of Allah and blow the place sky-high, taking everyone inside the warehouse with them.

Bobby sat in the back of the van, scanning the faces of the team as they headed for Ultramar. They were as ready as they could be. Still, his thoughts were in turmoil. They'd all trained countless hours on taking down bad guys, executing dozens of rescues over the years. From his experience, he knew that they probably had only a fifty-fifty chance of getting Meir back. Those odds hadn't been discussed in the briefing.

Dead and injured hostages were normally referred to as "breakage," but this hostage wasn't breakage. This was his son.

He glanced at Talia, who sat next to him. Silent. Tense. Resolute. Like him, she wore tactical-level body armor and gear identical to that of the rest of the team. While she'd have preferred her Glock, Nate had issued her a sound-suppressed 1911A1 pistol like the rest of the team. She wore it in a drop holster on her right hip; the sling of the M4 hung over her shoulder. He couldn't decide if the armor made her look like a badass warrior or small and vulnerable. She was still pissed about not leading the assault, and he wasn't happy about it, either. But Nate had made the right decision about not having them enter the Bunker with the rest of the team. They were too physically beat-up, too psychologically spent, and far too emotionally invested. A bad call on either of their parts, and they could get not only themselves but other team members killed. And Meir could become a casualty.

He wished, however, that they had better numbers, because the guys could use the extra firepower up front. Rhonda was now controlling the drone from headquarters stateside, because they needed Stephanie as their wheel man and lookout—much to her husband Joe's dismay.

One of his conditions for Stephanie coming along was that she was not to be involved in direct combat. That she wouldn't be subjected to line-of-fire casualties unless paper cuts and carpal tunnel were considered combat wounds.

But Stephanie had won this battle by default. They needed her behind the wheel and in constant radio contact with Rhonda, who continued to relay updates on the drone images. As of their departure from Royal Brit, none of the heat images had moved. Which was exactly what they wanted, for the tangos to be sound asleep, so it would all be over before they knew what hit them.

Nate's final words before they loaded up had been straight and to the point. "The timeline is this: Breach the warehouse, disable the alarms, kill the lights. Hit the Bunker hard and fast, take out the guards floor by floor, secure Meir. In and out in less than two minutes. Head for the airport. Mission accomplished."

Sounded great in theory. Now it was about to be tested.

He ran Nate's assault plan through his mind, visualizing how it would go down. Nate would be the site commander at the warehouse, overseeing and calling the shots.

Once the entire team was inside, Green and Jones

would come at the Bunker from the front. Black and Brown would be the second line of defense into the Bunker. Cooper and Santos would enter through the back. Carlyle would stand close by at the casualty collection and extraction point, at the west front corner of the Bunker. Bobby and Talia would provide backup at the warehouse door, watching for anyone trying to escape.

Stephanie would stand by in the van, ready to drive them the hell out of there when it was over.

Easy-peasy. Except for a few minor details.

Although they would know where the tangos and Meir were, they didn't know how the bad guys were armed or if any changes had been made to the building that might affect the assault. The assumption was that the blueprints were up to date, but it never paid to assume. It was the best they had, however, so they were going with it

"ETA sixty seconds," Stephanie said. "Final radio check commencing now." They all wore their radios on a pouch on the back of their armor. The voice-activated throat mike pressed against their necks, and the earpiece fit under their sound-deadening hearing protection.

Steph called out each individual's name, waited for a return "check," and pronounced them good.

"Rhonda, what are you seeing from the drone? We good?" Steph asked.

"You're clear. Nothing moving but the wind.

Break a leg, boys and girls. Kick some serious ass."

Stephanie pulled the van up to the gate securing the warehouse fence. Santos peeled out of the van, broke the padlock with bolt cutters, and opened the gate wide. Stephanie rolled the van slowly through, and Santos jumped back in on the fly.

She pulled up short of the warehouse, out of range of exterior security cameras. "You're on, Rhonda."

"Roger that."

Then they waited, tense and watchful, knowing Rhonda was manipulating her computer back home, keying in codes, hacking into the exterior security camera system.

Less than a minute later, Rhonda's voice came over their headsets. "Done deal, people," she said. "If anyone's awake and monitoring, they're now looking at a looped video of an empty parking lot. So unless they've got X-ray vision, they're not going to spot you out there."

Stephanie slowly pulled ahead toward the main warehouse door. Bobby fingered his rifle, double-checked that his helmet was strapped on tight, along with the thermal-imaging glasses clipped to the front of it. After the others were inside and shut down the power to the warehouse, he'd slip the glasses down so he could see to do his job.

A calm came over him as he closed his eyes and touch-searched his gear, making sure he could put his hands on any part of it without looking, knowing the rest of the team was doing the same thing.

Stephanie stopped the van next to the main warehouse door.

Jones and Green grabbed the breaching charges they might need to blow the Bunker doors, then climbed out of the van. They'd be the first through the door. Everyone but Stephanie followed and stacked up next to the warehouse wall. Talia hung tight behind Bobby, the two of them providing rear security. Santos used his bolt cutters again on the locked warehouse door. Once he broke the lock, he checked for alarm sensors or wires.

"Aren't you done yet?" Coop asked, impatience and nerves getting the best of him.

"We'll find out soon enough," Santos said. "Do-or-die time."

They knew that when Santos opened that warehouse door, there was no going back. They had to run almost eighty yards to reach the Bunker, take out the two ground-floor guards, then set and blow the breaching charges to get inside.

At the same time, Carlyle would go open the electrical panel and blow the power to the entire complex, then slip back into position. About ten thousand things could go wrong, and there was only one way that this would go right. Everything had to work exactly as planned.

Bobby reached back and squeezed Talia's hand. "Don't do anything stupid."

This was it.

On Santos's "Go," he followed the team inside.

They'd just cleared the exterior door when alarm bells went off, screaming through the cavernous warehouse like banshees.

34

Rami woke up with a start. Beside him, the boy, Meir, whimpered in his sleep.

He blinked, shaking off his confusion, and realized something was wrong. A noise. Something loud and shrill and horrible.

The door to their room flew open.

"Get up!" Amir stood on the other side, a rifle in his hand, fierce anger on his face.

"What's happening?"

"Someone has broken into the warehouse. They can only be after the boy. Take him, and hide with him in the closet. If anyone comes after him but Hakeem or me, shoot them."

He shoved the rifle into Rami's hands.

Just then, the alarm went silent. Soon after, the sound of automatic-rifle fire reverberated through the building.

"Do you understand what you are to do?" Amir demanded.

Rami nodded. "Kill them."

"Yes." Amir glared at Meir. "Then you kill the boy."

"What the hell, Santos?" Black yelled into the mike, as they all ducked for cover behind tall wooden shipping crates, large pieces of machinery, and whatever else they could find.

"You tell me!" Santos yelled back. "They must have added a secondary alarm system that wasn't on the blueprints."

And now they were squatting like sitting ducks on a lake surrounded by hunters, the screeching alarms rubbing their already raw nerves like sandpaper.

"Carlyle, kill those fucking lights," Nate ordered. "We'll lay down cover." *No battle plan survives contact with the enemy.*

The axiom rolled through Bobby's mind. This was what happened in rushed operations thrown together in bad conditions and without proper recon and surveillance. So much for a sneak attack.

Time for plan B, the *oh, shit* plan. All men on deck, a full-out assault on the Bunker as soon as Carlyle killed those lights and that damn alarm.

Muzzle flashes erupted from the Bunker—the bad guys clearly knew they had company—and Black's team lit up the warehouse with live rounds and tracer fire in response.

Suddenly, the warehouse went dark. The alarms stopped screaming. Score one for the good guys.

"Carlyle?" Nate barked over the radio.

"I'm good," Carlyle barked back, sounding out of breath.

Without surprise on their side, things got much more dangerous. And they couldn't use overwhelming firepower to shoot their way into the Bunker, or Meir could become a victim of friendly fire.

Another problem: they hadn't anticipated that the warehouse would be so full of crap. They had to maneuver around stacks of crates and machinery to get to the Bunker. While offering some protection, the obstacles cost them speed. And speed was their best weapon right now.

As one, the team ran the maze toward the Bunker, bullets whizzing all around them. Bobby flipped down his night-vision goggles, firing as he ran. Running beside him, Talia did the same. He stopped and hunkered down behind a crate about fifteen yards from the Bunker's front entrance, then looked around and counted. All six infrared lights that the team had secured to their helmets to identify one another in the dark were present and accounted for.

He ducked for cover when another round of gunfire strafed the warehouse and the flash of tracers lit things up like the Vegas Strip.

"Green's down!"

Out of the corner of his eye, Bobby saw Carlyle grab Green by the handle on the back of his body armor and drag him behind a stack of crates.

"He's just stunned, Steph," Carlyle said after several long, tense seconds.

"I'm fine," Green grumbled.

"You damn well better be." Steph sounded worried but strong.

"On one, two, three," Black said, and everyone but Green stood and laid fire in the direction of the ground-floor guard who'd been giving them grief.

"Tango down," Jones said.

"Ditto that," said Santos.

Two down, seven to go.

Then a machine gun started firing from a first-floor window.

Jesus. These guys were loaded for bear.

Bobby dropped to one knee and shone the laser sight on his rifle about a foot over the muzzle flash from the big gun. He fired a three-round burst, and the machine gun went silent.

"Tango down," he said into his mike, then glanced at Talia. "You okay?"

"No," she said. "They must know we're here after Meir. What if . . . what if they decide to ki—"

"They're not going to kill him," he promised her, praying he wasn't lying, then shut off his mike so the others couldn't hear their conversation. "These bastards think they're invincible. They plan to be the last men standing. And they're going to keep Meir as their prize until the last shot is fired. They want you alive. They want you to see that they're in control. And to do that, they'll want you to see that they have your son. *Our son*," he added firmly. "And I'm not going to let that happen."

Santos fired a 40mm flashbang grenade through the window the machine-gunner had been using, and Bobby clicked his mike back on, getting back into the game as a loud crack reverberated through his earpiece—more tango fire, distinguishable from the team's fire because the tangos weren't using sound suppressors. Then the muffled *whosh, whosh, whosh* of a sound-suppressed M4.

"Tango down," Jones said.

"Hoo-ah!" Brown whooped. "Give 'em hell, boys!"

The next several seconds were a clinic of a precision team working together as though their thoughts were connected. Cooper and Santos peeled off toward the back Bunker door, taking one of the breaching charges with them. Jones and Green, with the remaining breaching charge, belly-crawled to the front door while everyone else laid cover fire.

"Breaching in three, two, one." Santos's voice came over the mike, followed by the huge roar of an explosion.

"Ditto that," Jones said, as he and Green scrambled out of harm's way. Jones hit the firing clacker, and three seconds later, the Bunker's front door blew down with a jaw-rattling *boom* and fell inward in a cloud of smoke.

They were in!

As Santos and Cooper started clearing the first floor from back to front, Jones and Green charged in and started clearing from front to back, meeting them in the middle.

On Green's heels, Black and Carlyle rushed in, discarding their original plan on the fly. "Heading to the second floor," Black said, and got a "Roger that" from both Jones and Santos. Although this all happened in a matter of moments, Bobby felt as though time had stopped. Nothing moved fast enough to suit him.

"I can't sit here and do nothing," he said over his mike. "I'm heading for the fourth floor."

Beside him, Talia rose.

"No!" he said. "You stay put. We need someone to cover, in case anyone gets past us."

"I'm with Bobby." Mike Brown appeared out of nowhere.

Her face pale but calm, Talia nodded, then took a position behind a huge turbine. "Bring him to me."

Bobby gave her a clipped nod, and with Brown on his heels, he charged through the blown Bunker door.

The room billowed with smoke and the smell of plastic explosives. The fire sprinklers had gone off, and cold water drizzled down his back.

"We're inside, heading up the stairwell for the top floor," he reported.

"Roger that," from Black.

Based on the blueprints, there were stairwells leading up both the front and the back of the building. In theory, they should have cleared one floor at a time.

But the drone photos indicated that Meir was on the top floor, so that was where he headed.

His earpiece echoed with the sound of more flash-bangs, then a burst of M4 fire and a gargled scream that quickly went silent.

"Tango down. Second floor clear," Jones said.

Brown followed as Bobby ran up the stairwell taking two steps at a time, his adrenaline hitting an all-time high. They had entered the textbook "fatal funnel." No place to hide, and all a bad guy had to do was fire a burst into the well and be guaranteed to hit one of them.

His breath rasped, and his heart pounded. More out of concern for what they would find than from exertion.

A flash of light from muzzle fire had him dropping to his knees in defense. Behind him, Brown fired three distinct *snicks*.

"Tango down."

The two of them jumped over the body and raced up the stairwell, past the third floor and onto the fourth landing without running into more resistance. Taggart stood next to Brown by the stair door, a flash-bang in his hand.

As soon as Mike opened the door, Bobby tossed it inside. The two of them charged into the hall when it went off. Bobby's only thought was of getting to Meir before the bad guys had a chance to recover and decide to kill him.

In the strobe of the flashbang, he saw a man raise an AK-47.

He fired three rounds into the man's chest and followed that with two in the head. "Tango down," he reported grimly.

If his tally was right, Hamas was down seven. That left two standing in the way of getting Meir.

The odds were now better than good. But it only took one lunatic to fire a killing shot, so he kept moving. He and Brown quickly cleared the rest of the floor.

And found nothing.

No one.

Where the hell was Meir?

Bobby keyed in his mike. "Fourth floor clear. Anybody have eyes on the boy?"

"Negative," came a unison reply.

What the hell?

Nate jumped in. "Start a search in detail."

They'd have to look under every bed and table, in every closet and bathroom. Anyplace anyone could be hiding.

Rhonda's voice broke over the radio. "All teams, we're going to have company soon. I've been monitoring radio chatter, and the Omani police received a report of shots fired in the warehouse district. That would be us."

Shit. The last thing they wanted was to have to explain an unsanctioned U.S.-backed op on Omani soil, especially when he, personally, had already sent four dead Hamas in a crushed rental Golf to their morgue.

"I'll try to divert them," Rhonda added. "I'm thinking another bomb threat on the opposite side of the city will trump a suspected-shots-fired call."

Whatever it took. If Rhonda could buy them even five minutes, it could be the difference between pulling this off or not.

35

Rami didn't know what to do. Amir had ordered him to hide in this closet and to kill anyone who came in. To kill Meir.

All around him, he heard gunfire. Explosions. Meir had curled up in a corner, his eyes closed, his hands over his ears. He was so scared.

So was Rami.

The guns kept firing, and voices shouted in Arabic. "Kill them! Kill the infidels!" Amir shouted.

But Rami knew this was not about Allah. This was about revenge and money.

"What's happening?" Meir asked him, his eyes wide and afraid.

And again, Rami thought of his little brother back home. Of his mother. And he thought of how he hoped someone would protect them if anything bad happened.

He drew a bracing breath, picked up the gun, and stared for a long time at Meir, thinking of the orders Amir had given him.

"It's going to be all right," Rami said. "It's going to be all right."

The door flew open and slammed against the wall. Amir. "Give him to me."

Rami faced Amir, standing between him and Meir, the rifle in his hands. "You will not hurt him," Rami said, swallowing back a thick lump of fear.

Amir's eyes grew dark with rage. "You will give him to me. Now."

Rami backed a step toward Meir. "I will kill for Allah. But not for you."

Amir roared and leaped into the closet. He swung the butt end of his rifle at Rami's head, hitting him in the jaw.

Pain exploded through his face, and he tasted blood as he dropped the rifle, then fell to the floor.

Amir kicked him hard in the stomach. He doubled over in pain, then felt the mean edge of Amir's boot heel slam into the back of his head. Then he felt nothing at all.

Brown moved to the front of the building, and Bobby ran toward the back. The plan was to search every nook and cranny that they might have missed and meet in the middle.

Bobby jerked open a door to what looked like a closet. A flash of light stunned him, and something slammed into his chest plate. A bullet. He staggered backward and brought his rifle up, and the instant the laser hit the bad guy's face, he pulled the trigger.

Nothing. His rifle was jammed.

And then he saw Meir. Amir al-Attar had his hand clutched around his throat, holding the boy against him like a human shield.

And Bobby knew he would die before he'd let anything hurt his son.

He dropped the rifle and reached for his pistol. Another flash of light flared, and another bullet hit his body armor dead center in the sternum, knocking him over backward.

Pain knifed through his chest as the wind was knocked out of him. He gasped for air, groping for something to break his fall, and hit the edge of a desk with his FAST helmet on the way down.

The chin strap gave, the helmet flew off, and his head hit the floor with a *crack*.

Stars swam in a suddenly endless sky of black. Then even the stars burned out.

Talia heard the sounds of the battle as she crouched behind a large turbine that provided cover while she watched the doorway. Every flashbang explosion, every round of rifle fire, tore at her resolve to stay put.

Each somber report of a tango down gave her hope, and she itched to get into the Bunker to help them look for Meir.

But she'd given her word. She'd do her job and count on Taggart and the team to save her son.

"Taggart's down." Brown's voice boomed over the mike. "Carlyle, get your ass up here."

Oh, God. "H-how bad?" she asked, her voice trembling.

"Not sure." Brown grunted as if he was moving something heavy. "He's breathing. I don't see any blood."

"What are you . . . what the *hell*?"

That was Taggart's voice! She expelled a huge breath of relief.

Brown said, "I think he must have gotten his bell rung. Now, stay down. Damn it, Boom, just stay the hell down! Carlyle's on the way. Let him check you out."

"No time. Have to . . . have to get to Meir. Amir . . . has him."

Meir was still in the hands of the terrorist! Her fingers tightened on her rifle. They should have found him by now. Each moment that passed drove her a little closer to panic. Where was he? Had they already killed him? The thought ripped at her heart.

No longer willing to stay out of the fight, she stood—then quickly ducked back down.

A shadowy figure appeared in the Bunker doorway, the smoke backlighting him in a ghostly haze.

One of the team? One of the terrorists?

She couldn't see. Couldn't tell.

She quickly lowered her NVGs so she could see better in the dark, and she immediately knew.

The man stepping out of the doorway wasn't wearing team fatigues. He wore a dishdasha. He was one of the terrorists.

Her breath caught when he turned his head directly her way.

Amir al-Attar.

In one hand, he gripped an AK-74U short-barreled rifle. In his other, he had a death grip around Meir's neck and shoulder.

He was alive!

Heart slamming, she drew a steadying breath, and her years of training took over. Knowing she was more accurate with a handgun than with a rifle, she calmly wiped her sweating palm on her pants leg and reached for the pistol.

With the precision and steadiness of an automaton, she cocked the hammer back.

Amir whirled around at the sound, bringing his rifle to bear, pointing it straight at her head.

She fired first.

Hit him through his open mouth. And couldn't stop firing—three more rounds into the center of his forehead.

He dropped like a stone, taking Meir down with him.

Then she sprinted across the floor and pried Meir out from under the body.

"Momma!" His arms flew around her neck.

She scooped him up and ran back behind the safety of the turbine. "Yes, it's Momma!" she cried, hugging his warm, precious body which he'd wrapped around hers like a monkey around a tree trunk.

"You came."

"I promised, didn't I?" Crying tears of relief and joy, she hugged him harder. "I always k-keep my promise." Although she didn't want to let him go, she pried him away from her so she could check him over. Finding no blood, she patted him down for injuries and cried a few more tears once she was sure he was unharmed.

"Rami kept me safe," he said, and lunged back into her arms.

She buried her face in his neck. She was never letting him go. Never.

When she finally looked up, she saw Black and Jones flanking a trussed-up terrorist. Hakeem. They'd taken him alive. Then she saw Taggart standing right in front of her, his eyes full of joy, relief, and pain.

"Say it," he whispered—and only then did she realize the gunfire had stopped. "Say it," he repeated. "You earned the right."

She smiled through her tears, then keyed her radio. "Tango down. Hostage secure."

PART III

Redemption

"Love doesn't hurt. Expectations do."

—Pushkaraj Shirke

36

One week later

"Nate was in a good mood today."

Bobby, Coop, and Mike Brown were relaxing over beer and thick steaks sizzling on a grill in Coop and Rhonda's backyard.

"That's because his DOD briefing on the Oman op even put a smile on the head of the joint chief of staff's face," Brown said.

"Well, hell yeah." Coop flipped all three steaks. "We took out the Hamas cell responsible for the embassy bombing, gathered enough evidence at Ultramar to prove it was them, and got our hostage out without a scratch. *And* we provided enough intel on a terrorist money launderer to nail the bastard, plus, we took Hakeem al-Attar alive and he's talking his head off. We even brought the drone back. What's not to smile about?"

"And yet our friend here"—Brown looked pointedly at Bobby—"looks like he lost his dog. Did you lose your dog, Boom?"

Bobby tipped back his beer. He hadn't wanted to come tonight, but it was tradition. The three of them were the only living members of the One-Eyed Jacks team. Because they all knew how transient life could be, they'd long ago made a pact to gather after every op to celebrate the fact that they were still around.

"Never had a dog," he said, realizing the moment the words were out how dour and *poor me* he sounded.

"Indigestion, then?" Coop glanced over his shoulder, a spatula in his hand.

He knew they weren't going to quit until they got what they wanted out of him. "Ask your damn questions, already."

Brown glanced at Coop and, at his nod, let 'er rip. "How are things going with the boy?"

Now they were getting down to the nitty-gritty. "He's a sweet kid."

"And?" Brown prodded.

Bobby leaned forward, legs spread, elbows on his knees, and rolled the cold beer bottle between his palms. "And . . . I don't know what to say to him. How to act around him."

There. He'd admitted it. He was tongue-tied by a five-year-old.

"Because he's a kid? Or because he doesn't know you're his father?"

"Yeah." Bobby rose and walked over to the edge of the pool. "That."

It had been frustrating. And exhilarating. And his only choice in the matter was to follow Talia's lead.

"So when are you going to tell him?"

"I don't know. He's been through a lot. Talia wants to give him a little time to recover. Get past the abduction." He tipped up his beer, looked back at his friends. "I guess I agree with her. Has to have been a pretty traumatic experience for him."

"I get that," Brown said, nodding thoughtfully.

"He's scheduled to see a child therapist tomorrow," Bobby said. "We'll have a better idea after the session of how this has all affected him."

"Sounds like it could have been a lot worse for him, if not for the kid who was watching out for him."

"Rami? Yeah." Bobby looked back at the pool, watched the automatic cleaner move slowly back and forth. "He really came through for Meir. We're lucky Amir didn't kill them both. And Rami's lucky to be back home with his mother. Has a couple broken ribs and a broken jaw, but he'll be okay."

"What about Talia?" Brown asked, as Coop pronounced the steaks done, heaped them on a platter, and carried them into the house.

"What about her?" Bobby followed them inside. The table was already set, salads waiting, so he sat down.

"That's what we want to know." Coop made room for the steaks on the table. "What's the story with you two?"

"Which one's rare?" Bobby asked instead of answering.

Coop pointed it out and waited for Brown to fill his plate, too.

"What I don't get," Brown said, "is how you kept quiet about her all these years."

"What, like I'm some cowboy who brags about the notches on his gun belt?" Bobby grumbled.

"You know that's not what I mean. It was pretty apparent that besides making a kid together, there were some seriously heavy vibes going on between you two."

Bobby looked at his plate. "We had a thing in Kabul, all right? I thought it was more. She thought it was less."

"Less how?"

He glared at Coop. "Less as in she was Mossad, and I was her mark, okay? Less as in I got played, and she got gone. End of story."

Most men would have let it go at that point. Not his friends.

"Until you ran into each other in Oman and you found out you have a son."

"Yeah," Bobby gritted out. "Until then."

Coop shot Brown a concerned scowl, then got up and opened the fridge. He plunked another beer down in front of Bobby. "How many of these is it going to take to get the whole story?" he asked.

Bobby twisted off the cap and took a deep, long swallow. "Keep 'em coming, and maybe we'll find out."

The next morning, Bobby stood under a hot shower in Coop's guest bathroom, hungover and more than a little ashamed that he'd spilled his guts last night. He'd known going in that those two wouldn't leave him be until he purged it all.

Well, he'd purged more than his story. By the time he'd drunk the equivalent of a brewery, he'd lost most of the beer and all of his dinner. God, what a lightweight. He'd been in no shape to drive home, and even worse, he didn't remember half of what he'd said.

Maybe when his head quit pounding.

Five minutes later, he stumbled out of the bathroom and dressed, hoping to avoid the walk of shame and sneak out the front door unnoticed.

He made it as far as the foyer.

"Robert Taggart, you turn around and march right back in here to my kitchen."

Rhonda. His shoulders sagged. He was in for it now. "Thanks for the bed. Gotta go." He waved over his shoulder.

"Like hell."

He heaved a deep breath and slowly turned around to face the music.

"For God's sake, I'm not going to beat you," she said more gently. "I brewed a fresh pot of coffee. And if anyone can use some, it's you."

Rhonda Burns Cooper was one of the most gorgeous women he'd ever met. Given that Coop had once made his living as a model, the two of them together looked like Ken and Barbie come to life. Only there was nothing plastic about either one of them.

They were genuine and intelligent and had damn near as much integrity as the pope. He'd give his life for them, and he knew they'd do the same for him.

He just wished they didn't think they needed to look out for him. Especially where Meir and Talia were concerned.

When the coffee she placed under his nose actually smelled good, he thought maybe he might recover.

He huddled over the mug. "Don't suppose you've got anything for this headache?"

She opened and closed a cabinet door, then produced two tablets. "These should help."

God, he hoped so.

"Coop told me about last night."

Of course he did. "Where *is* the canary?"

She grinned. "Apparently, he didn't indulge as much as you did. He's out for a run."

Bobby nodded, then regretted it when a bomb exploded in his head. When the pounding settled down, he found himself slowly looking around the Cooper domain. It was a great house, and Rhonda had made it into a home. Classy décor. Potted plants. Grass. Pool. Neighborhood block parties. If the neighbors knew, however, that two of the world's most elite covert operatives lived next door, they'd think twice about letting their dogs drop lawn bombs in their yard.

"So," he said, suddenly curious, "did you ever see yourself here? Ward and June Cleaver? Planning on having a little Beaver of your own someday?"

"Never did." Rhonda sat down across from him at the island with her own cup. "But I've got to tell you, I'm loving it."

He grunted and sipped his coffee. Coop loved it, too. Bobby could see it in his eyes. In the proprietary way he "owned" that grill. In the way he talked about his damn lawn mower, like it was as precious as his car, for Pete's sake.

"What about you?" she asked.

He glanced up. "What about me?"

"Do you ever see yourself here?"

Ah. As in a Mr. to someone's Mrs. As in a father to his child.

There was no missing the subtext; she wanted to know about him and Talia.

"Nope. Never have."

"And Meir . . . Talia? No chance they could change that?"

A week ago, he'd have flat-out said no. But Meir's existence meant he had to look at his lifestyle a little differently now. Talia? He mostly felt sadness and regret when he thought of her.

I loved you.

I still love you.

No. He couldn't let himself go there. If a dog licks a wound long enough, not only doesn't it heal, but it gets more painful. He still felt like that dog. He wanted to make things better between them, but so far, he couldn't make the festering wound of their past heal up. "It's . . . complicated," he finally said.

"So I've heard." She was quiet for a while, then cut straight to the chase. "Do you love her, Bobby?"

He propped his elbows on the granite and dropped his head into his hands. "I did. Once. Then, for almost six years, I hated her. Now I honestly don't know how to get past what she did to me."

He lifted his head, looked up into Rhonda's sympathetic eyes. "She showed up in my life again a little more than a week ago. We survived a bombing together, rescued our child together—a child I didn't even know existed—and . . . hell, I don't know what to feel."

"Hatred?"

"No." He let go of a weary sigh. "I don't hate her anymore. But I don't seem to be able to forgive her, either."

"And if you somehow could? What then?"

"I don't know," he admitted honestly. "And *if* is a really big word right now."

The back door swung open then, and a very sweaty and winded Coop stepped inside, walked directly to the fridge, and downed about a quart of cold water straight from the pitcher.

He wiped the sweat from his face with the hem of his T-shirt. Then, seeing Bobby slumped over at the counter, he laughed. "Wanna beer, buddy?"

"Want me to trim that peach fuzz growing back on your bald head with your new lawn mower?"

Coop feigned a blow to his heart. "Low, bro. Threatening me with my own lawn equipment."

"I've gotta go." Bobby eased off the bar stool. If he stayed around any longer, Coop would gear up for a replay of last night.

"Stick around. We can cool off in the pool."

"I might end up drowning you. And while your lovely wife looks good in everything, black isn't her best color."

"Come on, sweetie." Rhonda walked around beside him and linked her arm in his. "I'll walk you to the door."

"Chicken," Coop taunted.

"Don't mind him," Rhonda said when they reached the foyer. "It's his way of saying he cares about you."

Bobby gave her a weak grin. "I'd still like to drown him."

"Some days, so would I." She leaned in and hugged him. "In the meantime, if you ever want to talk, I'm here—with or without the beer."

"I can see you out there," Coop shouted from the kitchen. "Unhand my woman!"

"Can I give you one piece of advice?" Rhonda said, ignoring her husband's theatrical shout.

He grinned. "And if I say no?"

"Wouldn't matter. Look. Anger is a burdensome emotion to carry. It'll wear you down, heart and soul. If you have feelings for Talia, even if you can't get past the pain or the betrayal right now, leave yourself open to at least consider the circumstances responsible for what she did, okay?"

He let go of a deep breath. "I hear you." And he

had considered. He'd even set aside his feelings to help get Meir back. But now it was "real life." Now he had the opportunity to think—really think—about the impact Talia's lies had had on his life. Especially her lie of omission.

He'd missed his son's first five years. His first smile. His first steps. His first words. Those were things he could never get back. And when he let himself run with it, the old, familiar, churning anger that had fueled him for so long gnawed on his resolve to let it go.

"Try to do more than hear me. Try to see and understand what she did, and why she did it, from her perspective."

He glanced at Rhonda. "You sound like her advocate."

"I hope I sound like your friend. Like someone who cares very much about you and doesn't want you going through the rest of your life carrying a load of regrets over things you could have changed. You didn't have the chance to make choices before. Now you do. I want to make sure you make the right ones."

37

Bobby grabbed his keys from the counter and headed out the door. Uri and Miriam Levine's longtime home was a grand restored row house close to Georgetown University, where they were both tenured professors. He could cover the nine miles from his apartment in McLean to the Levines' doorstep in just under twenty minutes.

So far, he'd made the drive exactly twice. Once to deliver Talia and Meir to her parents after they'd arrived back in the States and once for a brief five minutes to check on the two of them.

The Levines had wanted him to stay for dinner that evening, but he'd begged off, saying he had to get back to Langley for a briefing. The truth was, he simply hadn't had it in him to stay.

Instead, he'd made good on the promise he'd made to himself. He'd driven to New York and visited his mother in the Bronx. He'd felt really good about that and had left with a promise to come back as soon as he could.

Tonight, however, he'd accepted the Levines' second invitation. They'd given him little choice.

"Talia has told us so much about you," her mother had said when she'd called yesterday. "We owe you so much for bringing her and Meir home to us. And we very much want to get to know you. You'll be a big part of Meir's life now. I hope that means you'll be a part of our life, too."

How did he say no to an invitation as generous and kind as that? That the Levines, Talia included, had no plans to keep him out of Meir's life was a gift. He'd been concerned that once the fog of fear had lifted and life started to return to some semblance of normal, Talia might have second thoughts. She might decide Meir was better off without him. Better off without the influence of a man who was still, for all practical purposes, the same man he'd been when she'd met him. So yeah. It had been a gift. Now he had to figure out how to accept it.

He slipped behind the wheel of his black GMC pickup and backed out of his garage, his mind seeing Meir. And Talia. Put him in the front line against a swarm of tangos, and he'd feel fear, hell yeah. Anyone worth his salt would. But it was a fear he was used to. One he could control. He hadn't yet gotten a handle on the fear that gripped him when he spent more than five minutes in a room with Meir and his mother.

Oman no longer seemed real. Oman had been a nightmare of tension and frayed emotions and dan-

ger. So frayed he'd made love to a woman who had
betrayed him. He'd temporarily let go of an anger that
had simmered for years.

But fatherhood—that was real. And it scared the
hell out of him.

Most men got nine months of prep time to wrap
their mind around their new normal of fatherhood,
though. He'd gotten the equivalent of a short fuse on
a megabomb.

He pulled into a strip mall and bought flowers and
a bottle of wine.

When he pulled up in front of the house, he was
nervous as all hell. He made himself take three deep
breaths, then walked up the sidewalk and rang the
doorbell.

He had it pretty much together—until Talia
opened the door.

Holy, holy cow. She looked . . . amazing.

It was summer in Georgetown. Which meant
it was hot. He'd left his collar open, but he started
sweating in his white dress shirt and chinos, because
she looked beyond beautiful in a long, lightweight
teal slip dress. A dress that was a dead ringer for the
one she'd worn in Kabul the night he'd taken her
out to dinner. The delicate white shawl draped over
her shoulders looked familiar, too. Both brought
back the memory of that night, of how in love he'd
been, and it was all he could do to keep from reaching for her.

"For your mother," he managed, extending the flowers and the wine.

"How thoughtful. Come on in."

As he followed her inside, there wasn't a question in his mind; she'd dressed that way for him. She'd known he would remember that night. It had been the first time he'd seen her in anything but her khakis. The first time they'd gone out in public together. The first time she'd worn her hair down for him other than in bed. They'd laughed and teased, and he'd kissed her in a lantern-lit alley.

Later she'd made love to him as if he was the one man on earth she wanted to be with.

Then, in the morning, she'd been gone.

Now she wanted to fix things between them. She wanted him back in her life. A part of him wanted that, too, but how did he get one hundred percent past her betrayal? How did he get past five years of not knowing his son?

Rhonda was right. Anger was a burdensome emotion to bear. But when a man carried it as long as he had, it became a part of him. He didn't know how to be without it.

"Robert." Miriam Levine greeted him warmly as he followed Talia into the living room. "We're so glad you were able to make it."

The house was very much like Miriam: understated, warm, sophisticated, and quite beautiful. It was easy to see who Talia favored.

"Taggart." Uri stood and extended his hand. "Welcome back. Let's get right down to business. What can I pour you?"

Bobby returned Uri's smile. "Whatever you're drinking is fine by me, sir."

"Whiskey it is." Uri glanced back over his shoulder. "Neat or rocks?"

"Neat."

"Open this lovely bottle of wine Robert brought, would you, dear?" Miriam said.

"I can get that for you, ma'am." Bobby took the bottle from Talia, aware of the brush of their fingers during the exchange.

Miriam smiled. "Wonderful. Now, you three enjoy and relax. I'll just be a moment in the kitchen and be right back."

"She's a wonderful cook," Uri said, with a twinkle in his eye.

While he must be pushing retirement age, Talia's father was trim and fit and exuded energy and goodwill.

"I hope she didn't go to too much trouble." Bobby glanced at Talia, at the way her long dress hugged her slim hips and moved against her while she made herself busy selecting wineglasses.

"Oh, she did, but she loves it," Uri said, smiling.

"I'll go see if I can help," Talia said.

"No, dear." Uri handed Bobby his drink. "You stay here and entertain our guest. I'm much more familiar with your mother's kitchen than you are." Whiskey in hand, he walked out of the room, leaving them alone.

Bobby was suddenly grateful that he'd brought the wine. He set down his whiskey and went to work getting the bottle open.

"How are you?" Talia asked, moving up beside him.

She smelled like flowers. Something fresh and light and summery. "Good. All healed up."

"Even your head?" She was referring to the blow he'd taken at Ultramar when Amir's shot had knocked him to the floor.

"Barely a concussion."

Although he felt a bit concussed right now. The scent of her, her nearness, the way her hair tumbled softly down her shoulders. It took him back to the bed in a Kabul hotel where they'd spent hours making each other feel amazing. Where she'd made him fall in love.

"It's fine," he said, cuing back in to her question. "I'm fine. What about you?"

"I'm okay," she said softly.

And that pretty much dead-ended the conversation. But not his memories. And on their heels, that familiar burst of anger. It didn't have to be this way. She could have told him. She could have figured something out. She didn't have to leave him. She didn't have to crush—

Damn. He felt like a hamster in a cage. Constantly spinning, spinning, never getting where he needed to be.

He didn't know what to say to her. Apparently, she didn't know what to say, either. So now what?

He popped the cork on the wine bottle. "Would you like some?"

She nodded. "Please." And he filled her glass.

And the silence became another entity in the room.

"Meir should be down in a few minutes," she said, breaking the quiet but adding to his tension. "I'd just gotten him out of the tub when you arrived, and he's getting dressed."

"He takes care of that by himself?"

"Oh, yeah. He's very independent, insists he can get dried and dressed without any help."

Because she smiled, he figured she approved. And yeah, independence was a good thing. Even for a five-year-old. "How's he doing?"

"I wanted to talk to you about that before he came down."

"Something wrong?"

"No," she said quickly, and sat at the end of an overstuffed sofa, gesturing for him to take a seat. "Things are actually quite good."

He grabbed his drink and chose a chair directly opposite her. Not because he was afraid to get too close to her but . . . oh, hell. Yeah, that, he admitted to himself grudgingly.

"He had his first session with the child psychologist today. She was very pleased with his overall emotional health. She'd like to see him a couple more times, just in case there's some lingering trauma that hasn't surfaced yet, but she was quite astounded by his ability to analyze and compartmentalize and most of all to realize the danger was past and that he feels secure."

"Good. That's really good to hear. He's one tough little guy."

"I . . . I want to apologize," she said, after a moment's hesitation. "I should have consulted you about the choice of psychologists. I'm so used to making all the decisions when it comes to Meir, I didn't stop to think."

The concession caught him a little off guard. He *had* wished she'd consulted him, even though he would have deferred to her choice. So the fact that she'd apologized meant something. And while the next thought that tripped through his mind was *I could have helped you with those difficult decisions for five years if you'd let me*, he had difficulty mustering up the resentment. Mainly because she was no longer shutting him out. And she could have done so.

"It's all right," he said. "Frankly, I was concerned you might not want me to be involved in his life, once things settled down."

Her eyes grew misty. "I realize why you'd think that. I could tell you a hundred times—a thousand—how sorry I am that I didn't get in touch with you. And believe me, I am sorry. Now. But I believed the decisions I made back then were the right ones. Just as I now believe the only right decision regarding you and Meir is for you to be involved in his life. As his father."

Would he have taken her to court if she tried to keep him away from Meir? He didn't know. But the thought had been there, in the back of his mind, in those moments when anger wove around uncertainty and his feelings turned negative. Hearing her say she wanted Meir to know him as a father eased a lot of tension. Gave him a lot of relief . . . which was quickly overrun by a familiar anxiety. What did he know about being a father?

"Do I take your silence as relief or dread?"

"Both," he confessed. "A lot of relief, and I thank you for that. But I have to be honest. I don't know the first thing about kids."

She smiled. "Well, you're going to learn."

He smiled back. "Yeah. I guess I am." After a moment, he asked, "When—or maybe the word is *how*—are we going to tell him?"

"I spoke to the therapist about that. She suggested the three of us might go on a few play dates?" she said apprehensively. "Maybe to the zoo. Or the Smithsonian? A picnic by the river? The idea is to let him get to know you as a person before we tell him you're his father."

"That makes sense, I guess. How do you feel about it?"

"I like it," she said simply. "And *I* like zoos, too."

When she smiled, he found himself smiling again. But a question remained. "What *have* you told him—in the past, I mean—about his father?"

She looked at him, then away. "I told him his father loved him very much and that he wanted to be with us, but duty had taken him away."

Her admission shocked him. "He doesn't think I'm dead?"

"I don't know what he thinks. I'm not sure how he interpreted it. He seemed to accept my answer and draw his own conclusions. And he's never asked again."

Bobby heard child-sized footsteps bounding down the stairs. He jerked his head around. And there was his son.

Warmth flooded his chest as Meir jumped over the last step to land with a thump on the floor, grinning from ear to ear. His dark hair was slicked down and wet; a smudge of what looked like chocolate rode on the edge of his grin. He looked happy and loved and like an all-American child in worn jeans, lime-green tennies, and a Dallas Cowboys T-shirt.

"Hey, buddy." His mother opened her arms when he scooted into the room. "Look. We've got company. Do you remember Mr. Taggart?"

Suddenly shy, the boy lowered his head and leaned against Talia's legs. "Hi," he said to the floor.

"Hello, Meir." Bobby couldn't take his eyes off the picture they made together. "You're a Cowboys fan, huh?"

That brought his head up. "Yeah," he said, looking a little interested. "You like 'em?"

"If you like 'em, I like 'em," Bobby said.

That brought a grin. "I've got a football," Meir said, looking hopeful.

"Yeah? Maybe after dinner, we can go out and toss it around for a while. If it's okay with your mom, that is."

"Can we, Mom?"

The excitement in Meir's voice had Bobby's heart expanding. When he glanced at Talia, he sensed she'd been watching him during the entire exchange

A telling smile lit her face. "Of course."

38

It was as dark as a deep well. As quiet as a graveyard at midnight. Then Bobby heard a muffled chorus of whispers. The flashes of tracer fire grew closer as the enemy encountered the hidden trench.

Light. Weak. Distant. More of an afterglow, like lightning strobes flashing beyond a coal-black horizon. It wouldn't be long now.

They were coming.

He ducked behind a thick concrete wall, pressing his back flush against it. His finger poised on the trigger, he waited for the enemy to make their move.

"Stand down," he whispered to his team members. "Hold . . . hold."

Then they came. The shuffle of feet on concrete as the raspy breath of his enemy drew nearer.

"Now!" He sprang around the wall, leaning on the trigger. "You're a dead man!"

"Aw, geez." A boy of around sixteen glared at him. "Dude. You're *way* too old to be playing laser tag."

"Then why am I still standing and you're dead?"

With a roll of his eyes, the kid shuffled dejectedly back to his team's utility box to reset his laser gun.

"Nice shot, Bobby."

"What did you call me, soldier?" He scowled down at Meir.

The boy giggled. "Oops. Sir. Nice shot, sir."

"There ya go." He squatted down to Meir's level. "Next one's yours, Sergeant. Let's go smoke 'em out."

"Yes, sir," Meir said, with so much enthusiasm that Bobby laughed. Beside him, in the reflective light of the red sensor tags on her vest, Talia was smiling, too.

This was their third outing in as many days, and he'd been having the time of his life.

So had Meir, if the look on his face was any indication.

"We make a good team," Talia whispered, as they followed Meir down the dark hallway, on the lookout for the green and red enemy teams.

They made a damn good team, Bobby agreed. He may be biased—hell yeah, he was biased—and Meir was pretty young, but the boy had all the makings of a super operator. He really got it when Bobby taught him the hand signals. And now, taking point, Meir attacked the game like a born leader.

The kid was strategic and tactical and strong—like his old man. And sometimes, Bobby thought, as he followed Meir down the dark hallway, the way he smiled and the expressions he got on his face. Wow. He reminded him so much of himself when he was a boy. Like him, the kid was absolutely unstoppable.

Pride swelled in his chest—and then he spotted the lights of the green team coming straight at them.

"Take cover!" Bobby instinctively dived in front of Meir and took a bullet for him, taking out two enemy combatants as he fell, landing stretched out on the concrete floor with a thud.

"Wow," Meir said. "That was soooo cool!"

Before Bobby could get up, the room lights flashed on, glaring into the battlefield like strobes.

"Uh-oh." Talia grinned down at him when a door opened and one of the game managers walked in.

"Sir." He scowled down at Bobby. "I told you during the first game, it's against the rules to dive to the floor. I gave you a pass since it was your first time, but I can't do it again. I'm afraid you'll have to leave. And by the way, you're the oldest person I've ever had to eject."

They were still laughing when they pulled up in front of the Levines' house.

"Been a long time since I've been dressed down by a pimply-faced kid with a ponytail." Bobby got out, then walked around to the passenger side of his truck and opened Talia's door.

"The look on your face." Talia chuckled. "Priceless."

"Guess I didn't set a very good example, huh, bud?" Bobby opened the rear club-cab door so Meir could get out.

But he was sound asleep, his head lolling forward,

his chest straining against the shoulder strap of the seat belt.

"He's gone." Talia reached in and unbuckled his seat belt. "It was a very big day."

"Here, let me get him."

She stood back, and Bobby easily lifted around forty pounds of exhausted boy out of the truck.

"Man. When he's out, he's out," he whispered over Meir's head as he cradled him against his chest. "And he goes one hundred percent, one hundred percent of the time."

"He loves being with you. It's brought out a side of him I've been waiting to see. You're good for him."

That went both ways. The heat and the weight and the little-boy salt and sweat scent of his son triggered emotions he'd never known were inside him. It wasn't just that he felt protective of, proud of, or even love for his son. He felt . . . fuller. Like a part of him had been missing, and now he was whole. Like his reason to be was so much more significant than it had ever been before.

All his life, he'd protected first his buddies, then his country. Now . . . now he had this small, perfect little person he was responsible for. It added weight. It added purpose. It added meaning to everything he did. It was scary as hell but more gratifying than he could have ever imagined.

Talia let them into the house. "Mom and Dad are out for the evening. Bridge at the Emersons'."

"Sounds . . . exciting?" he said doubtfully.

"Oh, it is. That sweet little woman I call Mom? She plays cutthroat."

"Good to know," he said, laughing, and headed up the stairs.

He knew which room was Meir's. The boy had shown it to him yesterday before they'd left for the zoo. He'd felt a ridiculous rush of pleasure that Meir had wanted to share his private space with him.

"Just lay him down," Talia whispered, as she folded back a Dallas Cowboys sheet and bedspread. "He can sleep in his T-shirt and shorts tonight."

Bobby carefully deposited Meir on the bed, then took in the sight of his sleeping child's face as Talia made quick work of removing his shoes and socks.

"He's a miracle," he whispered, finding himself in another of those moments of wonder he so often experienced simply being around this child.

"Come on downstairs," Talia said. "If you've got a minute, I want to talk to you about something."

He gently brushed the hair back from Meir's forehead, then followed her down the stairs.

He'd been wanting to talk to her about something, too. He wanted to tell Meir he was his father. It was time.

"This morning, when we were waiting for you?" Talia turned away from the bar and handed him a glass of whiskey. "Meir told me that he wished you were his dad."

She watched his face. This rough, deadly warrior

who ate bad guys for breakfast, who walked into live fire, turned into an emotional wreck right before her eyes.

She sat down beside him with her wine. She'd fallen deeper in love each hour she saw him with Meir. So tough, so focused, and so in control in every way. Yet this boy could wring emotions from him she suspected no other living person ever had.

"Thanks. For sharing that. And . . . wow."

She let him have his moment. Meir was head-over-heels hero-worship in love with Bobby. That also was a first. He'd always been reserved around the men in her life. Not that there'd been many. Mostly family men with children who were playmates. There'd been only a few men she'd dated during the last five years. None much more than once. One, however, she'd made an attempt to get to know better.

Frank had been a nice guy. He'd liked Meir, and Meir had liked him. But he and she had never truly bonded, maybe because she hadn't really given him a chance. Because Bobby Taggart's memory had always haunted her.

"I want to tell him," he said, meeting her eyes. "What do you think? Is it too soon? I don't want to mess this up or upset him."

"I've been thinking about it a lot." She'd been thinking about *him* a lot, too. About how he was pleasant yet distant when he was around her. How he avoided any accidental contact between them. How he failed to pick up any signs she put out there that she wanted to be more to him than the mother of his child.

It was frustrating. And a little heartbreaking. But she was a big girl. And this time was all about Meir. The condition of *his* heart was what mattered most.

"How about the two of you have your own day together? Then you can decide whether you think he's ready. When you come back, if you think it's time, then we'll tell him together."

He looked at her long and hard, then reached out and covered her hand with his. "You could have made this all so difficult. I want you to know how much I appreciate—"

"He's your son, Bobby," she interrupted. "And if anyone has a right to be difficult, it's you. You missed so much. Meir missed so much. I have to live with that—and with myself, knowing I'm responsible for those lost years for both of you."

There were only so many ways she could say she was sorry. And there were only so many times she could look into his eyes and see how her decision to keep father from son had affected him. How it affected the two of them now. He said he wasn't angry anymore, but if that were true, he should have forgiven her. But he hadn't. And the longer time went on, the more she feared he never would.

She turned her hand into his, gripped it tightly. "You haven't asked, but I want you to know that I'm staying in D.C. It's not only about you and Meir, but your relationship does play a big role in my decision."

His clear relief told her this issue had been weigh-
ing on his mind. And she'd told a white lie. Her decision *did* hinge on his and Meir's budding relationship.
She didn't want to take them away from each other.
And she wasn't ready to give up on him yet, either.

"I've had enough drama in my life," she went on.
"I want to start over here, where Meir can be close to
you and to his grandparents. So they can enjoy being
with him."

"What will you do?"

"For now, my only job is looking out for Meir. I'm
in no rush to go back to work. With my background
and connections in the State Department, I don't anticipate any difficulty finding a position here when
I'm ready."

"You'll stay here? With your parents?"

"No. They enjoy having us, but they need their
space. We do, too. So I'll start looking for a place—
but again, I'm in no rush." She was dragging her
heels. Even though it seemed unlikely, she still held
on to the hope that if she gave him enough time, gave
him enough reason, when she moved out, it would be
someplace large enough for the three of them.

"Bobby." She looked at their joined hands, then
up at him. "You know I'm hoping there can be more
for us."

"Talia. Let's not—"

She cut him off. "Go there? I'm sorry, but I have
to. This is killing me. I meant it today when I said
the three of us make a good team. I need to know if

there's—" She stopped, swallowed. This was so difficult. "If there's any chance for you and me to start over."

He stood abruptly, let go of her hands, and snagged his drink. He tipped it back, downing it with one swallow.

"I know you care about me." She pressed. "I know you're still attracted to me—"

This time, he cut her off. "I do care. My God, you're Meir's mother. Of course I care about you. Attracted? Hell yes. I don't think that's ever going to go away."

"But the anger," she said, reacting to the rigid set of his shoulders as he walked to the bar and refilled his glass. "That's not going away, is it?"

"I've tried. I've lain awake countless nights and tried to talk myself out of these sudden rages that come over me when I think about what we had, about how you threw that, and me, away. About how you kept Meir from me. My God, Talia, you broke me. Something died. Right here." He pressed a closed fist to his heart. "Anger took its place, and I don't know how to get rid of that."

She watched him with tear-filled eyes, knowing she had no one to blame but herself.

"Look," he said, turning back to her. "Give me some time, okay? I'm still working through this. Hell, I'm still figuring out how to be a father. I've got to get that down first. Then . . . then maybe I can work on me. Figure out why I can't let go of this."

She lowered her head. "I understand."

"I've got to go." He sounded weary and even apologetic.

She pulled herself together and stood, forced a smile. "Sure. So tomorrow? Guys' day out?"

"If that still works for you."

"Of course it does. Meir will be thrilled. What time should I have him ready?"

"Let's say ten. Tell him to wear his guy clothes. He'll know what I mean."

"Ah. You two already have your little manly secrets," she said lightly.

"Don't worry, Mom. You're always going to be his number one squeeze."

Great. Now they were both pretending nothing was wrong.

"Thank you for today. We had a really fun time," she said sincerely.

"Me, too." He walked over to her and cupped her shoulders in his big hands.

She couldn't help it. Tears filled her eyes.

"Aw, God. Don't." He pulled her into his arms and held her gently against him. "I'll figure this out. Just give me a little time."

He pressed a kiss to the top of her head, then headed out the door.

39

"This is waaaay cool."

Bobby grinned down at Meir and tried like hell to stay on his feet as they made their first circle around the rink at the Anacostia Roller Skating Pavilion. Pancaking in front of his son wouldn't take him far in the hero-worship department.

"Way cool, huh? You don't miss your mom?"

"Nah. Well, sort of. But sometimes it's cool to do just guy things. Mom likes girl stuff."

"Yeah? What kind of girl stuff?"

"Oh, you know. Shoppin'. Huggin'. Cookin'. And she kisses me way too much."

Bobby laughed and steered them clear of some teenage girls who were whooping it up to music only they could hear through their iPod earbuds.

"Someday, when you get a little older, you're going to realize that's not such a bad thing," he said. "You're even going to like it when a girl kisses you."

Meir wrinkled his nose. "A girl other than my mom or Gramma?"

"Yeah. Other than them."

He seemed to think about that. "You like to kiss girls?"

"Sure," Bobby said slowly, wondering if he'd just stepped in it.

"Do you like to kiss my mom?"

Yup. Stepped in it up to his ankles. "Your mom's a very nice woman," he said, evading the question.

"I think she's pretty."

"You're right. She's very pretty."

"You know what would be way, way, waaaay cool? If you and my mom got married."

Oh, boy. "Look, they opened up the concession counter! And I bet they've got ice cream."

"For real?"

Thank God Meir took the bait. "So are you a chocolate or vanilla guy?"

"How about a scoop of each?"

"You got it."

Somehow Bobby managed to keep off the topic of Talia and kissing and marriage for the rest of the afternoon. Just like he somehow managed not to land on his ass, even when he lifted Meir onto his shoulders and they made a few passes before the rink manager blew the whistle and motioned for Bobby to put him down.

"Seems like you get in a lot of trouble," Meir said, after they'd had their fill of the rink.

Bobby chuckled as they walked side-by-side to his

truck. "I'm working on that. Most of the time, I try to play by the rules. That's always a good thing to do."

"Yeah," Meir agreed, and climbed up on the running board. "Unless it's a bad rule."

Bobby got him settled in the backseat and buckled into his seat belt. "And what would you consider to be a bad rule?"

"A rule that says my dad has to stay away because of duty."

The words stopped him cold. Sank a fist into his gut. And no amount of self-talk could make him feel like less of a heel.

He almost told him right then: *I'm your dad.* Then he thought about rules, about the agreement he and Talia had made to tell Meir together.

"I'll bet your mom is wondering what we've been up to," he said, then walked around the truck and settled in behind the wheel. "You're not going to tell on me, are you?"

"About getting in trouble?"

Bobby glanced at him in the rearview mirror. Oh, he had a devil look in his eye. "Yeah, about that." He couldn't stop a chuckle. "Remember, I bought you ice cream."

"Okay. It'll be a secret. Just between us guys."

Once upon a time, he'd have run a few red lights and broken a few speed limits when he was in a rush. And he was in a rush now, to get back to Talia and finally tell Meir that he was his father. But it was funny how priorities and attitudes changed when other lives were dependent on him doing the right thing. So he took his time driving, and they played "guess what animal I'm thinking about" all the way back to Georgetown.

"Let me guess," Talia said, after Meir burst into the house. "Somebody had ice cream."

"Aw, Mom. How'd you know?"

A smiling, sunburned Taggart closed the door behind them. He looked vital and happy and heartbreakingly handsome. He also had a smear of chocolate on his collar. "Yeah, how'd you know?"

"I'm a mind reader," she said. "In the meantime, both of you might want to take a look in the mirror."

Meir was already racing up the stairs.

"He's had to go for the last five blocks," Taggart said. "Man, that kid can eat. And guzzle down soda. But he only had one; I know soda is limited."

She smiled. "Did you think I was going to scold you?"

"Um, maybe."

"And would you deserve it?"

One corner of his mouth tipped up. "Maybe."

She crossed her arms over her waist and leaned against the newel post. "Good day?"

His entire face lit up. "The best. He's so amazing, Talia. You've done such a great job with him."

"There are genes involved, too. And he got some good ones from you."

"I'd like to think so." He looked expectant then. "I think it's safe to tell him tonight."

She nodded. "Me, too."

They moved into the living room, and a few minutes later, Meir came bounding down the stairs. "Can you stay for supper? Can he stay, Mom?"

"Sure. Bobby?"

"Who's cooking? You?" he asked, squinting at Meir.

"Heck no! That's woman's work."

"Excuse me?" Talia feigned outrage. "Where did you hear that?"

Bobby held his hands in the air, pleading innocence. "Not from me. I think you'd better run for it, bud. You've got a mad woman on your hands."

Before Meir could make his getaway, she grabbed him and started tickling him until he squealed. Bobby's phone rang. "Taggart," he said, answering as he smiled at them. Then he sobered abruptly. "Roger that. Yeah." He checked his watch. "Right. Give me fifteen."

"What?" Talia looked up at him, her arms still wrapped around Meir.

"I'm really sorry, but I've got to go. Can we have that dinner and that, um, conversation another time?"

She knew he was subject to rapid deployments, but she'd hoped one wouldn't come up so soon. "Will you be gone long?"

"No clue. Sorry."

Meir pulled out of her arms and walked over to Bobby. "You have to go?"

"I do," he said, squatting down to Meir's level. "But I'll be back in a few days, okay?"

"Why do you have to go?"

"They need me at work, buddy."

"But you can still stay for supper, right?" Meir moved in closer and wrapped his arms around Bobby's neck. The picture the two of them made together was both touching and heartbreaking.

"I'm sorry, buddy, but I can't. We'll make it another night. Soon as I get back, okay?"

"But I don't want you to go." Meir threw himself against Bobby's chest.

Bobby held him tight, buried his face in the boy's neck. "I don't want to go, either. But remember, we talked about rules? When my boss says I've got to work, then I've got to work."

"I don't like that rule."

Bobby looked up at Talia, his eyes bleak. "Sometimes I don't like it, either."

He gently pulled Meir away from him so he could look him in the eye. "You take care of your mom while I'm gone, okay? And I'll be back before you know it."

He looked heartbroken and a little helpless when his eyes met hers. And the truth was, she felt like crying, too.

"Come on, sweetie. Bobby has to go, now."

Meir hugged him hard, one last time, then whispered something in his ear. She couldn't hear it, but whatever it was, Taggart almost melted before kissing Meir's cheek and whispering something back.

Then he met her eyes with an intensity that shook her, before he hot-footed it out the door.

40

I love you.

Forty-eight hours later, Bobby rode shotgun in a gray 1993 Mazda, parked on a dark back street in Jobar, a suburb of Damascus, Syria. While a firefight raged four blocks away, Meir's whispered *I love you* stayed with him like a sweet breeze, calling him home.

I love you, too, buddy.

The lump in his throat had been so huge he'd had trouble choking out the words. And when he'd looked over Meir's shoulder and seen the intense concern in Talia's eyes, something had inexplicably shifted inside him. The sensation or revelation had been so powerful it had staggered him. He hadn't immediately recognized it for what it was then. Couldn't deal with it because of what he thought it might be.

So he'd bailed. Run like hell and gotten out of there.

With little else to think about during the long

transatlantic flight, he now had a handle on what had happened. And it gave him a damn good reason for wanting to get back home.

He squinted through the car's windshield, then looked left and right, searching. "Where's our guy?"

"Patience, Grasshopper." Coop lowered his spy-glasses, giving his eyes a break. "He'll show."

"He'd better." This from Brown in the backseat. "Or he's a dead man. And most likely, so are we."

They were all armed to the teeth and hoping like hell they wouldn't need to fight their way out.

"He's got"—Coop lifted his arm and checked his watch—"fifty-four seconds before this ship sails."

It was supposed to be a walk-in-the-park, in-and-out, two-day mission. Find the spy. Get the spy. Bring the spy to the States and out of harm's way.

But the trouble with war—especially another country's war—was that too often, things went FUBAR. This op had gone a little sideways from the get-go, and the signs weren't good.

First, they'd had trouble getting clearance at the airport. Then their contact hadn't shown up. When they'd finally located him, he'd lost touch with their target. After a lot of scrambling, swearing, and ass chewing, they'd eventually gotten a handle on the mission, tapped into a network sympathetic to their target, and made contact.

Now here they sat, a day late, an extraction window short. Waiting for him to show at the designated time and place. Two blocks east in the factory district, tanks lined the streets, and Syrian army regulars fought back the insurgent jihadists infiltrating the war-torn country by the thousands.

"What I want to know," Coop said, lifting the glasses again, "is how we know he's one of the good guys."

And therein lay the rest of the problem. In Syria, more than any other war zone on earth, it was almost impossible to tell the good guys from the bad guys. There was the moderate opposition, the radical opposition, the Al-Qaeda and ISIS insurgents posing as moderate opposition. Then there was the government itself, where corruption ran rampant. Even the top brass at the Pentagon argued over the effectiveness of their "good guy" vetting process, with estimates of up to seventy-five percent of the findings being inaccurate.

Supposedly, their spy, Betros Olikara, was a good guy. For the past eighteen months, he'd been passing information on to his CIA handler in Damascus. When the handler had turned up MIA, Olikara had gotten word to the U.S. embassy; he was certain his handler had been assassinated and was scared he'd be next.

That had been three weeks ago. It had taken this long for word to filter down to DOD that Olikara wanted to defect. Apparently, there'd been a lengthy dialogue when the CIA tried to persuade Olikara to stay on with a new handler, but Olikara wasn't budging. He didn't feel safe anymore.

So the team had been dispatched to get him out.

And maybe, just maybe, Bobby thought when he spotted a moving figure, that was about to happen.

An old man, in tattered jeans and a dingy gray hoodie pulled low over his face, appeared at the mouth of an alley half a block away. He limped heavily toward them.

"That's our guy." Coop shifted into gear but planted his foot on the brake. "Dressed exactly like he's supposed to be. Anyone see anything out of place?"

"Negative," Bobby answered, all his senses on red alert.

Brown keyed in his commo mike. "Bravo One? How's it looking back there?"

"All clear."

A block behind them, Bravo team—Santos, Carlyle, and Johnny Reed, a veteran Black team member— waited in an older-model Lada Kalina. Charlie team— Jones, Rafe Mendoza, another Black team veteran, and Josh Waldrop with the ITAP team—idled in a boat of a 2006 Chrysler, a block ahead.

"Charlie?"

"Nothing but night," Waldrop answered.

"It's tee time, boys," Brown advised. "Let's get this guy outta here."

Brown ended commo as the target approached the Mazda's rear door and rapped on the window. Brown rolled it down and asked the predetermined question, to which only Olikara knew the correct response. "Are you lost, traveler?"

The man glanced quickly behind him and then back. "Do you know the way to San Jose?"

Magic words.

Brown shoved open the door, and Olikara dived inside.

Without another word, Coop pulled out, the Alpha team moving out in front of them and Charlie coming up to guard their flank.

Just three old cars—with what Bobby hoped to hell had a lot of modified muscle under the hoods—heading home after a night at the local bar or a long day of work.

"Thank you." Olikara slipped the hood off his head and collapsed against the backseat.

Bobby glanced at him in the rearview mirror. Only the deep stress and fatigue lines surrounding his eyes suggested that he might be an old man. In truth, the limp was faked, and Olikara wasn't yet forty.

"We must hurry," he said.

"Were you followed?" Brown wanted to know.

"I . . . I do not know for certain. But . . . I might have been."

The sudden sucking sound of bullets hitting the rear panel of the Mazda—*thwup, thwup, thwup*—answered the question in spades.

"Punch it, Martha!" Bobby yelled above the gunfire. Shouldering his AK, he aimed out the window, firing toward the muzzle flashes.

Steady fire pelted them now. Alpha team picked up speed ahead, and Charlie pulled up on their bumper, guarding their six from the rear.

"Sit rep!" Brown requested.

"Yeah, we're in deep shit," Reed called back with his usual calm, over the sound of his AK firing multiple bursts. "Got four—whoa, nice work, Carlyle! Make that three tango vehicles moving up fast on our ass. Deadeye here took one of them out."

"What's the plan, Stan?" Jones, in the forward car, wanted to know.

Brown said, "Hope we don't run out of gas."

"Nice!" Reed laughed. "Care to build on that?"

"Keep shooting, and keep the pedal to the floor. If you see a way to ditch them, take it, but give us a heads-up."

"Roger that!" Jones shouted over the sound of more gunfire as a Toyota HiLux pulled up beside the Mazda.

Bobby drilled the driver, and the HiLux swerved into them, bounced off their front bumper, then rolled over, skidding down the street on its roof before slamming into a building.

Another HiLux pulled up on the driver's side, and Bobby hiked himself up onto the frame of the open window, took aim on the shotgun rider over the car's roof, and took him out as Brown got the shooter in the backseat.

"Pull up past him if you can!" Bobby yelled, still hanging out of the window.

The moment Coop pulled ahead, Bobby fired into the driver's-side windshield. The HiLux spun around, then rear-ended the tango car behind them, putting an end to that threat as well.

Bobby dropped back inside the car and quickly replaced his empty mag with a full one.

"We've got to get off this street," Brown said. "It's too wide. We're easy targets."

"Working on it," Jones said from the car ahead of them. "I think . . . yeah. Narrow side street two blocks ahead. Sharp right." No sooner had he said it than Jones cranked the lead car into a hard right, gunned it, and disappeared between the buildings.

"Hoo-ah!" Coop braked and swung the wheel right. "Shit! No brakes!" he yelled, attempting to correct the suddenly out-of-control vehicle.

"Brace!" Bobby yelled, as the passenger side of the Mazda went airborne.

The little car zigzagged several yards on two wheels at a wobbly forty-five-degree angle, before the laws of physics kicked in. He hung on as they flipped over and over and over, the world upending to the sound of metal screeching against pavement and the scent of gasoline filling the air.

No! he thought as he lay crumpled inside the wrecked Mazda. *I'm not dying here!*

Flames erupted close by, and smoke rushed into his lungs. Slicing pain consumed his chest and shoulder.

As he felt his world fade, he saw Meir's face.

I love you.

And there was Talia, crying as he lay there bleeding, dying.

Oh, God. How am I going to tell them I'm dead?

41

"You're not dead! Boom! Get with the program and help me, damn it!"

Coop. Yelling at him? What the hell? And what was with all the gunfire? And the smoke?

"We're going to have to lug him to the Chrysler. On three. Lift."

That was Brown.

And then he was airborne, and *fuuuuucuccckkkk*. The mother of all pain ripped through his shoulder.

Everything went black again.

Bobby came to with plugged ears, a raging headache, and the unmistakable sound of whining jet engines.

He worked his jaw until his ears popped. Then he looked around, feeling a little muzzy-headed. Yeah, he was in the jet. He started to reach for his seat belt and gasped when a knife blade of pain dug into his left shoulder. When he could breathe again without sweating, he took stock of himself.

Someone had covered him with a blanket. Beneath it, he'd been stripped down to his boxers. A white gauze bandage covered his right hand; another one wrapped around his bicep. His right arm was in a sling, the shoulder tightly bandaged.

Then he realized he was on oxygen. That soaked it; he wanted some answers.

He craned his neck so he could see out into the aisles. Everyone appeared to be asleep. Coop, Brown, Santos, Reed, and the rest of them.

He felt a presence behind him and looked up.

Carlyle smiled at him. "See, you *aren't* dead."

"What's that supposed to mean?" His tongue felt thick and desert-dry.

"You thought you were a goner."

"What are you talking about?"

Carlyle actually looked sympathetic. "Let's start with this. Do you know your name?"

"What the hell kind of question is that?"

"Just answer."

"Bobby Taggart," he grumbled.

"What's the date?"

He had to think a minute, but it finally came. "July twenty-four — twenty-fifth?"

"Close enough. How many fingers?"

"Three. Now, for God's sake, tell me what's going on."

"Do you remember being on an op in Syria?"

"Of course. We got this guy out of Damascus." He stopped cold. "We did get him out, didn't we?"

Carlyle nodded. "We did. He's on board with us. What's the last thing you remember?"

That took a little thought. "We were taking heavy fire. Trying to outrun the tangos. Hmmm . . . why don't I remember what happened next?"

"Most likely because I've got you pretty well dosed with morphine. When the haze clears, everything will probably come back. Or it won't."

"Thanks. That really cleared it up for me. In the meantime, can you fill me in?"

Carlyle sat down across the aisle, then gave him the CliffsNotes version.

"And none of our guys was hurt?"

"Cuts and bruises. Coop sprained his ankle, which I'm sure you'll take heat over, since he was lugging you away from a burning car at the time. You dislocated your shoulder again—if you hadn't already figured that out. But according to you, you died."

"Huh." If he dug hard enough, he could probably pull much of what Carlyle had just told him out of his memory. Right now, however, his head hurt too much. And he felt dog-tired.

"Why don't you get some sleep?"

"Do I really need this thing?" He pointed to the oxygen tubing.

"Yeah, you inhaled a lot of smoke. The oxygen should be making it easier for you to breathe."

"Any chance I could get some water? I'm bone-dry."

"Sure. Be right back."

By the time Carlyle returned, however, Bobby was sound asleep again.

● ● ●

"When can I get out of here?"

A serene-faced nurse wearing a powder-blue uniform and whisper-soft shoes smiled up from the notes
she'd been typing into a laptop. "That will be up to
the doctor, Mr. Taggart."

Bobby shifted and winced. "Is there any way you
could find out what's taking so long with those X-
rays?"

She finished typing and smiled again—the smile
he was sure she reserved for cranky patients. "Busy
night in the ER. I'm sure they're working as fast as
they can." She walked to his side, checked his water,
and fluffed his pillow. "Is there anything you need
before I go?"

"A get-out-of-jail-free card?" he grumbled.

"You keep that sense of humor, Mr. Taggart," she
said with another dry smile. "You'll be healed up in
no time."

He scowled as she walked out of the room. He
was hungry, he was tired, and he was sore from being
poked and prodded and moved and . . . crap. This
place was turning him into a whiny baby.

He closed his eyes. He hated hospitals. He didn't
do well on the disabled list, either, and he had a feeling Nate would bench him for a lot longer than he
had the first time he'd dislocated the damn shoulder.
If the doctors started talking surgery . . . Man, he
didn't even want to go there.

When he opened his eyes again, a whopping three

minutes had passed. "Time does fly," he muttered to the hospital walls.

After six long hours of waiting, he wanted out of this place. It was almost ten p.m. He wanted to get to Talia. There were things he needed to say to her, things they both needed to hear. And he missed Meir so much!

He didn't have a phone, and except for Nurse Cheerful, he hadn't had anyone to talk to since Coop had limped into his room on crutches. That had been two hours ago. Coop was home now, and no doubt Rhonda was babying him like a puppy.

Then he heard footsteps in the hall. They stopped outside his door.

Finally!

Be the doctor, be the doctor, be the doc—

But it was Talia, and he wondered if his elevated heartbeat sent the monitors racing.

She stood hesitantly in the open door, her dark eyes wide, her face filled with anxiety. "Is it okay if I come in?"

"Yes. Please. I'm dying of boredom here. How did you know where to find me? And what are you doing here this late?"

She rushed to the side of the bed. "Rhonda called. She told me that you'd been injured and they'd taken you straight to the hospital when you landed. Are you in pain?"

"Nah," he lied, then made the huge mistake of

trying to move, and molten fire burned through his shoulder. "I'm just . . . a little banged up."

"A little banged up?" She looked horrified. "You look terrible. And you're on oxygen."

"As a precaution, that's all. I inhaled a little smoke. They're double-covering the bases."

Unconvinced, she stared at his bandaged shoulder.

"Dislocated," he said, before she asked. "Carlyle was able to put it back in place. Not a big deal. It's happened before."

He didn't want to talk about his injuries. He wanted to talk about something much more important. But when she spun around and walked to the window, his alarm meter flipped on.

She was quiet for so long, something was clearly wrong. And when she lowered her head and brought a hand to her mouth, he realized she was crying.

"Talia? What's happening?"

She shook her head, still wouldn't face him.

His first thought brought sheer panic. "Meir? Is something wrong with Meir?"

"No," she said quickly. "Meir's fine."

"You're okay?"

Her laugh didn't sound happy. "I'm okay."

"Then for God's sake, what is it? This can't be about me. I told you, I'm okay."

She turned around, swiping the tears from her face. "This is *precisely* about you. I didn't know what I'd find when I got here. I was so afraid—"

"I'm sorry." He cut her off, hating to see her this way. "I'm sorry you got worked up over nothing. I'm sorry you came all the way over here for no reason."

Her reaction was sluggish, like watching someone take a punch in slow motion. He didn't get it, but her transition from anxiety to calm detachment was gut-wrenching.

"Of course," she said, her face now expressionless, and her tone suddenly measured. "I don't have any reason to be upset. It's not like you haven't warned me."

"Warned you? Warned you about what?"

"Look. I shouldn't have come. I'll let you rest. I'm glad . . . that you're all right."

"Why shouldn't you have come?" he demanded.

"Because I don't have the right. I'm not your wife. I'm not your lover. And other than sharing Meir, I have no reason to be in your life." She turned and walked toward the door.

"Talia. Wait."

She didn't look back as she kept on walking.

He couldn't let her go—not like this.

He ripped the oxygen tube off his face. Grunting through the pain, he managed to sit up and slide his legs over the side of the bed. His head started spinning, and he started keeling toward the floor face-first.

"Mr. Taggart!" Nurse Cheerful to the rescue.

She rushed to the bed, caught him around the waist, and set him right. "What are you doing out of bed?"

He let her help him sit back down.

What I'm doing is failing—miserably, he thought, as she settled him back against the pillows. "I want to see the doctor, now. If he's not here in five minutes, I'm checking myself out. Clear?"

"I wouldn't advise that," she said, holding his hard gaze.

"Five minutes," he repeated, checked the time on the wall clock, and then closed his eyes.

Her hands shook so hard Talia could barely fit the key into the ignition of her dad's Taurus. For long moments, she sat in the hospital parking garage, staring at the concrete wall in front of her.

I'm sorry you came all the way over here for no reason.

His words had hit her like a bucket of ice. *No reason . . . no reason . . .*

He didn't consider her a factor in his life, other than being Meir's mother. He was never going to get past the harm she'd done. No matter how much she hoped, how often she told herself he just needed time, it wasn't going to happen.

If she'd given it even a moment's thought, she'd have realized she had no business rushing over here. If he'd wanted her here, he'd have called her. He'd have asked her to come.

That was what people did when they were hurt or in trouble. They called the ones they loved, reached out to the people who were important in their lives.

But he hadn't called. And she hadn't thought. Her fear for him had rolled right over the fact.

She lowered her head to the steering wheel. He'd been surprised to see her, not pleased. Polite but not forthcoming about his injuries. You didn't lie to people you loved. You didn't cover. Not to someone important.

She lifted her head, refusing to give in to the tears. She'd shed enough over him. It was time she realized once and for all that he'd never find it in himself to forgive her.

With a deep breath, she started the car, then pulled out of the lot.

It was time to let him go. For Meir's sake, they would find a balance—but that was as far as things between them would ever go.

42

Bobby knew Talia's bedroom was at the front of the house, northeast corner. He stood outside on the freshly cut lawn at midnight, listening to his taxi drive off into the night and hoping like hell that the rock he was about to pitch wouldn't break the windowpane. The first one he'd thrown had hardly made a sound.

The doc had finally shown up, ordered one more X-ray, then pronounced him fit enough for release. He sent him home with antibiotics for the minor cuts and burns, pain pills for the shoulder, and an order to follow up with his own physician in a week or so.

"Go home. Stay there. Get some rest," were his parting words.

So far, he was zero for three on following doctor's orders.

He was about to haul back and chuck the stone when the light went on in Talia's bedroom.

The window slid open. "What are you doing?" she half whispered, half scolded. She must have heard his first attempt after all.

"I need to talk to you."

"Now?"

"Now."

She hesitated for a moment, then shook her head as if she couldn't believe what she was about to do, and disappeared. A few seconds later, the front porch light came on.

Then she was there. Opening the front door, slipping outside. And God, oh, God, did she look pretty. It was July, and it was hot. She wore a pale pink clingy tank top and loose boxer-type shorts. Her feet and legs were bare. Her long, thick hair fell across one side of her face and past her shoulders.

"Do you know how beautiful you are?" he asked, walking up the path to the porch.

"Are you medicated?" she asked, eyeing him carefully.

He grinned. "Maybe. But only a little."

She crossed her arms protectively over her breasts. "Which would explain why you're here at this time of night."

He held her gaze in the porch light. "It's the only place I wanted to be."

He hated that she looked so guarded, so unsure. She was one of the strongest women he'd ever met, yet he was the reason she felt such vulnerability.

"Can we sit?" he asked softly. "Talk for a little bit?"

She leaned back against the closed door. "Shouldn't you be in bed? You can sleep in the guest room if you want."

"I can sleep later. I need to talk to you." She had no response, so he nudged her a little. "But right now, I really need to sit down, or you're going to end up calling a crane to get me up off the ground."

"Oh, God." She rushed down the sidewalk in her bare feet, lifted his good arm over her shoulder, and wrapped her arm around his waist. "Can you make it into the house?"

"Let's go to the love seat first. It's closer."

She helped him up the three steps, then walked him across the wooden porch floor toward the white wicker love seat with its soft floral cushions. "You sure you're okay?"

"Yup." He caught her hand when she moved toward a nearby chair. "Sit by me."

She looked down at their joined hands before reluctantly easing down beside him. "If this is about my little scene at the hospital, you don't have to try to—"

"Make you feel better?" he interrupted. He shook his head. "That's not the reason I'm here. Wait. That's not entirely true. I *am* here to make you feel better—I hope. But not for the reason you think."

"You're talking in riddles."

He was so tired. His shoulder throbbed like a heartbeat. But he knew he couldn't sleep until he said what he'd come here to say. "You know what they say about some guys. 'He's a man of action, not words.' Well, that's me. I get things done. With action. The words part? Not so much. At least, not most of the time. But

I've got things I want to tell you. *Have* to tell you. And I'm so afraid I'll screw it up."

Her eyes softened. "You're doing fine so far," she said, before looking away.

He watched her profile in the porch light. Strong. Beautifully defined. "You know what I thought the first time I saw you?"

Her brows furrowed. "We're playing twenty questions?"

He gave her a look.

She looked down at their joined hands. "Okay. What did you think when you first saw me?"

"I thought, now, *there's* a distraction that could get me killed." It didn't take much to conjure up that memory and the instant attraction that had shot through his chest. "Yet I couldn't stay away. Now here I am, living proof that I was wrong about you."

"Not entirely," she said, seemingly enthralled with their hands. "I almost did get you killed."

"No, what you did was save me. Twice."

"Yeah, well, it seemed like the right thing to do at the time."

Because she gave him a little smile, he felt encouraged. "What was the first thing you thought when you saw me?"

"I thought this was about *you* talking."

"Humor me. I'll get there."

She expelled a deep breath. "All right. I thought, there's a hard man. And then you shocked me and smiled. And I knew I had a chance of coming out of Kabul alive."

He'd never looked at that time from her point of view until they'd reconnected in Oman. Not only had she been doing her job, but she'd been doing a dangerous job. Hell, he could have killed her if he'd found her out. At the very least, he could have turned her over to the U.S. military as a spy. The risks she'd taken had been monumental. No different from the risks he took.

"That night, after Meir and I had our day together?" he said. "I got the call about the mission before we had the chance to tell him that I'm his dad. When he hugged me, he whispered that he loved me."

"He told me," she said, in the gentle, loving tone she wasn't even aware she used when she talked about their son. "He said you told him you loved him, too."

Bobby smiled, nodded. "I do love him. But it was the honest and unfiltered way he just came out and said it that . . . somehow changed things."

She swallowed, then asked quietly, "Changed things, how?"

"Well, that took me a little while to figure out. Because I was digging too deep. Thinking too much."

Careful of his shoulder, he turned to her, clasped her hand tighter, and felt a rush of uncomplicated joy when she didn't pull away.

"When he threw himself into my arms and whispered those words, that little five-year-old boy showed me that love is much simpler than we make it out to be. It's life and circumstances—some within our control, some out of our control—that gum up the works.

"On this last mission," he went on, "I was in a car, and we got hit. We rolled, and I thought it was all over for me." He met her eyes. "I saw Meir. I saw you. And I thought, how am I going to tell them that I'm dead? It was going to hurt you so much. The guys said I even yelled it when they dragged me out of the burning car."

"Oh, God."

He felt her shiver, and he squeezed her hand even tighter. "I didn't tell you this to upset you. We both know that what I do is dangerous. But it's what makes me tick. And after seeing you in action in Oman, I think it's what makes you tick, too. I think it might even be part of the 'juice' we feel for each other. We understand each other so much better than someone who hasn't been in our shoes.

"Anyway, in those moments, I realized like never before that life is short. That there's no time for complications and that I need to keep it simple. So here's the simple truth. I love you, Talia. I have always loved you. Even when I thought I hated you and could never forgive you."

Her eyes glittered with unshed tears. "And now? Now you think you can?"

"Sweetheart, I already did, a long time ago. But it was Meir's gift of unqualified love that made me realize it. My ego stood in the way for six long years.

Because you were gone. That hurt much more than the betrayal. The simple truth is, I didn't like my life without you in it. So I conditioned myself to get through it on hate and anger."

"I never ever wanted that," Talia told him. "Not from the first moment I met you. Going through with my mission was the hardest thing I've ever done. That and leaving you, knowing you'd hate me."

"I know that now," he said. "But maybe I needed these six years to heal. Maybe we both did."

The hope in her eyes grew even brighter than her tears.

"Talia, there's no doubt in my mind that we were meant to be together. And I think the time is now."

She leaned into him and kissed him with lips that tasted like her tears. "I love you."

He cupped her cheek and pressed his forehead to hers, feeling like the luckiest man on earth. "Thank God." He smiled. "Can you help me to a bed now? I think the word *upright* is about to fall off my 'can do' list."

43

With Bobby relying heavily on her for support, Talia walked him up the stairs toward the guest bedroom.

"Not your room?" he asked, as they passed her bedroom door.

"You'd like that, wouldn't you?" she whispered, smiling up at him. "Bet you've sneaked into a lot of girls' bedrooms under their parents' noses over the years."

"We'll talk about my misspent youth another time," he hedged. "I want to sleep in your bed."

"Not tonight, Romeo. There's a little boy sleeping right across the hall who has a tendency to rush into my room some mornings, to make sure I'm awake and ready for breakfast."

"Sweet." He pressed a kiss to the top of her head. "I like the sound of that."

And she loved the warmth and anticipation in his voice. "You wouldn't like it much if he came bounding up onto the bed and your shoulder ended up under his bony little knees."

He winced. "Good point. But someday soon, right?"

Her heart squeezed in the sweetest way. "Yeah. Someday soon."

She'd truly thought their someday would never come. Even after she'd heard the taxi pull up outside, heard the car door slam, and finally gotten up to look outside and seen him standing there in the dark in the yard, staring at her window. Even then, she hadn't foreseen this.

I love you, Talia.

Damn right he did, she thought happily, as she led him into the guestroom and helped him down onto the bed.

"Oh, God." Bobby's moan fell somewhere between gratitude and pleasure. "The therapeutic powers of being horizontal are highly underrated. And being naked. There are supreme healing benefits in that, too. Especially being naked with you."

It had taken a bit of persuasion to convince her to undress and come to bed with him. No funny business. He just needed to feel her beside him for a little while, needed that skin-on-skin contact to make this feel real.

"You know you need to rest, to limit your physical activity, and I wish you'd take a pain pill."

She'd had to try. He'd known that, but his next words had broken her.

"*You're* my pain pill."

"I'm such a sucker."

Beaten, she'd pulled her tank top up and over her head. By the time she'd shimmied out of her boxers, he was wishing to God he could make love to her in a hundred different ways.

She'd stood naked by the bed, letting him look his fill. He'd forgotten how the peaks of her small dark nipples turned up so slightly, how perfectly round her apple-sized breasts were, how her hips flared from her tidy waist, and how her ass—Lord, he loved her ass— was high and tight and filled his palms in the most delicious way.

"Lord, I've missed you," he'd whispered when she pulled back the sheet and crawled in beside him, molding her warmth against his.

Missed the silk of her skin, the feel of her hair trailing through his fingers. He didn't care that it was past four in the morning, that the double bed in her parents' guestroom was too short for him. In fact, he liked it that the two of them had to snuggle close together because the mattress was so small.

Most of all, he loved that she was finally lying beside him, where she belonged.

For long, leisurely moments, he floated on a stream of contentment, his fingers trailing up and down the length of her bare thigh, over the gentle curve of her hip, their breath in sync, his heartbeat matching hers in rhythm and speed.

"I could lie with you like this forever," he murmured, turning his lips into her hair.

"And I wish we could." She sounded sleepy as she pressed a kiss against his collarbone. "But Dad's an early riser." Her soft breath fanned his neck, both soothing and stimulating. "I'd better get back to my room."

"In a little while," he cajoled. "Do something for me first?"

"Hmm?"

"Touch me." He'd hardened to steel the moment she'd lifted her top. "I need to feel you touch me. I've needed it for so long."

She pushed up on one elbow. Her eyes were dark and brimming with desire, but she shook her head. "Not a good idea. You know what that will lead to. You're in no condition to—"

"Let me worry about my condition." He reached up, gently gripped a handful of her hair, and tugged her down to his mouth.

Familiar yet new and everything in between. Her mouth was heaven, her lips soft and tentative at first, until the kiss took on its own energy, and she opened her mouth over his, inviting him inside.

He groaned low in his throat and thrust his tongue into her mouth, loving the way she sucked him in and lapped him up, then turned the tables. She slipped her tongue between his lips on a sensual glide in and out that mimicked the way he wanted to move inside her.

"Please." He was begging and didn't care. He'd

never been so happy to grovel for something in his life.

"I don't want to hurt you."

He pushed out a pained laugh. "Sweetheart. You're killing me already."

Up on her elbow again, her hair falling over her eyes and tickling his shoulder, she locked her gaze with his, slowly shook her head in defeat, then tormented him with the leisurely glide of her fingertips down his chest, then into the concave of his belly.

Finally, after skimming her fingers over and around his pulsing cock, she enclosed him with a soft fist.

He closed his eyes, fought to control his breathing as she alternately played the tip of her thumb back and forth over his glans, then squeezed him and worked her hand down to his root and back again.

He let out a low moan and indulged in her generosity until the need to take her with him overrode anything else.

"This is not just . . . about me." He could barely breathe for the deep, sensual pleasure. "I want . . . I need you along for the ride."

She glanced up at him through the veil of her hair, then slid lower on the bed, grazing the tip of him with her lips and then her tongue, before she took him all the way into her mouth and damn near destroyed him.

"Inside," he pleaded. "I need to be inside you." He reached down, touched her where she was slick and wet and so, so ready for him. "You're so amazing."

She straddled him then and stood on her knees over him as he caressed and finessed her swollen flesh, loving the soft, earthy sounds she made, the way she moved against his hand, before he finally urged her down and over him.

She eased onto him, taking care not to jostle him and cause pain to his shoulder, but he was beyond caring. Beyond pain. Being one with her, being surrounded by her—hot, slick, gloving—being loved by her erased the physical pain of his injuries and the emotional pain that had kept them apart for so long.

"I . . . love . . . you," he gritted out between clenched teeth, as she moved over him, wringing molten sparks of physical pleasure too explosive to control, too amazing to comprehend.

Above him, she closed her eyes, let her head fall back, and rode with him to an end that was cleansing and cataclysmic and new.

With a muffled moan, she came, taking him with her. Eyes closed, breath catchy, she sat above him, stretching out the ride, taking in the thrill. When she finally opened her eyes and met his, a slow, satisfied smile spread across her beautiful face.

"Hey," she whispered, leaning down to kiss him.

"Hey, yourself." He cupped a hip in his hand, sated, spent, and renewed.

"Don't think that you're always going to get your way."

He chuckled. "Was that a warning or a dare?"

"That, Mr. Taggart, was me trying to retrieve some of my pride. I made that way too easy for you."

He pulled her down against his good side with a smile. "It's about time *something* we did together was easy."

She sighed in contentment. "Amen."

"Let's try another easy fix."

"Yeah?"

"Yeah. Marry me."

44

"Mom says I have to be quiet and not make you tired."

"She does, huh?" Bobby turned his head on the pillow to see Meir standing gravely in the doorway of the guestroom. "You know the thing about moms?"

"What thing?"

"They worry too much." He patted the mattress, inviting Meir to join him on the bed. "Come on in."

Meir relaxed then and eased into the room. "Mom says you were in an accident."

"I was. Had a little fender-bender. Banged up my shoulder a bit."

"Does it hurt?" His eyes were solemn.

It was on the tip of his tongue to deny the pain, but he thought better of it. "Sometimes. If I move wrong. But I'll be good as new in a few weeks."

The boy seemed to think about that. Which was fine. He was too young to know the whole truth about what Bobby really did. And he'd had enough to deal with lately anyway.

"You really can come sit with me," Bobby said.

"You're not going to hurt me. Now, tell me what you've been up to while I was gone."

Meir clambered right up beside him on the bed. "Grampa took me to the aquarium one day."

"Was it cool?"

"Pretty cool, yeah. But it was stinky. Like fish." He made a face. "The sharks were cool, though."

"Someday you'll have to take me. I've never been to an aquarium."

"Sure. Maybe Mom can come, too."

"Of course. Where is your mom?"

"Right here." Talia walked into the room, carrying a bed tray with coffee, juice, and a plate full of scrambled eggs and toast. "Thought you could use some nourishment."

"I'm not an invalid," he said, smiling, secretly pleased that she'd gone to so much trouble. "I could have come down and eaten at the table."

"Now you don't have to."

She set the tray on the top of a bureau, then turned back to the bed. "Do you need to get up first?"

"Took care of that a while ago."

It hadn't been easy; in addition to his shoulder, he was beginning to feel all the other bruises and strains and cuts and burns from the roll-over. Still, he'd managed to get out of bed and use the bathroom. Getting settled again had been another story.

"Let's prop you up a little better. You want to help me, Meir?"

Meir scrambled to his knees, and when Bobby

leaned forward, he helped his mother fluff up the pillows and add an extra one behind his back.

"Thanks, buddy."

"Eat before the eggs get cold." Talia settled the tray over his thighs.

"Does she boss you around this way, too?" He winked at Meir.

"Sometimes." Meir grinned from his mother to Bobby as if they'd just shared a guy moment. "But it's okay. She *is* the mom, after all. She usually knows what's best."

"You're right about that," Bobby agreed. "She's real good about keeping an eye out for you, huh?"

Meir nodded.

"I was thinking. Maybe I could help her look out for you. In fact, maybe we could all look out for each other."

The child was no dummy. His eyes told the story. It was clear that he sensed something was happening here. Something big.

"How would we do that?" he asked, his gaze jumping between the two of them.

"Well, if we all lived together," Bobby said, "it would be pretty easy."

Talia was watching her son's reactions carefully.

"You mean . . . live together like a family?" Meir asked, up on his knees again.

"Yes," Talia said, joining them on the bed. "Like a family."

A slow smile spread across the boy's face. "Does this mean we're getting married?"

Bobby laughed, and Talia smiled tearily as Meir glanced hopefully from one to the other.

"Yeah," Bobby said. "That's exactly what it means."

Meir's dark eyes widened with hope. "Then you'd be my dad?"

The lump that suddenly lodged in his throat kept Bobby from answering. He nodded and finally managed a whispered, "Yes. I'd be your dad."

"Wow!" Meir bounded off the bed. "I've got to go tell Gramma and Grampa!"

Laughing, Talia caught him just before he headed out the door. "Whoa, partner. Hold on a sec. There's something else we want to tell you."

She glanced at Bobby, and he knew with everything in him that the love in her eyes and the boy in her arms were the best gifts a man could ever hope for.

Beyond excited, Meir squirmed in Talia's arms. "What else do you have to tell me?"

Talia nodded at Bobby. *Go ahead. It's time.*

"Something good, buddy," he told his son. "Something really, really good."

45

"Somebody want to tell me what that was all about?" Bobby asked into the lazy quiet.

It was after nine p.m. on Sunday, a week after his mishap in Syria. Around five o'clock, every member of the ITAP team and their wives and kids had trooped into the Levines' Georgetown home to see him.

"How's the shoulder, Boom? And who is this vision beside you?"

"Can't keep a good man down—especially when he's got a nurse who looks like this taking care of him."

It was ridiculous. One corny—not to mention leading--line after another, as they arrived carrying casseroles, cakes, pies, or salads to add to the "impromptu" potluck.

Impromptu? Hell, it had been a setup from the get-go. And he'd felt like a bug under a microscope as they'd all filed by him.

The entire Black Ops team—Black, Jones, Reed, Mendoza, Green, Wyatt Savage, Luke Colter, and even Sam Lang, who was retired—had dropped by, and Bobby had gotten the distinct feeling that they'd all gathered for something other than well wishes.

Even Carlyle, Santos, and Waldrop—the only bachelors left on the ITAP team—had made an appearance. They'd brought the keg.

The crowd was gone now. The kitchen had been cleaned up, the kids had played until they dropped, and their parents had carried them to their cars. Meir, who now had a raft of new friends, was sound asleep in his bed.

Only Jamie and Rhonda Cooper and Mike and Eva Brown remained.

The evening had cooled off, so they'd moved to the front porch to enjoy the night sounds and the soft summer breeze.

Bobby sat on one end of the wicker love seat, Talia close beside him. He still had to wear the damn sling, but his shoulder was feeling better each day.

Coop and Brown were sitting on the top porch step, each nursing a whiskey. Their wives were nestled between their thighs on the step below them, Eva sipping wine and Rhonda enjoying a beer.

No one answered his question, so Bobby tried again. "I repeat. Somebody want to tell me what that was all about?"

When they still remained suspiciously silent, he looked pointedly from one to the other. "*No one* has an answer for me?"

Coop looked at Brown, then shrugged. "That was about your friends coming to wish you well."

"Right." Bobby turned to Talia. "You buying that?"

She grinned. "They *were* concerned about you."

"Not as much as they were concerned about *you*. So who let the cat out of the bag?"

"It wasn't me," Mike said quickly.

Coop asked, "What cat? What bag?"

Rhonda gave her husband a look. "Man up, or I'll do it for you."

"You're a hard woman." Coop grinned at his wife and turned to Bobby. "I might have accidentally mentioned that you'd proposed to Talia. It was a slip, okay?"

Brown snorted. "Accidentally. Right."

"Anyway, next thing I knew, the rest of the guys wanted to meet Talia. So did all the wives." Coop lifted his hands. "What better way than a potluck?"

Bobby grunted in disbelief. "Next thing, you're going to tell me you baked a casserole."

Coop looked a little wounded. "What if I did? Turned out pretty good, if you ask me."

Eva chuckled.

"He's been trying to get in touch with his feminine side," Brown said helpfully.

"Stop teasing him," Rhonda scolded. "I love a man who cooks. It's sexy."

"So—did I pass?" Talia cut straight to the heart of the matter.

Rhonda smiled at her. "With flying colors. But the truth is, none of them could imagine Bobby in the role of dad. *That* was the real draw."

Bobby smiled. "Well, I guess they know now." He still had a lot to learn about fatherhood, but the love had come naturally. He was filled with it.

They all fell comfortably quiet then, and Bobby closed his eyes in contentment. The woman by his side, the little boy sleeping upstairs—he was one lucky SOB. He had it all. More than he'd ever hoped for. More, probably, than he deserved.

Cooper and Brown—his brothers in every way but blood. He'd lost them once. Never thought he'd get them back—or be as close to their wives who he considered sisters.

And he had the girl. He'd lost her once, too. Lost a part of himself when she'd left him. But she was here now, and so was their son. He had it all.

"So," he said, feeling full and rich and settled, "I'm getting itchy, sitting around this house so long. How about we go out for breakfast tomorrow morning? Just the six of us."

"Fine by me," Coop said.

"I'm in," Brown added.

"Want to draw to see who's buying now or wait until morning?" Coop dug into his hip pocket for his wallet.

Mike, who always seemed to lose this contest, did the same. "Let's get it over with."

Mike carefully slipped out his tattered and torn jack of hearts. A bullet hole pierced the center of the card, a reminder of what he had been through.

Coop eased out his own one-eyed jack, the edges blackened by fire.

"I need a little help." Bobby smiled at Talia, who helped him remove his jack of spades from his wallet, the fragile card sliced through the middle by a combat knife yet still holding together.

"The stories these cards could tell," Brown said, his expression a little melancholy as he rose and walked over to Bobby.

"I'm glad they can't talk." Coop stood and joined them.

"I'm just thankful I'm alive to remember." An unexpected swell of emotion took Bobby by surprise. He looked up and met his friends' eyes. "And I'm thankful to be here with all of you."

Their gazes held for a brief, intense moment of brotherhood. They were all that was left of the One-Eyed Jacks. They'd been betrayed and estranged but never beaten. And their bond had never been stronger.

Breaking the spell, Mike gathered the three cards and gently shuffled them. "Talia, you do the honors. Close your eyes, and pick one."

Bobby met Talia's smiling eyes and could see she'd already made her pick. She'd picked him. Eyes wide open.

"No need, gentlemen." He held her unwavering gaze. "Winner buys, and I feel like the biggest winner who ever walked the earth."